Midnight Menagerie

Edited by Carol Hightshoe

WolfSinger Publications ⸸ Brackettville, Texas

Table of Contents

The Ring Master Invites You to Visit the Midnight Menagerie

Ladies and gentlemen, and, of course, all you 'sweet' children daring to see what, up until now, only existed in your dreams. Or perhaps your nightmares.

Behind me, lurking in the blue-black darkness on the fringes of the unknown are the stars of the show.

Creatures waiting to be seen, anxious to meet you…creatures from so many galaxies you never knew existed. And I, as the master of the show cannot wait for the entertainment to begin.

Section One
The Carnival Arrives

Ladies and gentlemen, daring souls and dreamers, and those who teeter on the tightrope of curiosity and dread—welcome! Welcome to the Midnight Menagerie!

Here, beneath the striped canopies and the whispering winds of the carnival, wonders awaken! The strongmen flex their might, the acrobats defy gravity, and the fortune tellers spin futures like gossamer thread.

But perhaps it is not the glitter and grandeur you seek. Perhaps you are drawn to the shadows, to the hushed corners where curtains shudder though no wind stirs. To the tents where the line between spectacle and sorcery blurs, where each act carries a cost, and every gaze may be met by something that stares back.

So come, buy a ticket and take a step beyond the ordinary. The show is about to begin.

Tunnel of Lust

Fin Patiliu

Come hither and teeter awhile en route to carnal fascination
Unrelenting acts of pleasure and little death within
Stay vigilant beyond the gate
Sights unfathomable will sink in
Wickedness comes with prying eyes
Body heat helps light the way for escaping

~

Pay heed, creatures of ritual are never escaping
Wantons lacking quench here get devoured by fascination
Soul meets soul on lover's lips while lustful intent travels between
the eyes
Keep your faith hidden within
Desire not to fit in
Divine love may yet open the return gate

~

Fear calls dark winds to conceal the gate
Aspire not towards escaping
The nebulous vestibules of Paradise welcome us in
Desires can poison, but not the antidote, which rules a lifelong
fascination
No words of love escape tormented tongues within
Their sweet nothings blister loins and boil floaters across the eyes

~

Precious eyes
Blind to every gate
Yearn to see more from within
Nothing but mutual heat escaping
Longing reprieve from excessive fascination
Porous flesh invites the fallen in

Midnight Menagerie

~

To me blend in
Share mine eyes
Keep sound mind and release your fascination
You shall get the gate
You shall experience unashamed, paroxysmal escaping
Faith a leap curious one, and spiral further down the bowels
within

~

We all change within
Some change so much all they want is further in
Emotional incontinence keeps the worldly from escaping
By all means indulge your temptations, and feast your eyes
Poets are known to frolic for days by this dimension's gate
Welcoming ye misguided, cold feet in heat yet full of carnal
fascination

~

Eyes of eternal *fascination*
Escaping vice means abandoning elation
The tunnel *gate* chooses who cometh *within*, and stay *in*.

~ * ~ * ~

Fin Patiliu has fiction published in Strange Days Books: *Dreams* anthology, *MiNDFOOD Magazine*, and SpecFicNZ's *Artificial Sweetener: Tales of AI 100% written by humans.*

One of Fin's earliest written word discoveries was seeing the name Cameron under a strikethrough line on his own birth certificate. Date night circa 1982, two sweethearts cozied up in front of David Cronenberg's Scanners, which suffice it to say, scared one canoodler well enough not to consent to naming their first born after the film's protagonist. Fin strives to reclaim his fictional legacy, of blowing people's minds.

Born in Papua New Guinea. Raised in New Zealand. Lives in Auckland.

Keeping the Tradition Alive

Annie Percik

"I want to put together a travelling show," Grandma Louise stated without preamble as she walked into the room.

I looked up from the daily news bulletin scrolling across my palm screen to see her fixing me with her iron stare. Her face was a mass of wrinkles but those grey eyes looked out at me with piercing acuity. Hands on hips, she radiated an energy that belied her advanced age and tiny stature.

I dropped my hand into my lap, palm down to show she had my full attention, and pasted an interested expression on my face. "A travelling show? What do you mean?"

Grandma Louise was known for her hare-brained ideas, often coming up with something outrageous, which the rest of us needed to approach with care. Usually, whatever she got enthusiastic about was wildly impractical, or sometimes downright hazardous, but nobody wanted to crush her enthusiasm. And presenting resistance could easily enflame her dangerously stubborn streak, especially if anyone suggested there were things she shouldn't or couldn't do.

She sighed. "The traditions are being lost, Helen. Out here on the ring, nobody understands what our family used to do."

I chuckled. "Well, you can't exactly get a performing elephant on a space station."

The only reason I even knew the word 'elephant' was because of Grandma Louise's stories. She wasn't really my grandmother, but there were too many 'greats' in the accurate description of the relationship to use on a daily basis. She was the oldest person in any of the colonies, and the only one who could actually remember the travelling circus she grew up in. She was also the only survivor of the earliest longevity trials. None of her peers or even her children or real grandchildren were left alive to help tell the stories or share properly in her reminiscences.

"I'm sure you and your cousins can help me come up with something," she said. "You're all bright kids. I want to bring the circus to every space station in the ring. And you're going to help me do it."

And that was that. For Once Grandma Louise had got an idea firmly in her head, and this time there was no shaking it loose. No matter the obstacles and arguments any of us put in her way, she kept coming up with solutions and counterarguments to keep the idea alive. And gradually, her passion started to infect the rest of us. One by one, we came around to her view and started arguing in its favour. She put together a team to handle the project. I was on holograms, my sister Julie did the costume design, and our cousin Petra worked on the marketing. Grandma Louise oversaw every detail, correcting us at every turn, whenever anything we produced didn't exactly match her vision. It might have been annoying if it hadn't been for the light that shone from those piercing grey eyes, every time she got lost in the images spilling from her mind.

"No, Helen, the horses' gait needs to be smoother. They're meant to be graceful. Leave the galumphing to the elephants."

I went back to the control panel for the holograms and entered new parameters to tweak the different animals' movements.

"The top hat needs to be taller, Julie. I want to be imposing, so the kids see me as someone to look up to. Literally."

My sister scrubbed out the offending headgear from her 3D sketch and added more height until Grandma Louise was satisfied.

"Bigger, Petra! All the lettering should be bigger! With curlicues and bold shadowing. The circus is a major event and the posters need to reflect that."

The tip of my cousin's tongue stuck out of the corner of her mouth as she applied herself to redesigning the marketing materials for the event.

After two months, we were all exhausted, but Grandma Louise's eyes were bright as she looked out at her first audience. Petra had done an excellent job getting the word out, and the station had been buzzing with anticipation and curiosity for days. Now, the gallery around the zero-g dome was packed with people of all ages. Grandma Louise straightened her incredibly tall top hat, shook out the tails of her bright red jacket and grinned at me.

"How do I look?"

She stood as straight as she could and gave an elaborate flourish with her arms, her theatrical background shining out from every pore.

"Amazing," I said. "But didn't you tell me once the ringmaster was always male? I thought all you were allowed to do was wear a spangly leotard and look pretty, while the horses galloped round you."

She winked at me. "That's a part of the tradition we don't need to keep alive."

With that, she strode out onto the platform that extended into the dome, clicked out of her magnetic boots and pushed off into the air. She executed a perfect somersault and used her manoeuvring jets to come to a stop at the exact centre of the dome, spinning slowly to survey the crowd.

"Roll up! Roll up!" Her magnified voice echoed around the chamber and a hush fell. "Welcome, one and all, to the first performance of the Galactic Circus! Have we got a show for you today! You won't believe your eyes!"

The crowd gasped as my holographic elephants materialised at the edges of the dome and started stomping majestically around the path in front of the gallery. They waved their trunks and trumpeted at the crowd. I saw more than one small child reach out to try and touch them, mouths agape in wonder. The adults too were transfixed, their faces suffused with a joy not often seen amidst the daily drudgery of keeping the station running. I felt a smile tug at the edges of my own lips at being a part of bringing this spectacle into their lives. In the centre of the circus ring, Grandma Louise spread her arms wide and reclaimed her heritage.

~ * ~ * ~

Annie Percik lives in London, writing novels and short stories, whilst working as a freelance editor. She writes a blog about writing on her website, which is where all her current publications are listed, including her novels, *The Defiant Spark* and *A Spectrum of Heroes*. She also hosts a media review podcast, *Will You Still Love It Tomorrow*, and publishes advice and meditation videos featuring her teddy bear Stanley on Instagram (@wisebearstanley). He is much more popular online than she is.

Visit her website at: https://alobear.co.uk/

The Menagerie of the Milky Way

Harriet Phoenix

Tom and Amanda stepped off the shuttle that had carried them into high orbit and joined the crowd of other winners. One young man had evidently given his plus-one ticket to his mother, and a woman standing at the viewport chatted excitedly to a teenager who could only be her sister, but mainly it was couples in their mid-twenties like themselves.

No wonder, Tom thought. *Any guy who wins* this *ticket and doesn't take his girlfriend better expect to be single by tomorrow.*

Despite their calm stroll across the lobby, Tom could feel Amanda buzzing with the same excitement that bubbled through him. With every soft impact of his trainers on the floor (not metal, not plastic, not anything he recognised) he felt it; *this is alien. I'm in space, on an alien space station, where an alien is going to take me on a tour to see more aliens.*

Of course, over the last three years seeing aliens had become commonplace, but that was on TV. This would be *live,* not just the k'Bleeki but species from all across the galaxy. Royalty, heads of state, tycoons and Nobel winners had all had this tour, but the k'Bleeki wanted to meet a healthy crop of regular people as well. And so a lottery had been created, with seven thousand plus-one tickets sent to seven thousand lucky, randomly-selected citizens of planet Earth.

And one week ago, a ticket for this, the very last night before the Menagerie of the Milky Way (its Earth name) left orbit to continue on its expedition across the galaxy, had arrived with his name on it. He, Tom Crofter, who never won anything, who'd attended his third-choice University so he could get a low-paying job in data entry, had been *chosen.*

He felt underdressed, like he should've rented a tux or something. But the invitation had specified a casual dress code, and warned them to be prepared for lots of walking. So he'd cleaned his trainers and donned his best version of the jeans and fandom T shirts he wore every day. Amanda had edged closer to smart casual, and he noticed she'd found time to touch up her roots; there'd definitely been a pale stripe among the purple three days earlier when he'd invited her.

He tore his gaze from his girlfriend's hair as they waited for their turn being photographed. Couples posed, prom-photo style, in front of the station's enormous clear wall before passing through a nearby door to meet their guide.

"What does it say about what we're about to see," he murmured to Amanda. "That the sight of Earth from space is only the warm-up act?"

Amanda smiled, not taking her eyes from the blue and white orb hanging in the blackness beyond the window.

"Do you think it'll look different to us?" she asked. "Next time we see it, on the way home?"

Tom felt his lip tighten. "I hope so."

Just then the couple in front finished their photo and Tom and Amanda stepped forward. At the human photographer's direction, Tom slipped his arms around Amanda's waist while she leaned her head back, fanning her hair out across his shoulder.

He thought of what was ahead, and as the camera flashed he managed to conjure a grin someone might assume to be for the girl in his arms.

~ * ~

The flash ended, and Amanda blinked. "What…"

"Okay, that's great!" The photographer waved them towards the door. "Have an amazing time!"

"Wait, what…"

"C'mon, Amanda!" Tom's arm moved up around her shoulders, hurrying her along. "Let's go and see the aliens!"

"Tom," she hissed as they approached the door. "Did that flash seem *odd* to you?"

"What?" He looked at her as the double doors hissed open and they stepped forward into a solid white waiting room with another set of doors ahead. "A little, I guess. Usually flashes make me blink, but that one didn't. And maybe it went on a second or two longer. Why?"

"Just…" She struggled for a way to explain the feeling, like a subtle penetration across every inch of her skin, that wouldn't sound hysterical and dumb.

"Did it feel, somehow, like…*more* than light?" she finished lamely.

He considered, then shook his head.

"Even if it did, why *shouldn't* it?" he challenged. "We're on a spaceship made by an alien civilisation so far past us it's gone right back around to being funny. They handed out the technology that saved our arses like it was nothing. They probably had to make a new camera dumbed down enough for some human intern to use, and it'll probably be the highlight of that guy's whole career just to touch it. So, seriously, why would the flash on that camera be the same as ours?"

She shrugged, before he could start waxing too lyrical. "Just seemed odd, is all."

The double doors in front of them hissed open, and Amanda got her first look at a k'Bleeki.

On TV, they stood inches above all but the tallest humans, and so she'd imagined their presence would be intimidating. But TV didn't communicate their delicacy; up close, it seemed incredible a stray breeze didn't whisk them away. Something about the way they moved made it seem as if they were just gliding with every step.

Like humans, the k'Bleeki had limbs surrounding a torso with a head on top. Convergent evolution was the term being thrown around by scientists; nature finding the same solutions to the same problems. The k'Bleeki were a little like insects, with six legs jointed *differently* than anything from Earth. Like crickets, they spoke to each other by vibrating parts of their exoskeleton, but that exoskeleton was closer to cartilage than chitin, translucent and sturdier than it looked.

The process *could* be used to imitate human speech, but this was uncomfortable and exhausting. k'Bleeki who interacted with humans therefore spoke using surgically grafted speakers that translated their thoughts into whatever Earth language they pleased, sounding *just* lifelike enough to dip a toe into the Uncanny Valley.

"Thomas Crofter and Amanda Hale?" the k'Bleeki asked.

The pair of them nodded, and the k'Bleeki's sunset-orange form tinged with shades of lilac.

"Wonderful!" They said, beckoning them out into a corridor as white and featureless as the room they'd left. Identical white walls curved and branched from where they stood. "My name is Darmin, and I will be your guide this evening. If you'd like to follow me, we'll get started!"

Tom and Amanda headed down the corridor with Darmin, who hesitated before adding, "Ah, may I just clarify…which is Tom, and which is Amanda?"

"I'm Amanda, this is Tom," Amanda replied, cutting off Tom who closed his mouth with a snap.

"And you are the female, correct? And Tom is male?"

"That's correct." Amanda worked to keep the irritation out of her voice. Human gender norms were not universal, she knew that. She'd seen documentaries; k'Bleeki changed genders pretty much on a whim, and each possessed both sets of equipment, tucked away inside the exoskeleton when not in use. They wore clothes, the styles of which had nothing to do with an individual's current gender; Darmin's pale grey tunic with many pockets was likely pragmatic, while the green sash across their chest probably denoted their rank. Their names were the closest approximation to their k'Bleeki names the first human they spoke to could manage.

It was, in short, just about impossible to tell a k'Bleeki's gender by looking, which was why humanity had decided to cut through the whole problem by assigning them all 'they/them' pronouns, and also why it was stupid to get offended when they weren't clear on anyone's gender. Even if Tom had made a stupid sniggering noise when they asked.

Darmin made another lilac blush. "Ah, good! I know the basic signs, of course—body structure, differences in presentation, the keratinous fibre on your scalp and other ornamentation—but there's so much individual variation that it's as well to check. It's all so fascinating!"

Introductions over, Darmin's talk turned to the facility. The corridors, they explained, could be adjusted to cater to the atmosphere of any species that visited the Menagerie.

"What if you'd found intelligent life on, say, Venus?" Amanda asked. "Could you cater to beings who live in an atmosphere of sulphuric acid?"

"It would present a challenge," Darmin admitted. "But not the greatest one we've faced. We've had visitors who lived in ionised plasma! The facility can handle it; the challenge lies in protecting the guides as we move through that environment. Earth's atmosphere is comparatively simple. However, I will need to change my gas cylinder at some point during the tour, for which I beg your indulgence."

As they walked, a nook appeared in the wall, leading to another door. Darmin waved them in and turned to face them.

"This is the first stop on your personal tour," they announced, indicating the door. "The beings you're about to see are from a planet some forty thousand light years away, and your scientists have named them *Lupus cercopithecidae exo*."

Amanda frowned. "Wolf monkeys?"

Tom chuckled. "Well, why not? We have wolf spiders and we have spider monkeys. Why not wolf monkeys?"

Amanda forced a laugh, biting down on a retort. *Oh, Tom, do you have any idea how* boring *you are when you try to be interesting? You haven't crawled under any big rocks yet, so I guess not.*

"Although these creatures appear intimidating," Darmin continued. "I assure you the habitats you'll be seeing are entirely self-contained. Each habitat is a perfect replica of the exhibits' natural environment, with the viewing ports disguised using holograms as normal features of the landscape. They won't even know you're there!"

~ * ~

Through the door, a small lift took them up into the wolf monkey enclosure. Rather, a small viewing point disguised, as Darmin had said, as a large rock inside the enclosure.

At first, Amanda thought there'd been a mistake. How could a *viewing port* be so dark?

She glanced around, blinking, and as her eyes adjusted to the almost non-existent light, Darmin's voice reached her in the gloom.

"All the view ports are kept darker than the enclosure, for ease of viewing," they explained. "In this case, that is very dark indeed. The atmosphere of the wolf monkeys' planet reflects almost all visible light, meaning…"

"...They live in near-total darkness," Amanda finished.

She stepped closer to the thin film of energy between her and instant death. As she started to pick out details, she realised with a start she'd been watching a tribe (troop? Pack?) of *aliens* without realising.

They had six legs arranged around a central torso with a face protruding from the centre, a face that seemed to be mainly teeth and jaws. It wasn't hard to imagine how human scientists had seen that face and immediately thought "wolf." Watching the nimble way those six legs propelled them around the stone spires of their enclosure, the "monkey" part was no mystery either.

"Amazing," she breathed.

Darmin's electronic tones drifted over her as she peered into the gloom. She took in the complex hierarchical structure as she tracked movement, trying to match the pack's roles to the individuals.

"Oh, is that their cub?" She pointed to a smaller figure near the centre, clinging to the rock.

"That's correct!" Darmin somehow managed to sound pleased. "The youngest pack member is currently pre-adolescent. However, one of the adults is soon due to deliver their own cub. When that happens, this cub..."

Tom followed Darmin as they pointed out the pregnant wolf spider and explained how the new addition would impact the current youngest's role, but Amanda was distracted. Something was clutched in the cub's claws, with surprising delicacy. Something spindly, with six spokes radiating from a central...

"It's a *doll!*" she gasped. But it came out as a shriek, and as the others turned to stare at her she pointed.

"The cub," she stammered. "The cub, it, uh...it's playing with a doll. So, uh, one of the adults made a doll and gave it to their kid, or the kid made a doll, and, well...is that normal?"

Even in the gloom, she saw Tom's eye roll.

"It's not uncommon," Darmin said.

And they continued their talk. Amanda tried to pay attention, but that wolf-monkey child and its doll gave her the chills.

~ * ~

"What was all *that* about?"

Amanda raised her eyebrows at Tom as they followed Darmin

down a corridor. "Excuse me?"

"All that back there. Freaking out over a doll made of sticks. What was *that* about?"

"You didn't think that was odd?" she challenged. "A being making a facsimile of itself for their kid to play with…that doesn't seem, I don't know, sort of oddly sapient behaviour to you? I mean, *we* do that. Animals don't."

"Dogs play with sticks, Amanda. You don't get all spooked over that."

"Dogs don't tie bundles of sticks into pretend dogs and give them to their puppies, Tom."

"Well, no. No opposable thumbs, for one thing."

"Be serious!" she snapped. "I just…didn't expect to see that kind of behaviour from an animal in a zoo. Surprised me a little, that's all."

He smiled at her, one of his humouring smiles.

"Oh, just forget it," she snapped.

"So, is this human 'bantering' behaviour?" Darmin asked. "Where you exercise your bond with verbal sparring and pretend to argue?"

"Uh…yeah, sure," Tom said. "Bantering. That's it."

"So fascinating!" Darmin's hand-analogues fluttered. "Many species engage in some form of ritual combat in their mating behaviour, but it's always interesting to observe!"

"I imagine you've seen plenty of couples interact this past week," Amanda observed. "It's mostly couples coming in, right?"

"Yes, mostly." Darmin rustled their exoskeleton irritably. "But sadly, a fair number of ticket holders have brought friends or relatives as their guests, rather than mating partners. Most unfortunate."

"What?" Amanda asked. "You mean, like that guy who brought his mum? I thought that was sweet."

"Yes. Sweet. Appealing." Another exoskeletal rustle. "But not really *useful*."

Amanda blinked. "What do you mean, 'useful'?"

"So," Tom said loudly. "What about this next exhibit, huh?"

"Just along here," Darmin said. "By the way, would it be alright if I let you both enjoy it without me for a few minutes?"

They patted the small gas cylinder grafted to their side. "I won't be long."

Although Earth air wasn't toxic to the k'Bleeki, it was lacking in certain compounds their species needed to survive. Amanda had seen a documentary comparing it to a human breathing pure nitrogen; the nitrogen itself was harmless, but the lack of oxygen would kill within moments. Therefore, k'Bleeki who interacted with humans did so in Earth or Earth-like air, but were fed intravenously by a cylinder containing those compounds.

"Oh," Tom said. "Yeah, sure!"

"Yeah," Amanda said flatly. "We'll be just fine."

~ * ~

Amanda was in one of her snits.

"That was weird, right?" she asked. "With Darmin?"

"You're seriously thinking about the tour guide right now?"

The creatures that darted around the viewpoint were not fish. *Acraspeda noctiluca exo* were closest to a cross between a jellyfish and a squid, each a little bigger than his pinkie. Hailing from an ocean planet with no natural predators, they had evolved with no need for camouflage and nothing to fear from even the most elaborate bioluminescent displays. Thousands of tiny forms darted around them in formations of astounding complexity, blazing with every colour imaginable. It was dazzlingly, beguilingly beautiful, utterly transcendent.

And *still*, Amanda wasn't happy.

God, he wished Chrissy had said yes.

"Tom, I'm not kidding." She looked around, checking that Darmin was still changing their cylinder. "Did you notice how they were over people bringing friends and family? Why would that bother them?"

"They want to learn about regular humans," he recited irritably.

"Then shouldn't they be just as interested in observing family and social bonds? Aren't those just as significant as romantic ones? Why get annoyed some people didn't bring their partner? And what did they mean by, 'not useful'?"

"Maybe their thesis is on pair bonds. What's it matter?"

Better question: why hadn't *he* been one of the lottery winners to annoy Darmin by bringing someone other than their bae?

Tom and Amanda…since their second year of University they'd been a single unit, Tom-and-Amanda as if they were one being, just like their friends Jake-and-Chrissy. But last month Jake-and-Chrissy had become simply Jake and Chrissy, while Tom-and-Amanda… Tom and Amanda…

When Tom had won this once-in-a-lifetime ticket, his mind had gone straight to Chrissy. That was how Tom-and-Amanda were doing.

They'd always had vibes, unspoken. Tom-and-Amanda could just as easily have been Tom-and-Chrissy; they both knew it. There'd always been that understanding between them. Or so he'd thought, until he'd told Chrissy about the tickets and invited her along.

"Tom, did you think I broke up with Jake to be with you?" she'd asked, her expression turning flat, flat as her voice had been when, reading her answer in his face, she'd told him, "You are unbelievable."

And then she'd just left.

He'd waited a couple of days, in case she reconsidered, or told Amanda. When neither of those appeared to have happened, he figured he'd got away with it and invited Amanda along. What else was there to do?

Somehow he *knew* she'd manage to suck the fun out of a zoo full of aliens.

Even now, instead of marvelling, she peered out at the amazing display with a frown.

"This viewpoint just looks like a rock, right?" she asked. "No different to, say, that rock over there?"

"I guess." If he'd had the nerve to go to art college instead of listening to his parents, was there even a hope he'd be good enough to communicate the slightest bit of the wonder he was seeing? Probably not, but he could have spent a career trying.

"Then why are they only dancing around *this* rock? Why not that one, or that one?"

Tom looked, and saw she was right; the creatures were ignoring the other rocks looming in the ocean, focusing their display on the one rock that was secretly a viewer.

"That's not a coincidence," Amanda said. "They know we're here. They must."

"Darmin said they can't," he replied. "They're the expert."

But he lacked conviction. They were so clearly being flocked, the display growing ever brighter and more intricate as he watched.

"Maybe the forcefield buzzes, and they can feel it through the water?" Amanda murmured, staring raptly at the not-fish. "Or emits a wavelength they can see, or maybe they have senses the k'Bleeki didn't know to account for…"

Of course, Tom thought. Now *she's interested; when there's a chance to show off.*

"All done!" Darmin appeared in the viewport with them, patting their fresh cylinder. "So much better! I appreciate your patience. How are you enjoying the *Acraspeda noctiluca exo?*"

"They're amazing!" Tom gushed.

"Oh, they've stopped!" Amanda said. "No, wait, they've just spread out. They were right up by the forcefield a moment ago."

"Magnificent, aren't they?" Darmin drifted closer. "We've recorded over twelve thousand distinct patterns, even allowing for varying numbers of individuals within the shoal."

"Is this how they communicate?" Amanda asked.

Darmin flushed lilac with pleasure. "Yes, it is, well done! Right now, they're sharing facts about their environment with each other."

"Wonder what they were saying a moment ago?" Amanda mused.

"What do you mean?"

"Just that, right before you came in, they were doing a much brighter, more complex formation. I just wondered why."

Tom rolled his eyes. *Watches a few nature documentaries, thinks she's David Attenborough. At least I know I'm not an artist.*

For the thousandth time, he wished Chrissy had said yes.

Or that—having been turned down by Chrissy—he'd left Amanda, and invited Jake instead.

~ * ~

The *Acraspeda noctiluca exo* had been breathtaking, but Tom had ruined it as usual, rolling his eyes every time she'd dared show a moment of curiosity. And it hadn't stopped, all evening. He'd *snorted* when she asked Darmin a question about the *Formicidae cuniculus exo*'s burrowing habits, annoying her so badly she hadn't even registered the answer. So, she hadn't had the maths grades to take the A Levels she needed for the Zoology degree she wanted; did that mean she wasn't allowed to show an interest? In anything, ever?

Can I be a little bit curious about the aliens, please?

The truth was, the aura of negativity that hung around Tom like a dark cloud became more exhausting every day she had to deal with it. She hadn't started going to the gym after work for her health at all; it had been to delay the moment she had to go home to that energy drain.

And if he thought she didn't *know* it had been three days between his winning the lottery, and inviting her, then he was in for a *big* shock. A mathematician she wasn't, but she knew those tickets came a week in advance and she could count on her fingers just fine, thanks.

Was it stupid, that deep down she'd hoped this once-in-a-lifetime trip would be some kind of second wind for them? Maybe, maybe not, but it hadn't taken her long to realise her mistake. Right around the time he'd *tsked* at her for asking about the life cycle of the *Chiroptera pterodactylus exo* the conviction had taken hold; this was the final stop for Tom-and-Amanda.

Tomorrow morning, she'd invite him out for brunch, somewhere nice and public where he wouldn't make a scene, and end it. Instead of a second wind, tonight would be a sendoff.

Perhaps it was a little heartless, dumping Tom right after what should have been the date of a lifetime, but Amanda knew she was making the right choice as she felt her footsteps lighten on the alien flooring. What would she do once she'd cut out the deadwood? The usual things people did, she supposed, like try a new hairstyle and change her wardrobe, but what else? She didn't feel like seeking out another relationship, because it felt like she'd *always* been in relationships, so maybe it was time to try being single.

Amanda was roused from her thoughts as they passed another tour group; the young woman and her sister they'd seen in the Atrium. The humans waved at each other and made excited faces while the k'Bleeki made a series of odd gestures, and then the two groups passed each other and disappeared from view.

Darmin's speaker made a noise halfway between a sigh and a *tsk*. "What a waste."

"What do you mean?" Amanda asked. Darmin didn't answer. "Really? She brings her sister on the trip of a lifetime, and…what, you're annoyed? Why?"

"Leave it, Amanda," Tom murmured.

"I merely wonder," Darmin said. "Why so many brought family members or friends rather than their mate. Out of nearly a thousand per night over the last week, almost twenty percent. It is not a *problem* per se, but given what we know about human behaviour, that seems odd."

"Maybe she doesn't have a...mate," Tom suggested.

"No, she must," Darmin answered. "All the lottery winners were in a long-term, opposite-sex relationship."

"Maybe they've broken up," Amanda suggested.

Darmin stopped and stared at her.

"Broken up?" they asked. "As in...ended their pairing? Is that something humans do? We thought you were monogamous!"

"I mean, like...officially?" Tom said. "But not everyone wants that."

"And even those who do," Amanda said. "Well...sometimes it's hard. Finding the right person. There's some trial and error involved."

Unwillingly, she found her gaze straying to Tom until their eyes met.

"And even when you *think* you've found that person," Tom said slowly. "Time goes by and you realise you don't work anymore."

"You don't fit," Amanda elaborated. The softness of her voice caught her by surprise. "There's nothing wrong with you and there's nothing wrong with them, but *together* you're really, really wrong."

"Maybe you were fine together once," Tom continued. "But since then you've grown up, and...you've grown apart."

"You've outgrown each other," Amanda agreed.

There was a silence as they regarded each other.

"And when that happens," Amanda said, slowly. "There's only one thing you can do. If you both want to be happy."

"You have to let each other go." Tom's voice was almost a whisper.

"Exactly."

Amanda blinked, not breaking eye contact. Her eyes felt unexpectedly heavy.

"Really?" Darmin's speaker somehow sounded chipper. "That is fascinating information! Plenty to unpack there. That is *exactly* the kind of insight we invited ordinary people along to share! In our experience, no matter what species you're dealing with, the leaders and the scientists would never think to explain such a facet of every-day life, but that's exactly the kind of thing we want to learn!"

Amanda felt herself smile.

"And, may I say, the two of you communicate it so well! It's fascinating to observe how attuned you are to each other."

"Yeah," Amanda said. "I guess we are."

"Well! Shall we continue the tour?"

"Good idea." Tom held out his hand. "Let's finish this."

Amanda took his hand. "On a high note."

~ * ~

It *was* a high note. He wasn't sure when it had happened, but Tom had forgotten what it was like to feel peaceful in Amanda's company. But since the talk with Darmin, it seemed they'd both relaxed. Amanda no longer seemed interested in finding fault with every wonderful thing they saw, and he no longer seemed to mind her endless questions, now that they'd cleared the air.

Now that they'd let go.

Tomorrow, he figured, they'd part ways. They hadn't really dis-cussed the details, but he knew Jake was looking for a flatmate...

He pulled out his phone to send Jake a quick text, only to remember there was no reception in space.

"Woah!" He held the phone out to Amanda. "It's nearly midnight!"

"Really?" She leaned over to look. "Wow! We've been here nearly three and a half hours."

She turned to Darmin. "Aww! We must be near the end of the tour."

Darmin's peach colours tinged at the edges with verdigris.

"We *are*! In fact, the *Plasmonis coronii exo* were, technically, the last stop on your tour. However, since you've been such pleasing guests and I've had such a wonderful time showing you our exhibits, I wonder if you'd be interested in seeing one last, rather *special* habi-tat that's not on the official tour?"

"Backstage pass?" Amanda said. "Yes please!"

"I'm game," Tom said. He hadn't noticed how tired he was, but since he'd seen the time he felt a little punch-drunk. But what was he going to do? Turn down an extra, so he could go home and sleep a little sooner? "What's special about this one?"

"It's a new exhibit," Darmin explained. "In fact, it's so new it's not really open to the public yet, and the viewing port isn't even finished. You'll be going into the enclosure itself!"

"Really?" Tom gaped. "Is that safe?"

"Perfectly!"

"Are you sure?" Amanda looked worried. "We won't contaminate their environment or anything, will we?"

"Of course not!" The pale green tinges at the edges of Darmin's chitinous armour deepened. "The safety of our exhibits and our guests is our overriding concern. Don't worry, I'm not breaking any rules. We guides have been given leave to show this particular exhibit to our guests, at our own discretion."

They gestured to a section of blank white wall, which opened. The enclosure beyond was dimly lit, gloomy in contrast to the bright corridor.

"We would love to know what you think," Darmin said, gesturing them inside.

They stepped through, moving into the space as their eyes began adjusting.

"Where are the exhibits?" Amanda whispered to Tom, who shrugged.

At the far end was a large rectangle of light, and they made their way towards that, shuffling carefully around objects that loomed at them in the semidarkness. Under their feet, the texture of the flooring changed.

"Wait a second." Amanda crouched, running her hand along the floor. "This is tile. But back here, this is carpet."

Tom passed her, realising as he did the change in flooring coincided with an archway the approximate size of double doors. He crossed over to the light source, pressing his hands to the glass and looking out.

"Tom!" Amanda leapt to her feet.

Ignoring her, Tom peered out through what he realised were French doors—locked, he found. He looked out over a grassy area with picnic benches and a basketball hoop, but before he could wonder about that a movement caught his eye.

Across the grass from him was another French door, and inside was a girl his own age, hammering on the glass with both fists. Seeing Tom, she waved both arms above her head, mouth working as she shouted something he couldn't hear. A boy appeared next to her, making frantic shoving gestures as he shouted along with the girl. They were shouting the same thing, one syllable over and over, and it took Tom a second to realise what it was.

RUN!

"TOM!" Amanda screamed from behind him. "Tom, *the door's gone!*"

He whipped around, just in time to see Amanda sprinting into the first room. Tom tried to follow, but crashed into a wooden structure that skidded along the tile floor with a groan. Extricating himself from what he realised was a kitchen table, he hurried after Amanda, who stood at the opposite wall, slapping and banging her fists on the blank space where the exit had been.

"NO!" she screamed. "No, you can't do this! No, no, *no!*"

The room lit up as Tom entered, revealing a living room. He now clearly saw the objects they'd dodged around were armchairs and a coffee table, and two closed doors to his right presumably led to a bedroom and a bathroom. As he watched, patches lit up on the blank wall, becoming windows appearing to look out over a meadow that couldn't possibly be there.

Amanda turned to him, her face blotchy and red.

"We're the exhibits," she told him blankly. "It's us."

He stared at her.

"We can't be," he said. "That wouldn't be allowed. No, our governments would…"

"They'd do what, Tom?" she asked him softly. "We're in *orbit*."

He gaped, mouth working as he tried to find the holes in her logic.

"They're probably in on it," she added, blanching as if working it out even as she said it. "The technology that saved the planet. We kept asking what they wanted in exchange. It was *this*. More exhibits for their zoo. They'll have deniability, I guess, claim the k'Bleeki tricked them, but come on; they made a deal. A few thousand humans, to save the rest."

A chime sounded throughout the space Tom began to realise looked very much like a high-end apartment.

"On behalf of the k'Bleeki Zoological Committee, welcome to our new 'Homo sapiens sol' attraction." The voice was k'Bleeki, although not Darmin's. "We hope you enjoy your new habitat.

Socialisation with other pairs will soon be possible. In four hours, communal areas will become accessible as the station leaves the Sol system. In the meantime, please feel free to explore your enclosure. We look forward to having you as part of our family aboard the Menagerie of the Milky Way!"

Amanda sagged against the wall, sliding down to the floor.

"That's why they wanted couples," she said. "Darmin was annoyed when people brought their mother or sister, because that's not what they wanted. They wanted romantic partners. *Breeding pairs.*"

Her head dropped onto her knees.

Tom stood mutely in the archway between the kitchen and the living room, gaping around the space that was to be their new home.

He wondered where the viewing port was.

~ * ~ * ~

Harriet's brain does odd things, and sometimes she's able to write them down in a way that other people find entertaining. This is lucky, because she's wanted to be a writer since she was old enough to understand books are written by people.

Being a massive nerd, Harriet mainly writes science fiction, fantasy, and speculative fiction. She's been described as "a nice person, but with a sinister streak," a description that makes her immensely proud. On occasion, however, a story will slip through that is both wholesome and pleasant, to her surprise and alarm.

She studied Creative Writing and English at Aberystwyth University. She now lives in Wiltshire, where she reads a lot, bakes, works on her allotment, and watches entirely too much TV. Deep Space Nine is her favourite Star Trek, which should tell you all you need to know.

Harriet's short fiction has appeared in numerous odd little places, including *The Screw Turn Flash Fiction Competition 2020*, *Terrors from the Toy Box* and in *Swindon Writing*. She's also appeared in previous WolfSinger anthologies *Never Cheat a Witch* and *Space Brides, LLC.*

In spring 2023, she began the journey to seek a diagnosis of autism. In 2024, she finally got around to asking about Inattentive ADHD as well. Find her at harrietphoenix.com.

Dark Mist

Robert Miller

As the giant cage filled with a dark swirling mist was brought forth, the Ring Master approached with exaggerated caution, seeking to draw the beast inside into revealing itself. When her fingers were only a few inches from the heavily reinforced bars, the mist darkened into a solid form and she jerked her hand away as the creature behind the bars snarled in hunger. The bars were strong, but some risks were not worth taking even for her show.

"Long ago, millennia before any of you present tonight were born, on the plains of Ebenen, a world of endless night, the nebel preyed on the people who roamed on the plains. The lone predator would turn into a mist, pass over the herds of livestock, and descend upon the sentries who stood guard outside the tents. As you saw it would solidify and then…"

With the audience hanging onto her last word, the Ring Master quietly triggered a small electric prod in the cage, and while the device was small enough not to be seen by anyone, it still packed quite a punch. The nebel howled, the hunting howl that spelled doom for so many on the world of its' birth. The audience members instinctively backed up, their survival instincts telling them to get away from the unfamiliar alien predator.

"Then the sentries would be devoured, leaving only their weapons and footprints as proof they had been there. The pattern continued for centuries, with no one ever having harmed much less slain the dread beast. That is until one of the young warriors assigned as a sentry managed to survive the onslaught of the nebel both alive and with all of his limbs attached."

As the lights dimmed, the nebel became more visible as the mist finished coalescing. It was roughly spherical in shape, looking like a sea urchin the size of a hover transport. Instead of spines, there were hundreds of heavily muscled limbs ending in grasping paws with curved claws pulsing with ultraviolet light. There were no eyes, unsurprising for a creature evolved on a planet of endless night, but there was no mouth visible either.

"This young warrior swore to hunt down the monster that slaughtered the other warriors from his age group and left his clan to track down the beast. Immediately after he left, his family held his funeral, certain they would never see him again."

From one of the pockets of her coat, the Ring Master pulled out a piece of raw meat and threw it through the bars of the nebel's cage. The spherical monster split into two hemispheres, connected by strands of muscle at the apex of the sphere. Inside the sphere were tens of thousands of tiny stalactite like teeth that whirred as they rotated. The hemispheres fused back together as the mouth closed and the Ring Master approached closer to the cage, teasing the predator with the tantalizing prospect of more fresh meat.

"The young warrior followed the tracks of the nebel from where it had eaten his friends. The only weapon he carried was a stone axe, for his people had not yet learned how to work metal. While there were no sunrises or sunsets on Ebenen to track time as most of you are used to, the planet's rings would become briefly visible at regular intervals and could be used to count time."

The nebel growled in the cage then reverted back to mist, the dark foggy cloud moving in a gaseous approximation of pacing. Realizing when the beast turned back to mist rather than a pulsing mass of claws and muscled limbs she would lose the audience's attention, the Ring Master pulled something else from a pocket of her coat. The artifact had an unadorned handle of alien wood and a stone head so dark it appeared to absorb the light around the Ring Master. The edge was so sharp, that if the Ring Master had wished, she could have used it to shave some of the other creatures in the menagerie.

"I hold in my hands here, recently unearthed by archaeologists, the very axe used to slay the first nebel to die by human hands on Ebenen. Even after all these millennia, it is still as sharp as the night it was made."

Several of the audience members gasped in awe at the ancient artifact. The Ring Master twirled the axe in her hands before holding it up for the audience to see more clearly. When she held the axe up high above her head with both hands, the nebel snarled and solidified again. The grasping claws strained against the bars. Something about the stone seemed to drive the predator mad.

"After the young warrior had spent several rings tracking the nebel that had eaten his friends, he finally found the nebel's burrow. He stood at the entrance, waiting for the nebel to emerge. Fighting a monster made of mist in a tight burrow would be suicidal. He waited for days until the predator emerged to hunt. As the predator emerged, or so the stories of the tribes of Ebenen say, a great meteor shower began and the sky was lit up for the first time in the planet's history. The nebel and warrior alike were both blinded."

While the axe was still held above the Ring Master's head, one of her assistants who was perched above the audience pointed a special light at the axe head. The light was meant to mimic the color and intensity of a meteor shower and reflected off the stone in an almost blinding flash, even though every other kind of light was absorbed by the rock. The nebel shrieked, a cry of not just anger but pain tinged with fear. Something about the reflected light was terrifying for the apex predator of the night planet in a way the mere stage lights of the menagerie simply weren't.

"The stone and the light from the meteors reacted to weaken the nebel. The more cynical may attribute this to simple blind luck, but the tribes of Ebenen say it was fate the young warrior weakened the nebel. The light from the meteor shower forced the creature to stay solid. And with his foe now solidified the young warrior charged."

The Ring Master brought the axe down in a dramatic slash, her assistant directing the light so it continued to reflect off the axe. The nebel howled as the light shining from a different angle struck its' limbs that had previously been shielded.

"The fight lasted for almost as long as the journey to track the nebel had. The howls of the nebel and shouted oaths of the young warrior were so loud the tribe who lived at the mouth of the valley sent their stealthiest hunters to determine what was happening. None of them had ever heard the predator that had hunted them for generations roar in fear. The cynics among the tribe said an even worse monster was displacing the nebel while the more optimistic thought someone would finally end the terror they had lived in for generations."

The assistant shut the light off and the stone of the axe head returned to its' naturally dark state, again seeming to absorb all of the light around it.

"Eventually, the young warrior triumphed. While the fight had been long and arduous, he was still standing afterwards and his foe was not. He had slain the dread beast that had hunted his tribe for centuries. He had proven that which was deemed invincible could be slain. While his name has been lost over the millennia since that great hunt, the tribes of Ebenen still tell his story every year. The story of the greatest hunt on the darkest world."

~ * ~ * ~

Robert Miller is an until recently aspiring author who has begun to publish fantasy and science fiction short stories with Raconteur Press, Three Ravens Publishing, and WolfSinger Publications. He lives in Davis County Utah.

Neolithic Park

Chris Clemens

The juvenile stegosauruses roaming the Visitor's Center sneered at the life-sized dioramas depicting how humans had once lived: sitting in circles, rutting, devouring squirrels.

"Look how puny they were!" Akatos gloated, pretending to sit on the humping skeletons. But the juveniles—some of them closer to hatchlings, really—hadn't come all the way to Isla Anthropocene for bones. Many years ago, sequenceable human DNA had been recovered from ancient, amber-trapped mosquitos; successfully incubated. For the first time in history, an extinct species was back.

"What a waste of dino-science."

"Wait and see, Akatos," the Director said indulgently. "Wait and see." The esteemed stegosaurus adjusted his gold-rimmed glasses with a loud snuffle before resuming the tour. "Next display, please. From our excavations, we always assumed humans were covered in feathery scales, but look: out they popped, smooth as eggs!"

"Ew!" The hatchlings wriggled.

"They even grew disgusting tufts of fur. A real surprise, and a delight as well."

"Gross!"

The Director smiled. "They aren't much to look at, it's true. But they're interesting. Very interesting little shrimpkins."

"But these are just pictures. Where are the real humans, uncle? When can we see them?"

"Soon enough, impatient ones. They're out in the preserves, still getting used to everything. The park is still under construction."

"Wasn't it supposed to be finished already?" Akatos asked.

The Director scowled, but only for an instant. The mid-day sun was pouring through the enormous windows of the Visitor's Center, and his theme park sprawled across the lush valley in a panorama of ambition. Lumbering work crews dug ponds, packed walkways, and reinforced enclosure walls. Teams of long-necked sauropods slowly hauled pieces of the great stadium into place. The lazy river through the center of the island was almost complete, and the constant status requests from the investment group were needlessly panicky. Neolithic Park would open in early summer, as planned.

"Uncle?"

Of course, dragging his older brother's brats and their overprivileged friends around the half-finished park wasn't part of that plan, but sometimes family was more important than work. Particularly rich family, of the investor variety.

"Hel-lo?"

"The park is essentially finished, Akatos; now hush. I can see we've spent enough time enjoying the displays. Down the ramp, children. Don't touch that. We'll need to take a roundabout path to the enclosures, but we can visit our Chief Executive Anthropologist along the way, I suppose."

"That sounds boring."

"Yes," the Director sighed. "It certainly does."

~ * ~

"...And that's why human mothers don't use eggs." The C.E.A., an elderly pterodactyl, concluded her lecture with a brisk nod to the juveniles, dozing in their seats.

"Gross!" Akatos, of course, had remained awake to ask annoying questions.

"Indeed. A matter of biology, yes, but a social fractalization as well."

The group was in the Hatchery auditorium, with a painted ceiling of enormous, grotesque human babies stretched across its expanse: babies smiling, crying, toddling, holding hands, babies soaring across the blue sky on incandescent white wings—which, the yawning group had learned, was a fascinating topic of dino-scholarly debate, as fragments of painted imagery depicted flying infants, while no human remains with wings had yet been unearthed. The park's humans hadn't sprouted wings thus far, but the Director remained optimistic.

"Boooooring." As expected, the nephews were uninterested by the Hatchery's impressive incubation chambers, tall vats of nutrients, cool, nurturing caves, and grassy training grounds where the first generation of babies had grown up in secret together, learning to be human again in a strange new world. Akatos might mock their crude finger paintings, proudly framed in the reception gallery, but those paintings would soon fetch millions each–billions, perhaps—when the novelty of owning mammal-created art was offered to influential collectors. Once the park opened, the Hatchery would become a hallowed place of resurrection, of stewardship, of history, of wealth creation.

With his fiduciary duties back on the mainland, the Director rarely found reason to visit the island, but each member of the executive team had sponsored a baby, of course. He'd selected a beige-colored female with a fluffy crown of black hair, and named her Lumpy, after a particularly loved-but-not-forgotten house iguana from childhood. He had hoped to meet Lumpy here—the progress reports ambiguously described her as "creatively challenging" and "a natural leader to watch for" —but her group had already been released into the preserves. So many moving parts! So much to keep track of, so much work, effort, and capital!

The rousing juveniles didn't appreciate any of it, of course. "So where are they? The real ones, not those weird sleeping pod babies."

"Yeah! We want to see the real humans *now!*"

The Chief Executive Anthropologist cleared her avian throat. "Actually, I'd like to once again raise my concerns. We are prematurely releasing the first generation of subjects. The walls—"

"I know all about the walls," the Director interrupted. "I'm assured we're working overtime to address your issues with the walls."

"The walls are the least of our problems. Are you aware Group Two has disappeared into the eastern forest? We have no way of knowing what they're up to."

"We have a robust flying squirrel surveillance network, which, once in place—"

"But it *isn't* in place yet, is it?"

"Isn't it?" echoed Akatos, who was watching the exchange with interest.

"Hush, Akatos. It's practically finished. We'll locate our shrimp-kins, don't you worry."

The C.E.A. flapped her leathery wings. "Oh, wake up, Director! We're rushing, cutting corners, and it's clear we don't understand the situation, don't understand them. Why would they just vanish, all together? Why would—"

That was enough for the Director. "Thank you very much for

sharing your wisdom with us today, Chief Executive Anthropologist. It has certainly been…interesting…to hear your perspective. I look forward to your performance review.

"Now," he turned grandly, "Who's ready to see some humans?"

~ * ~

The group strolled down a manicured dirt path flanked by spiky ferns and broad emerald leaves. It was a gorgeous sunny late afternoon. As they descended into the valley, the path became rougher, and shadows crept in overhead with the tree canopy. The Director guided the younger hatchlings away from steep embankments, but he was running out of human stories to distract them with.

"Let's see…oh yes. The groundskeepers were telling me the other week about a funny furry red one who wasted his whole morning bashing one rock into another."

"Maybe he came out wrong? I can't wait to see him!"

"Are we close, uncle?"

"I'm tired of walking."

"I think I stepped in human poop."

The Director almost sighed, but caught himself. "Almost there! The viewing platform is just up ahead. You can see it up through the trees: look. It'll be much nicer, of course."

At the base of the earthen ramps they met a grizzled raptor.

The Director beamed. "Ah, a welcome surprise! Here's our game warden. And how are our wild friends today, Mr. Raptoroon?"

The raptor's tan hat and utility vest did little to conceal the scars criss-crossing his muscular, diminutive body. "Vicious," he scoffed, snapping his razor teeth. "Clever. Aggressive. It was a mistake to ever bring them back from extinction."

The Director was taken aback. "I…see. Well, we were just hoping to have a quick peek, if you don't mind pointing us in the right direction."

"You'll point yourself straight home if you know what's good for you. I can't guarantee your safety out here, not anymore. I can't even guarantee *my* team's safety."

"Come now, Mr. Raptoroon. I don't think it's so bad as all that. Humans are very interesting creatures, as we were just discussing."

"Interesting? Tell that to Gary! Three of the little monsters waited until he was alone yesterday, hit him with a swinging stick contraption they rigged up. Gouged his eye right out!"

At this the hatchlings shrank into a terrified huddle, and the Director wrapped them in his comforting tail. "I'm sure that was an unfortunate accident. They're clumsy, experimenting—"

"Oh, they're experimenting, all right. They're dangerous, I tell you! That stick thing—they sharpened it on purpose. They're using *tools*. I know you can't understand what that means, back in your fancy office in Saurus City, but these aren't the funny apes you dreamed of. They're changing, learning, and faster than we ever imagined."

"They're certainly about to change our fortunes. Now, if you'll excuse us—"

"They're digging under the walls day and night! We filled three tunnels this morning alone. I've already asked for more resources twice, and nothing."

"We expected growing pains as we continue to adapt to their unique needs and requirements. We'll sink the footings deeper. Engage our humans elsewhere. Provide more fulfilling distractions."

"Provide distractions! We need to purge them all, start again. Gobble them up while we still have the chance."

"Mr. Raptoroon! We certainly won't be eating our investments. You'll have to wait until the restaurants open next year."

"Suit yourself," the game warden snarled. "But don't say I didn't warn you." He turned and skulked away up the path.

"My!" the Director said, shaking his armored head, and adjusting his glasses. "What a temper." He tried his best to sound confident. "I *am* getting hungry, though, aren't you? Akatos? A quick climb, a quick peek, and then dinner."

~ * ~

As the small group plodded despondently onto the platform terrace high above the treeline, a brilliant orange sunset was unfurling beyond Isla Anthropocene's volcanic peak.

Huffing and puffing, the Director surveyed the breathtaking vista with satisfaction. Soon tourists would be arriving on daily Dactyl Air flights, soaring above dozens of giant turtle cruises docking at the island's bustling port. Denizens of the sea swimming up for a nice day with the family, lodging overnight if they'd traveled from colder climes. Hotels, excursions, hunting preserves for political elites…the profit potential of Neolithic Park was immense.

"Where are the humans? I want to seeee."

The aging stegosaurus scanned the horizon; surely their trek hadn't been for nothing. "Yes, yes. Stay together, please. Don't fall over the edge. Oh!" Not far from the foothills beneath the volcano, several diminutive figures crouched by the eastern woods. "There— look. Three big ones, out by the treeline."

"Where? It's too bright!"

"There!"

"I can't see! What are they doing?"

The Director's reptilian eyes narrowed to slits. What *were* they doing? Certainly not playing and singing and performing. Was this furtive sneakiness their true nature? Certainly the observation decks would need to be rethought, the squirrel network prioritized. But it was madness to purge the entire lot, waste years of potential, just because of a few minor snags.

"I can't see! They're so boring! Stupid!"

"Make them dance for us, uncle!"

The director ignored his kin, focused on the humans, trying to understand. After creeping along through the tall grasses, the slender creatures had settled around a tall tree. With startling coordination, the humans at once attacked the trunk with a great thwacking sound that echoed throughout the valley. The rhythm reminded the Director of recordings he'd listened to, again and again, of the haunting music they'd supposedly drummed on their water troughs at night. Thwack, thwack, thwack. But the beatific smile froze on his face as he squinted, blinked, saw the sharpened stones lashed to each branch, and perceived the damage done.

Thwack, thwack, thwack, and the tree began to list, lean, topple.

Akatos appeared beside him. "Are they pulling down that tree to eat?"

"I don't think humans eat—"

"Well, I still think they're stupid."

"Quiet!" the Director roared, his patience finally depleted. He was startled when one of the humans roared back.

She stood straight and proud, a familiar beige-colored female with wild, dark hair, staring up at them, uttering a high, bestial scream that carried and resonated and soared; a challenge, a threat.

The other humans began to sharpen one end of the trunk with their stones.

"It's fine," the Director told his nephews, not quite knowing why. "It'll be fine. Dinosaurs will pay for interesting things. We're going to make an absolute fortune." He grinned reassuringly, squinting into the sunset as they watched Lumpy join her companions at the fallen tree.

In the cooling evening air he almost imagined he could see, rising from deep in the forest, a thin wisp of smoke.

~ * ~ * ~

Chris Clemens lives and teaches in Toronto, surrounded by raccoons. Nominated for Best Microfiction and Best Small Fictions, his writing appears in *The Dribble Drabble Review*, *JAKE*, *Dreams & Nightmares*, *Apex Magazine*, and elsewhere.

Your Own Risk

Caitlin Barbera

Warning! This tent contains an extremely dangerous creature. Enter at your own risk, and whatever you do, do not step off the path.

Mellie stared at the sign; her eyes narrowed. The attendants at the tent flap, three faceless silver automatons with articulated limbs, stared back at her. She was the only patron of the menagerie who seemed inclined to enter this particular tent.

But isn't this what she'd come to the menagerie for? She'd wanted to prove her courage, test her nerve against the strangest creatures from the most dangerous dimensions. This tent was exactly what she'd come here to find.

She took another step toward the entrance to the tent, the heavy canvas flaps hanging closed, letting only a slight hint of light out beneath. She looked at the attendants, wondering if they would stop her, say anything to her, try to talk her out of it. They didn't move except to turn their faceless heads to follow her steps.

She took a deep breath and pushed open one of the tent flaps, stepping into the dim interior. The top of the tent was lined with little hanging bulbs illuminating the carpeted path down the center but they did little to chase the shadows away from the corners. One of those corners contained an enormous cage, with a hulking shape crouched at the back, away from the light. Mellie felt her heart pounding with anticipation as she stepped closer to the cage.

She could see a glitter where the low light reflected off dark feathers that seemed to swirl from black to blue to red. There was a slight movement from the creature within, like the flutter of a songbird's wings scaled up to something enormous. Mellie took another step, so her feet were just at the edge of the path, and found she was so close she could reach out and touch the bars. She lifted her hand, inching it closer and closer.

"Be careful," someone hissed from deeper in the tent, and Mellie was so startled she drew her hand back quickly. An instant later, the thing at the back of the cage moved faster than she would have thought possible, launching itself at the bars that separated it from her.

With a cry, Mellie leaped backward and only barely kept herself from falling on her ass. The thing in the cage crashed into the bars, which looked almost like metal except for the way they reflected absolutely none of the light from above. The beast's talons, each of which was as long as Mellie's forearm and tipped by a curved claw the length of her hand, curled around the bars, but the almost-metal didn't budge. It folded its enormous wings and turned its head to the side to regard Mellie balefully out of one huge eye. It was not golden, like the eyes of the birds of prey Mellie had seen; instead, it was pure black from eyelid to eyelid.

Its feathers changed colors with the changing angles of the light in a way that was dizzying, making Mellie think of the swirl of galaxies. Each feather was long and narrow coming to a sharp point. The feathers layered over one another from the creature's knees to the crown of its head, where they gave way to a bare face that looked unsettlingly humanlike, except for the wickedly curved black beak in the place of its nose and mouth. It even had mobile brows over its eyes. As she watched, it furrowed its brow like it was considering a mild irritant. It flapped its wings slightly again, sending a rush of air over Mellie's face that smelled like cordite and woodsmoke, then cocked its head, opened its beak, and made a low, raspy sound disturbingly similar to a human voice saying the word, "When."

"When what?" Mellie whispered, unable to look away from the thing's black eyes and the shifting colors of its feathers. It released the bars and settled to the floor of the cage, lifting one eyebrow.

"When," it croaked at her. "When."

"It won't say anything else," a voice said, bitterly. "I've been here long enough, I should know."

Mellie had been so caught up in staring at the huge bird she'd forgotten the whispered warning that had kept her from getting her arm shredded. She turned toward the voice and saw another cage, a much smaller one, tucked away in the back of the tent. She'd completely missed it.

"Who are you?" Mellie asked, watching the bird warily as she maneuvered around its cage and toward the smaller structure. There was something sitting in it, huddled in a heap on the floor. No, not something. Some*one*. The closer Mellie came to the cage, the more sickly certain she was it held a human being.

The person in the cage lifted her head, revealing a woman about Mellie's age, maybe even a little younger, with tangled hair, a tattered shirt and pants, and bare feet. "My name's Sarah," she said, her voice wobbling. "What's your name?"

"Mellie. What are you doing here? Why are you in a cage?"

Sarah shrugged. "I don't know. It's been…months. Maybe even years. Since they took me."

Mellie felt her stomach twist with sympathy. The poor girl. They were keeping her in this menagerie, to entertain patrons. Patrons just like Mellie. No, this couldn't be allowed to continue.

"When," the horrible bird croaked again, the word warbling and coming out a bit garbled. "Wwwwwhen."

"I have to get you out of here," Mellie said firmly, taking a step toward the cage.

"Are you sure?" Sarah asked in a hushed voice, darting her eyes down to the floor of the tent. When Mellie followed her look, she found she was at the end of the little carpeted path. There was no way to get closer to the cage without stepping off of it. The canvas floor of the tent looked very dark, as though the light barely touched it.

Mellie hesitated, her heart pounding. She had no idea what would happen to her if she ignored the sign's warning.

But, she told herself, after all, hadn't she come here to the menagerie for just this purpose? To prove her courage and test her nerve.

And really, what was the point of testing her nerve and proving her courage if she couldn't use them to be a hero? Perhaps that was what she had been looking for all along: a chance to prove she was something more than a daredevil.

Sarah's eyes were so wide and frightened. Mellie breathed in, then out, then stepped off the carpet and toward the cage.

Now that she was closer, Sarah's eyes were beautiful and dark and Mellie couldn't look away from them. She couldn't even draw a breath as she made her way to the cage, hand lifting automatically to reach out for the locked door. She would find a way to open it. She would find a way…

"When," the bird insisted behind her. Mellie ignored it. "When."

"Thank you," Sarah said, her voice so sweet and soft, her eyes huge and utterly, lightlessly, black. She reached a hand through the bars of the cage, toward Mellie, and Mellie reached back. She had to. "Oh, thank you Mellie. Thank you so much."

"When," that horrible bird said again, but it sounded different now. Now, it almost sounded like it was saying... "Run. Run."

Then her hand touched Sarah's, and everything went black.

~ * ~

When it was over, there was nothing but a pile of empty clothes for the attendants to clean up. The skin thief never left a mess when she ate a meal.

The attendants swept up the clothes, as the skin thief watched from her cage, whispering to herself in her new voice. "My name is Mellie," she whispered. "What's your name? Will you help me?"

She glanced up at the omen bird, which was watching her with a raised eyebrow, looking decidedly unimpressed. The skin thief grinned widely, and the bird huffed and looked away.

Beyond the tent, the menagerie bustled, and perhaps there was even someone else looking at the sign outside, preparing to enter at their own risk.

~ * ~ * ~

Caitlin Barbera is a lifelong lover of reading and writing science fiction and fantasy. Her first story was about a girl velociraptor going on an adventure and fighting androids. She is currently a student in the Genre Fiction concentration of the Graduate Program in Creative Writing at Western Colorado University. A native of Colorado, she currently lives in the Denver metro area with her spouse, child, and dog, and spends much of her time coming up with more story ideas than she could possibly write in a lifetime.

She can be found at caitlinbarberawrites.wordpress.com.

Overlords

Petina Strohmer

The captive creatures waited restlessly inside their cramped cages. Some sat quietly, accepting their lot in life. Others screeched, roared and bellowed, pacing the wire floors of their enclosures or biting at the bars. Bright red fins flashed, scaly blue wings stretched, and huge, serrated claws scraped against the metal.

"Pipe down," Jack, the circus assistant, muttered. "You know the drill."

They did. All of these weird and wonderful beings understood that they were expected to sing for their supper, to perform in front of a fee-paying audience in return for food. No display, no dinner. It was as simple as that.

"Excuse me," a voice called from the back.

The assistant rolled his eyes. Most of these creatures, collected from the four corners of the known universe, couldn't converse. However, the few that did, more than made up for the others.

"Is that you again, Gremlin?" Jack said with a sigh.

"You know very well that is not my name," came the reply.

"It is now."

The usual exchange.

"Listen to me, lowly assistant," the scratchy alien voice said.

"You will address me as sir," Jack instructed the creature.

"I will when you use *my* name properly."

From the circus ring, behind the thick red curtain, Jack could hear the clowns winding up their show. Only one more act before the collection of cosmic creatures took the limelight. Any insurrection from these extra-terrestrial animals would need to be squashed before the ringmaster introduced them to the public. If not, her assistant would go to bed hungry too.

He sighed and made his way between the cages. A small grey fleen from Tramox 5 was fanning and preening its technicolour plumage, ready to show it off to tonight's appreciative audience. A bristly quinx from Outer Zecland flashed all six sets of its scarlet fangs at Jack as he passed, while the pudgy manon from Albria Minor appeared to have fallen asleep while waiting for its turn.

"Oi!" Jack called, poking his taser stick through the bars. "Wake up, you stupid animal."

The manon jumped at the electric shock, turning its signature fluorescent green in surprise.

Finally, Jack made it through to the indignant creature at the back of the line. The fact this little deon from Spraxal, a particularly far-flung location, could talk to humans, made it something of a showstopper. It also made it a major pain in the arse.

"What do you want, Gremlin?" Jack snapped. "You're due on in a minute and the ringmaster won't want to wait."

The deon was unimpressed, though it kept all three of its large orange eyes on the taser stick. It had been on the receiving end of that thing more than once. "The ringmaster is a hard taskmaster," it said ruefully.

"You brought me all the way back here to tell something I already know?" Jack tapped the taser against his thigh.

"Not exactly." The deon shook its head. "The ringmaster is as hard on you as she is on us."

"So?"

"So, do you think that's fair?"

"Fair?" Jack snorted. "Is life on *your* planet always fair, Gremlin?"

"My name is Groxon, as you well know."

"Groxon, Gremlin, whatever. Life here on Earth is very definitely not fair. Never has been, never will be. Live with it, space boy."

"Why should you?" Groxon asked.

"What?"

"Live with the unfairness of being treated no better than a non-human 'brute.'" Groxon paused. "Unless, of course, your master sees you that way."

"I don't live like a dumb animal," Jack protested.

"Don't you?" The deon raised its three eyebrows. "You have to do exactly what you're told, when you are told to, otherwise you, too, are starved—and beaten."

Jack rubbed the scars on his arm uncomfortably. "At least I'm not kept in a cage."

"Not one you can see," Groxon replied.

Suddenly, the air was split by the screams of two dratwins, squaring up to each other. Each held its dozens of gigantic flippers wide and spat stinking black goo at its rival.

"Knock it off!" Jack shouted. "You lost your supper yesterday by starting that crap. You wanna go hungry again?"

The dratwins bared their purple teeth at him and each other, but at least they stopped screaming.

"They're very territorial," Groxon said. "If you house them so close together, what did you think was going to happen?"

Jack scowled. "And you're suddenly an expert, are you?"

"Hmmm. What I do know is; if you are going to keep a creature in captivity, you had better keep it content, to make sure it doesn't rebel against its master."

"Shut up, Gremlin." Jack snapped. "What do you know about anything, you stupid, stinking, space monkey."

"I might bear a passing resemblance to an earth monkey," Groxon said, stretching out its long, hairy arms and legs. "But I'm certainly not stupid. How much do you know of your own human history?"

"What's that got to do with anything?" Jack demanded.

"If you did," the deon said patiently, "you'd know that long before you started capturing space creatures and forcing them to perform for your amusement, wild, terrestrial animals were banned from Earth's circuses."

"So?"

"And before that, your society outlawed the practice of humans paying to see other humans suffering from mental illness. It was called "laughing at the loonies" in Bedlam."

Jack just shrugged.

"And a century or so before *that*, humans enslaving other humans based simply upon the colour of their skin, was prohibited."

Jack yawned loudly. "And your point is?"

"My point is these galactic circuses are a backward step in the evolution of your species, aren't they?"

Jack yawned again.

"How would you like it if it was done to you?" Graxon asked.

"But it isn't, is it?"

"Isn't it?" The creature pointed towards the thick red curtain. "What's going on, out there, right now?"

"The clowns—and we'll be on soon enough so you'd better get to the point, Gremlin."

"Are the clowns human?"

Jack smirked. "Sort of. Most of 'em are burnt out circus performers, too old or too drunk now to do anything else."

"Who's on after them?"

"The Special People. Why?"

"And are they human?"

"Again, sort of."

"In what way?"

"Well," Jack paused. "They're called 'special' ... 'cos they're certainly not normal! Some are really tall, or really short, really fat or really thin. Many are malformed. A few have extra limbs, and one even has a single eye, right in the middle of his forehead. The one thing they all have in common is they're all so damn weird!"

The deon cocked his head. "Yet they are *all* human and, like the clowns, they're vulnerable people being exploited for the amusement of others."

"Hang on, Gremlin. If it wasn't for the circus, they'd have nothing."

"And that makes it okay?"

Jack looked at his watch. "Look. I've been standing here for ten minutes now and I'm *still* waiting for the point of this conversation."

"The point is, as I've already told you, keeping captive exhibits to parade in front of a paying audience would be a retrograde step in the evolution of the modern human."

Jack shrugged. "Everyone has a good laugh."

"And I'd say that was rather *inhumane*, wouldn't you? Most species, even humans, rarely devolve. So what's really happening here?"

"Zip it, Gremlin, and get ready to be 'exploited'. We're on in two minutes."

Jack turned towards the curtain.

"Is the ringmaster human?"

Jack stopped. "What? Of course she is."

"Are you sure?"

"Look, Gremlin, I've had about enough-"

"Because, even with their terrible reputation, humans have been moving, albeit slowly, from barbaric to more civilised beings over time. Outdated forms of exploitative entertainment, such as down-and-out clowns, freak shows and exotic caged creatures, hardly represents progress. What do you think?"

"I'm not paid to think." Jack snorted.

"Precisely. All I'm saying is just because something looks human, it doesn't mean that it is."

"Oh, so I suppose that nutter, David Icke, was right after all, and we've all been secretly enslaved by reptilian overlords in human disguise."

Groxon sighed. "Well…"

"Enough!"

The red curtain was pulled aside.

Jack smiled. "It's show time!"

"Open your eyes," Groxon called, but its warning was lost in a cacophony of squeaks, shrieks and squeals as the space creatures were wheeled out into the main ring.

Only as the lights suddenly went up did Jack notice, for the very first time, that the ringmaster's crocodile skin gloves looked amazingly lifelike and, in the glare, for a split second, the audience all closed their third eyelids.

~ * ~ * ~

Petina Strohmer is a traditionally published novelist who has also had thirty (mainly speculative) stories published in different anthologies, one of which was a #1 Amazon bestseller earlier this month. She lives in the magical Welsh mountains with a raggle-taggle assortment of rescued animals.

For more information, go to www.petinastrohmer.com.

In a Glass Cage

Deby Fredericks

"Is this even true?" a muffled voice asked.

"Is what true?" a gruffer tone replied.

Vayle was drifting in aer natural state, as a gently swirling cloud of water vapor. Whoever was speaking sounded quite close to aer cage. Ae concentrated, solidifying enough to see who it was.

The glass globe where ae was imprisoned hung far at the back of the side show, behind a barrier of threadbare velvet ropes. Seligrav's Spectacular Extravaganza was a small circus, and it had moved once again. Vayle had been aware when aer prison was wrapped in heavy fabric, and ae had recognized a wagon's rumbling motion. From what ae could see, the goblin carnies were setting up the sideshow. Vayle didn't care where they were, because it was nowhere near the island home ae longed for.

Based on the light outside the tent, it was afternoon. Performances wouldn't begin until the next day. The tent walls may once have been brightly striped with orange and green, but now they were faded and shabby. The floor was mowed grass, already somewhat trampled. Oil lamps on posts revealed the stands where taxidermied beasts stood poised eternally. Nearer at hand, the small stage was set up to look like a human residence. When the carnival was open, the two freaks advertised as the Drakaina and the Lion-Man would act out a parody of domestic life. Their stage lay empty now.

"Deceiving minx of many shapes," one of the carnies read from the garish sign he was washing. The sign also proclaimed Vayle as 'deadly zephyr of the Firebreath Archipelago!'

Deadly. As if Vayle ever had the chance to do anything like that.

"Misty? Sure, it's real. I've seen it lots of times." The second goblin dragged a short ladder closer to Vayle's cage. "Not for a long while, though."

The ladder creaked as the goblin climbed. Soon his gray face was level with aer vapors. Vayle's prison was a gleaming glass globe with ornate brass fittings. It was suspended amid an elaborately carved wooden frame, which was painted gold and studded with fake gems to match match the gaudy sign. Leaning in close, the second goblin started to polish the glass.

Vayle swirled a little, both irritated and amused by the effort. Misty was what the carnies called aer, when they bothered to think about aer at all. Much as he might shine the glass, the carney couldn't do anything about the thin film of algae building up on the inside surface. Neither could Vayle. The glass was perfectly smooth, both inside and outside. There were no edges or corners ae could push against. The cage was completely sealed, preventing aer escape. It also trapped increasingly stale air which encouraged the algae's growth.

"It could have died, I guess." The goblin carnie shrugged, not much bothered by the idea. Gaalor, she thought he was called. Bright red, protruding eyes concentrated on his task without really caring.

"How would you know?" the first goblin scoffed as he scrubbed the sign. Some of the gold paint was rubbing off. "It just looks like a bit of fog in there. Could be a spell to do that."

Vayle didn't know that one's name. His head was shaved except for a crest of coarse black hair done in short braids. Even his voice was muted by the thick glass, and anyway, ae had resolved not to take any interest in the circus that put aer on display against aer will.

So ae was surprised to feel a gust of real annoyance. Ae didn't often solidify anymore. It was such a chore to decide what shape to become. Elf, goblin, human? Male or female? Skin, scales, feathers, clothing? And what color should any of it be?

More importantly, what did such details matter to a cloud spirit? Changing didn't help aer escape. But it was irritating to be talked about as if ae wasn't even real. Ae drew in aer mist to imitate a short, knobby-kneed biped with gray skin, prominent fangs, and a hooked nose. Aer eyes bulged, bright red and slit like a frog's. Coarse black hair bristled rebelliously. Ae copied their clothes, too—dull-colored tunics over short sarongs to the knee. Worn leather boots slouching around skinny ankles.

Both carnies jumped when ae appeared. Gaalor wobbled on the ladder, but then barked a laugh. "Oh, there you are, Misty. I was starting to wonder."

"That's pretty good." the other one stopped polishing the sign and came over with an intrigued frown. "You need to have a clan tattoo, though." He ran a hand over the row of circles inked into his forehead.

Vayle scowled. Ae didn't need anyone's approval. With a long, knobby finger ae wrote in the film of algae: "I want out."

"Don't we all." Gaalow gave a rough yet sad laugh. He held up his left wrist, which was enclosed by a tight metal band. "Two more years til my debt is paid."

"Four for me," his fellow grumbles, plodding back over to the sign. "Mucking humans snatched us up all at once. Didn't care whether we actually did anything…"

"Careful, Sarjac," Gaalor cut in. "Don't let the sorcerer hear you."

The two of them grunted sourly and turned back to their chores. Despite aer vow not to care, Vayle watched them try to polish the weathered fixtures. Seligrav's Spectacular Extravaganza didn't live up to its name in any way. In fact, it served more as a mirror of the world's injustice.

The sideshow, where Vayle was held captive, offered only three living acts: Aleon, the Lion-Man; Javetta, the Drakaina; and Vayle. It was filled out by a handful of taxidermied exotic animals: a two-headed goat called Billy and Willy; a crocodile named Smiley; a so-called harpy Vayle knew was a vulture sewn together with an ape; and the skeleton of an unfortunate baby rhino that hadn't survived the rigors of circus life.

The actual performers—jugglers and fire dancers, minstrels and fools—all were human. Even Aleon and Javetta, strangely mis-formed as they were, counted as humans. Although, Seligrav did lock the two freaks up in their trailers at night. He said it was to protect them from curious or malicious intruders. Still, they were free and well paid. It was only the goblin carnies and Vayle aerself who labored by force.

"What do you think it means, though?" Sarjac asked after a while. "We've come all the way to Toberlyn, with the crowds getting smaller all the way. I don't know how Seligrav is paying the troupe."

"That's because Seligrav doesn't invest in the operation," Gaalor answered dourly.

"And the food is lousy," Sarjac complained.

"I hear he's going to sell out," Gaalor said.

The circus might be sold? Vayle tried not to wonder about the future, but ae couldn't stop aerself. How long it had been since those peaceful days! Ae had roamed the warm islands with aer fellow cloud spirits, from the rugged shore, where steam gushed up from magma streams, through the dense thickets of the jungle, to the throats of the volcanoes where scalding gasses surged forth, and down to the gentle lagoons where the island folk build their bamboo huts. The humans there had been kind and respectful, offering thanks when the cloud spirits brought them rain or softened the impact of storms.

But then the sorcerers came, on their big ships full of soldiers and steel weapons, and worst of all their cruel spells. Vayle had been too shocked and disoriented to see if any of the spirits or humans escaped. Ae had been trapped in this horrid glass ball ever since.

"Hey, Misty." Gaalor leaned in confidentially. "You should change yourself, the way you used to. Maybe the new sorcerer will like it, and he'll pay more."

"Yeah!" Sarjac exclaimed. "Help us out."

Ae stared at the goblins reproachfully. Then ae burst into a swirling cloud of vapor and tinged it dark with anger. The two carnies backed away, grumbling together.

Vayle sulked, too. For a while, ae had changed aer form quite often. After the shock of captivity, anger had taken hold. Humans came to stare at the 'deadly zephyr' who had never offered harm to any of them. Ae had shaped aerself to mock them. Ae exaggerated aer heavy frames, or their skinny frames, too. Their hair styles or their baldness, their noses and their clothing, all were ripe for taunting. Ae magnified small flaws into grotesque imitations.

But instead of being insulted, the humans found it hilarious. More and more of them came to laugh at aer caricatures. For a time, ae had become a big draw. Majia Seligrav brought special guests in person to show off aer talent. When ae realized what he was doing, Vayle had stopped participating. The sorcerer might bluster and threaten, but he couldn't do anything to Vayle without opening aer cage. They both knew it.

For a time, ae drew satisfaction from thwarting him. But it was very little, and it didn't last. Since then, Vayle had retreated into aer cloud form. Silent resistance didn't get aer any closer to freedom, but ae did not relent. Ae would do nothing to help those who held aer captive.

"What are you useless mudskippers doing?" Seligrav himself burst into the sideshow with dramatic swirling of the tent flap. "Get out there and help set up the stands, before I add to your debt of time," he roared at the goblin carnies.

Or the sorcerer tried to roar. What came out was a rasping yell that ended in harsh coughing. Two of the human performers were close behind him, trying to soothe him.

"Take it easy, majia. You'll wear yourself out." That was Ninkaya, the lead fire dancer, lithe even in the sturdy tunic and trousers she wore to help the carnies set up.

"Let us deal with this." Chauss, the strongman, spoke with a gentleness at odds with his great size.

Other staff crowd in behind them. From their worried expressions, they were either concerned about Seligrav or coming to see what the shouting was about. Vayle had no sympathy for the one who claimed to own aer, but even ae was startled by the changes.

The human sorcerer, Seligrav, was the owner and ringmaster. His magic created the circus's most dazzling effects. At center stage, he wore a long sleeveless coat of vivid purple velvet over a crimson satin tunic. Its flared sleeves glittered with sequins. A string of sorcerer's medallions glinted among the other charms and ornaments that blanketed his coat. Black velvet trousers were tucked into soft snake scale boots, with gloves to match. When he performed, costume wizardry made Seligrav seem almost as big as Chauss.

Now, in person, Saligrav was shrunken. He was too thin even for an embroidered linen tunic and trousers with a rust-red coat over it. The brown face was lined, with a tightness around the eyes that spoke of constant pain. Dark hair, normally worn in an extravagant pompadour, barely stayed in a faded ponytail. The tall gold staff he gestured with on stage now seemed more necessary to help him stay upright. When he swiped at Gaalor, he nearly lost his balance.

"Yes, Majia. Right away." The goblin carnies hastily bowed, staying clear of the staff.

Seligrav whirled, looking for someone else to yell at. Brown eyes, fevered with rage, squinted into Vayle's prison. "As for you…"

Ae remained a darkened fog. Seligrav sputtered as he found nothing tangible to focus his anger on. "Do your part, damn you! I didn't hand over a hundred silver for nothing. Make yourself useful!"

The suspended globe wobbled and swayed as he jabbed it with the metal staff head. Vayle quickly looked to see if he had made a crack, but there was none. Ae grudgingly solidified into the shape ae had worn most often on the islands. Ae was small, like a human child, wearing only a short batik sarong. Aer skin was dusky, with a massive cloud of curly black hair filling most of the globe. Matching aer stormy gray eyes with Seligrav's brown ones, ae pointed at the words written in the algae: *"I want out."*

"Aagh!" Seligrav threw his hands up and turned his wrath back on the cowering goblins. "Pretty it all up, you damned mudskippers. And the rest of you, set up for your best act. Trovere is coming. She'll be here tomorrow! And if we're all lucky, she'll buy me out. So make it shine!"

More of the performers had been coming in behind Seligrav. Startled glances flew between them. They were worried, yes, but some were also excited at the prospect of a new owner. If Vayle had been free, ae would have turned into wood smoke and made them all cough.

"Come, majia. You need rest," Chauss urged him out. "The goblins know their job."

Seligrav did go, bulling his way through the onlookers. The other performers jumped out of his way, then hesitantly began to follow. The two goblins had a brief discussion about whether Seligrav wanted them to help set up the stands or keep polishing the sideshow. They soon hurried out of the tent, taking the lamps with them.

Vayle resumed aer cloud form and churned restlessly. Ae didn't know who this Trovere was, and anyway, what did it matter who bought the circus? Ae didn't owe them anything.

~ * ~

Despite aer defiant resolve, Vayle wasn't able to return to a peaceful drift. Scant daylight faded away, leaving the sideshow tent dark. There was nothing to do but wait, endlessly, in aer glass cage.

At some later point, ae came to alertness. Human voices were shouting, followed by what sounded like cries of anguish. Lamps were lit, and they moved to and fro. Voices kept sounding, though ae couldn't pick out any words. There was a thudding rumble of feet, and it was definitely coming closer. Vayle condensed aerself a bit and watched the lights approach.

The tent flap billowed open again. A crowd entered slowly, carrying those lamps. In the front, Vayle saw the two freaks, Aleon and Javetta, followed by the hulking Chauss and the lithe Ninkaya. Then came the jugglers and fire dancers, the minstrels and fools, and even the hostler. Down by their knees, the five goblin carnies came in, too.

In fact, nearly the whole troupe was there. Vayle's attention sharpened when ae realized who wasn't there—Seligrav himself. Some of them were arguing. Some were downcast and tearful. Others comforted each other, or crossed their arms anxiously. Only the carnies were more curious than distressed.

"Aleon, this is ridiculous," Chauss protested.

"Misty isn't going to help us. You saw how it acted earlier," Ninkaya said, exasperated.

That name again, Misty. They meant it to be friendly, but Vayle didn't like it.

"That's not fair," Javetta retorted. "Seligrav yelled at it." The supposed Drakaina wasn't a reptile at all. When she was working, Javetta had a gown cleverly constructed to suggest she had a serpent's tail matched to a woman's body, but Vayle knew she was just a human woman whose skin grew in rough. If ae squinted, it might look scaly.

"Let us talk to Misty," Aleon said to Chauss. "We've spent more time with it than the rest of you."

"I told you," Ninkaya began, but the lead juggler, Theoris, cut her off.

"What do you suggest instead? Just all of us break apart?" He threw up his hands in a gesture of frustration. "With no prospects and a lot of questions from the guards?"

Artegne, the lead minstrel, said, "Let them speak to it. It's worth a try."

"We can still impress Trovere. Seligrav was trying to get us in with her," Marcas, the lead fool, reminded everyone. "Misty can help."

Vayle glared through the glass. There was no reason for 'Misty' to help them

"What do we have to lose?" Gaalor piped up, and the other goblins said, "Yeah."

"Then quiet down, everyone." Chauss seemed sure that, whatever their plan was, it was a waste of time. Ninkaya stuck her hip out and rolled her eyes.

Aleon stepped over the threadbare velvet rope. Despite being called "Lion-Man," Aleon was no animal. He was just a human with unusual hair growth. Silky red-brown locks covered his entire body instead of just his head. It was true, he and Javetta, with their act in the sideshow, were closer to Vayle than the others. When business was slow, they brought cups of tea and stood near aer cage. They had encouraged Vayle to do the caricatures and congratulated aer on especially clever ones. When ae stopped doing them, Javetta had been the only one to ask why.

So when Aleon got close to the glass globe, Vayle solidified into aer human form, the dusky child with massive thundercloud of hair.

"Misty, my friend, there have been events." Anxious brown eyes peered out from Aleon's luxurious curls. "We need your help."

They all kept saying that. Ae hovered, cross-legged, and tilted aer head in a way that encouraged more information.

Javetta said, "You saw Majia Seligrav this afternoon. You must know he was ailing. He was going to make a deal to sell our operation to Majia Trovere." Her shoulders moved in a shrug. "But now he's died."

There was a little pause. Vayle could see why the performers were upset. Seligrav gave them work, paid them, and organized everything in the circus. Ae just couldn't see what they meant for aer to do about it.

Javetta and Aleon peered at aer hopefully. Ae leaned closer to the glass. "I can't bring back the dead." Aer voice echoed inside the globe as ae half-shouted to be heard through the glass.

From their stricken expressions, the performers took this for mockery. Aleon rested his hand on the outside of the globe.

"But you can, Misty." Aleon's his eyes gleamed with stress and trust. "We know you're a great mimic. You can imitate Majia Seligrav. You can lead the circus."

Vayle instinctively leaned away from where his hand would

have touched aer shoulder if he could. Ae crimped aer brow to express confusion and disbelief.

"Just for one performance," Javetta quickly inserted. "If you can pretend you're Seligrav long enough for us to show Trovere our skills, then maybe she'll still buy us out."

"Then the troupe can stay together," Artegne pleaded..

And they wouldn't all be out of work. Vayle understood that, but ae had to point out the obvious problem. "I'm a spirit. I can't do magic and illusions."

"You don't have to." Theoris, the juggler, waved a casual hand. "We're circus folk. We do illusions all the time."

"With costuming and cosmetics, a little flash powder," Marcas agreed. There were nods and rueful smiles all through the sideshow.

"That's true," Ninkaya relaxed a little. "We already have a full script. We've rehearsed it and performed it dozens of times."

Chauss also brightened. "We'll have to cut out Seligrav's parts, but if Misty can imitate his voice—"

"We can add in a section of ballads to fill the time," Artegne suggested.

A general babble was rising. Chauss gathered with the jugglers and dancers to plan something out. Marcas reminded them he had been managing some of the operation as Seligrav became more ill. He could keep doing it for a while longer. With growing irritation, Vayle listened to the muffled talk penetrating the globe. Even now that they were desperate, nobody was asking what ae wanted. They probably assumed, since they liked working in a circus, that ae must like it, too.

Vayle returned to cloud form and changed aer rotation to rub and strike sparks inside the globe. After several bright flashes, Aleon raised his hands.

"Wait, friends! Misty hasn't agreed to anything."

The troupe paused, turning to look at the sparks reflecting around the interior of Vayle's cage. Side conversations lulled as they looked at aer expectantly. Ae solidified enough to point at the words on the inside of the glass.

"I want out," Javetta read helpfully.

"Naturally," Aleon soothed. "Don't worry, Misty. Of course we'll let you out."

"Hold on," someone called from the back. "We can't let it out.

It'll fly away, and then we can't sell it to Trovere."

Rage and despair drove Vayle into a churning cloud, blacker than wood smoke and thick with sparks. The globe wasn't big enough for aer to make real lightning, but angry sparks flashed mightily.

"We can't sell Misty," Javetta cried, indignant. "It isn't one of the horses, you know."

"Well what about us goblins, then?" Sarjac tried to protest. The humans talked over him.

Aleon was more polite than Javetta, but equally upset. "If we want Misty to impersonate Seligrav, it can't do that inside the globe."

"But it hasn't said it will help us," Ninkaya snapped back.

"It has to promise," Marcas said.

Aleon looked at Chauss, who folded his arms resolutely. "I think we'd all feel better."

Vayle churned and shot sparks inside the globe. Why was it so important the humans feel better? What about aer feelings?

"Please, Misty." Aleon turned back to Vayle, speaking softly. "We'll all be thrown out of work. Some of us have skills, like the fools, or a reputation like Ninkaya and Chauss. But for freaks like me and Javetta, there's no place else in the world that's safe. We need the circus."

Gaalor piped up again, "Nobody else wants to hire us goblins, either. We'll be stuck in Toberlyn with no money and no work. They'll sell our debt to a mine, or worse."

Vayle fumed in aer cloud form, but Aleon's plea did touch her. It reminded aer of the villagers who survived the sorcerers' first invasion. So many were cut down or bound in chains. A few survivors had begged the spirits for help, and they had tried. That was how Vayle had been captured.

From what ae understood, the sorcerers had thought ae was a wind spirit. They wanted aer to move their ship, even when there was no natural wind. But Vayle was a cloud, not wind. Ae was useless for that purpose. The obvious thing would have been to set aer free. But sorcerers didn't follow logic. They were too accustomed to reshaping the world for their own whims. After they found out Vayle couldn't do what they wanted, they sold aer to Seligrav's Spectacular Extravaganza.

Ae hated being confined, of course. These circus folk kept demanding things, when ae owed them nothing. Yet, they reminded aer of the villagers who had once been her friends. Despite everything that followed, Vayle did not truly regret trying to aid them.

If she didn't help the circus, and their troupe was split apart, wouldn't she regret it afterward?

While ae thought it over, ae lost track of what the humans and goblins were doing. Suddenly aer glass prison lurched and swayed. Ae was startled to realize the goblin carnies were back with their ladder. Humans crowded around as they unhooked the fittings. There was a lot of babble, people calling advice or warnings.

"Get back, you'll only get in the way," Marcas cried.

"Look out, you're going to drop it," Javetta warned.

Vayle wouldn't have minded that. With even a small crack, ae could have escaped more quickly.

"A little room here." It was Chauss whose big hands grabbed the unwieldy glass globe. With a jolt the cage was down on a surface of grass and dirt. Vayle coiled inside the glass ball, eager to be free. But the carnies gave a groan of disappointment.

"There's no stopper?" Aleon demanded.

"How did they get Misty in there, without a hole?" Sarjac asked.

"They were sorcerers," Ninkaya was exasperated but also disappointed. "They used magic."

"Well there has to be another way," Theoris cried.

The crowd babbled suggestions. One of the fire dancers wanted to do a flip and kick the globe, but Ninkaya said he could cut his leg. Marcas told Chauss to punch it, but the problem of cutting his hand was the same. Artegne said the jugglers could throw their pins at it. Vayle didn't care what they did, as long as it got aer out of this cage.

"I have an idea," Chauss finally said. "Bring it along."

Working together, the goblin carnies rolled the glass globe out of the sideshow and back behind their main tent. One of the gaily painted wagons was parked beside a large rock. Performers with lamps surrounded the area while Chauss climbed up to the driver's seat. Vayle's globe was passed up to him.

"Everybody get back," he warned.

A heave, and Vayle plunged downward. Impact echoed like a blast of thunder as the globe struck the rock. There were groans from the performers as the globe rolled down intact. Except, Vayle felt a shift in the air pressure. Ae searched frantically, and lantern light flared off a spider-web of cracks. Ae solidified and pushed aer heels into the weak spot.

Carnies were crowding around, exclaiming the globe hadn't shattered.

"Because it's magical?" Javetta asked anxiously.

Vayle pushed harder, desperate to be out of aer hated prison. They all heard the sharp crack of glass breaking. Circus people jumped back, warning each other to be careful. The shining glass gave way, creating a ragged, heel-sized hole.

Someone cried, "Watch out, it's sharp!"

What did sharp edges mean to a cloud? Vayle dissolved and surged through the gap. Freedom! Ae paid no attention to the cries of alarm, and one yip of celebration from Aleon. Ae billowed eagerly, soaring as ae hadn't been able to do in forever. Farther, farther! Ae stretched and spread, rising like a bank of fog above the circus tents. The cool night air shifted with a breeze, and Vayle trembled with the need to follow it. To be free, to drift where ae wished, traveling without limit until ae returned to the Firebreath volcanoes once again.

Circus folk were below her, looking up with exclamations of alarm and fear. "It's leaving us! I told you so."

"Get another jar. Try to catch it!"

As if they could. Vayle allowed aerself a moment to enjoy their helpless dismay. But then came Javetta's plea, "Misty, are you there?"

It was not aer name, but it pulled at aer all the same. Frustration mingled with the joy of flight as Vayle condensed aerself. Ae mimicked Seligrav as best ae could on the spur of the moment. The long coat and spangled tunic, the pompadour, and the gold rod that sparkled with fake gems.

"That is not my name!" Ae added a small crackle of lightning to aer simulation of Seligrav's booming delivery. "Do not call me that."

The shape was still vague, the colors hardly there and details fuzzy. But there were relieved cheers and much back-patting as the simulated Majia Seligrav hovered just above the gleaming ball of aer former prison.

"Well, what is it, then?" Ninkaya demanded.

"My name is Vayle," ae answered. Even as ae spoke, ae solidified more, bringing out the colors and details. "I will help you, this time only. And I have a lot of questions."

Seeing aer seemed to spur all of them to action.

"All right, yes, that's wonderful." Chauss stepped up to take control. "We'll break into teams. Artegne and the minstrels will adjust the script. Ninkaya, Theoris and the other jugglers check to be sure Seligrav's equipment is all there..."

How they took aer for granted! Annoyed, Vayle folded aer arms and mimicked Seligrav's arrogant manner. Javetta saw it and exclaimed loudly, "Thank you Mis—Vayle."

And Aleon prompted, "What did you want to ask about?"

The humans quieted enough for Vayle to ask, "This human, Trovere. Does she know Seligrav? Or will anyone else know there's a difference?"

The idea of another sorcerer coming around made Vayle wary. Ae had no intention of being captured again. But if ae failed, the human performers could still be hurt.

Aer words made them stop and think. Worried glances passed among them.

"I don't know," Chauss admitted. "Seligrav and Trovere are both sorcerers. They might know each other from training together." The strongman looked uncertain, but the goblin Gaalor jumped up on the rock to be seen among the taller humans.

"What does it matter? You're making this way too complicated," he scolded.

"What do you mean, goblin?" Ninkaya was immediately hostile.

"Nobody will know if the script has changed," Gaalor insisted. "Nobody here has seen it before. All you have to do is put on a great show. Make the audience happy. Impress Trovere. Us carnies will have everything in place for you to do it."

"He's right," Marcas immediately jumped in. "They don't care how we make them laugh, or dazzle them with our tricks. They just want to have a good time."

"As long as they do laugh," Theoris nodded. "We don't have to tell anyone what happened with Seligrav until after Trovere makes an offer."

Vayle boomed out, still imitating her former enslaver. "If I can't copy all his illusions, we can say this is a new act. Something special he developed just for the audience in Toberlyn."

As ae spoke, ae shifted from form to form, from the human sorcerer to a goblin carney, to the sultry fire dancer, to a cloud that shimmered with sparks, and finally back to the dusky island child.

"That's brilliant!" Aleon said. "I've never heard of a sorcerer doing that."

Javetta said, "Maybe Trovere will be distracted trying to figure out how you did it, and we can get a better deal."

"What if she doesn't make an offer?" one of the jugglers asked.

"Marcas has been helping with a lot of the management" Chauss said. "Maybe we can reorganize another way. But for now, let's get to those working groups. Tomorrow is coming soon, and we'll need the morning for a rehearsal."

Vayle hovered, watching them scurry to new tasks. Aleon and Javetta gazed up at aer with gratitude. "Thank you so much, Misty. I mean Vayle."

"We'll see if it works," ae replied.

This could be an interesting challenge, not just to mimic Seligrav but to exceed him. It was just like aer old streak of mocking impressions, but for a better purpose. And on aer own terms.

~ * ~ * ~

Deby Fredericks has been a writer all her life, but thought of it as just a fun hobby until the late Nineties. Since then she has published twenty fantasy novels, novellas and novelettes, either with small presses or independently. Her short fiction has appeared in *Andromeda Spaceways*, selected anthologies, and small magazines.

In addition, Fredericks writes for children as Lucy D. Ford. Her children's stories and poems have appeared in magazines such as *Boys' Life*, *Babybug*, *Ladybug*, and *Spider*. In the past, she served as Regional Advisor for the Inland Northwest Region of the Society of Children's Book Writers and Illustrators, International (SCBWI).

Her latest work is a middle grade fantasy duology, *Cleodora*, about a bold young girl who must learn why the nature spirits have stopped it from raining.

The Pain Artist

E. Florian Gludovacz

The pain artist blinked slowly, shading his purple eyes behind heavy lids. His gaunt face appeared sallow in the subdued light of his enclosure, the ears just a bit too pointed to be entirely human. His smile showed an immaculate row of white, shiny teeth, which were numerous, pointy, and curved slightly inward.

"Ladies and gentlemen," he said in an unexpectedly pleasant voice rich in warm overtones. "Welcome to our little carnival, our sideshow of wonders."

A hush fell over the crowd as they watched the figure intently. They had been awed by the transparent aliens from Baltoid 9, whose bones and internal organs stood out in stark contrast to their translucent skins. The blobby form of the high-g monster from Santrek had been astonishing in its unexpected agility and easy, controlled movement, and the trans-dimensional energy entity had been startling in its own way, but the attention lavished on the pain artist was different, immediate, and intense.

Of all the creatures the visitors had encountered in this tawdry second rate travelling show, the artist had been the first to address them directly, to speak with them, and to engage them in meaningful articulation of his thoughts. In this strange, surreal world of the exotic and outlandish, he stood at the centre of attention. This was the main attraction, after all, the rumour that made the audience pay the price of admittance. This was said to be a show of extremes, of depravity, and of transcendence.

"Welcome to my world, which is filled with wonder and pain. Pain! Ah, yes, pain is my medium and pain is the muse that shapes and guides my art in everything I do."

They hung onto his words with a mixture of unease, fear, and lust, of hope and disgust for what they expected to experience.

He rose abruptly from his stool and strode up to the metal bars that divided his enclosure from the audience. His amethyst gaze swept over the people before him, studying each member of the audience intently, making eye contact and drawing the deepest secrets out of their unresisting souls.

"Attend!" he cried, as he took a step back. A moment later, he lunged forward and slammed his face into the iron bars. There was an audible sickening crack as his nose broke and front teeth shattered, spraying an old lady in the first row with a mist of spittle and blood.

The audience gasped in shocked surprise, but there was some nervous laughter, a titter, and a guffaw. True to peoples' nature the emotions and reactions ran the complete spectrum of human experience and a small helping of schadenfreude and sadism could always be counted upon in any audience.

"Ah, yes, here comes the pain," the artist swooned. "But remember pain is my medium, it's the emotional clay I shape with my vision, the very centre of my creative being! Pain lies at the beginning and the end of all art!"

Even as he spoke, he ran his hands over his face and within moments the bleeding wound on his forehead had closed, the nose straightened, and his broken, bloody smile became whole before the stunned audience as his teeth regrew themselves.

"Oh, yes," he moaned in quiet pleasure. "Growing teeth always hurts. They hurt at least as much as broken teeth do, so I get to enjoy them twice!"

He made a complicated gesture with his hands that suggested things disappearing, signalling the opening act of his performance was concluded, and this exhibition was ready to enter the next stage.

"For my next trick I will require a volunteer. Is anyone in the audience brave enough to submit to my art?" He smiled winningly. "I promise it won't hurt a bit! Well, at least it won't hurt you! That is the only guarantee I will give, it's all I can commit to tonight," he added with a wink as he stepped to one side of his enclosure and pushed a hotly glowing brazier to the fore. The metal was an angry cherry red and his fingertips sizzled as he touched the contraption. Wafts of acrid smoke, of burnt flesh, of disconcertingly appetising roasted meat touched the audience in the front row.

"Now, ladies and gentlemen, boys and girls, who is brave enough to assist me? Who possesses the courage to participate in my art? Does anyone share my creative passions? Who will help me achieve art through suffering?" He peered at each face intently before gesturing in a sudden burst of enthusiasm. "How about you, young man? Do you have what it takes to create art?"

The members of the audience pulled back uneasily to reveal the young boy the artist had pointed at. He was perhaps thirteen years old with a mop of blond hair falling into his eyes and he still retained baby fat on his rosy cheeks.

"I...I don't know?" he whispered uncertainly. He was obviously fascinated by the strange being with an affinity for agony, yet also afraid of what might happen to him, if he involved himself in the artist's actions.

"Ah, but of course you can do this, dear child. I promise no harm will befall you." He beckoned again and this time the kid stepped forward, mesmerised by the steady, violet gaze that held depths of knowledge, sadness, and compassion.

"Please slide your arms through the bars of my gilded cage," the artist cooed. The boy did as he was told and in moments his hands were shackled. The handcuffs appeared in the artist's hands as if by magic and clicked into place behind the bars, which prevented the child from withdrawing his hands.

Gasps and murmurs of outrage greeted this act, yet the artist was undeterred, smiling cheerfully and waving a finger from side to side to dissuade further criticism.

"Watch very closely, ladies and gentlemen. Don't be afraid, my dear boy," he winked. "And don't flinch if you can help it!" He shrugged. "Or do if you can't!"

He grabbed the brazier and swung it into place so the hottest flames roared beneath the helpless child's hands. The boy flinched involuntarily, but after a moment, his expression changed to one of wonder and perhaps even delight. He began waggling his fingers inside the flames, yet to everyone's surprise nothing happened. Even though there was obvious heat radiating off the brazier, his flesh remained unmarked and there was no sensation of pain. He looked over his shoulder and grinned at the audience.

"It doesn't hurt!" he exclaimed.

"Voilà!" the pain artist cried in ecstasy, as he waved the burnt stumps of his hands for effect. "The boy is unharmed, hale, and healthy!"

In a flurry of motion, he swept the brazier aside and undid the shackles with rapidly healing hands.

"And now, please, give this brave young man a generous round of applause!" He clapped his hands which were unblemished once more to demonstrate and the crowd followed along obediently.

"Now, for my final trick! It is simultaneously the smallest and greatest achievement in my arsenal of arts. And in order to demonstrate, I will once again require a volunteer who has the capacity to be brave in the face of pain!" He eyed the people in front of him and finally settled on a strong young man in his early twenties. He was obviously fit, perhaps even an athlete, and very different from the previous subject in every regard.

"You have witnessed me reeling in my own pain, you have experienced the powers of my art in taking away the boy's pain and making it my very own. Now, you will witness my final feat, which is quite possibly the greatest achievement of them all!"

He locked eyes with the man, smiled thinly and fished around inside the pocket of his coat. He withdrew a thin, sharp needle and held it up to the light. The silvery steel caught the light at just the right angle to flash a wicked gleam towards the audience. The point was thin and razor sharp and it was quite obvious to everyone in the crowd the implement could cause some serious pain.

"Behold! Behold! Behold this tiny needle and the power it can possess in my capable hands! Please, sir, if you would stretch out your hand?"

Somebody winced in anticipation of what was to come, a woman scoffed under her breath at the anticlimactic revelation of seeing the small implement. The man simply shrugged and complied. The artist stepped closer and held out the needle, waving it back and forth in front of the volunteer's eyes. Then, in a quick and decisive motion he stepped back and jabbed it into his own finger.

The man yelled in surprised pain and jerked his hand back. He had expected a variation of the earlier trick with the brazier and had guessed the artist would absorb the subject's pain. Yet this was the exact opposite! The artist began jabbing his hand repeatedly, causing little droplets of blood to well up on his skin, while the man's hand remained unblemished even as he shook it in obvious discomfort. The artist turned around and jabbed the needle deeply into his own buttocks. The man squirmed and squealed, jumping up and down in pain and embarrassment.

"Thank you!!! Thank you very much!" The artist cried with a

flamboyant bow. "Thank you for being such a good sport," he said to the man with a disarming smile. "I thank you all for attending me as I performed my humble art for your entertainment and pleasure! But now I must rest! I wish you all a pleasant day!" He stepped back from the steel bars and into the shadows just as a slightly tattered velvet curtain dropped from above, obscuring the strange creature from further view.

There was hushed silence, confusion, and perhaps just a bit of anger from the young man who had been the butt of the artist's joke. Then the applause started. At first it was hesitant, a quiet staccato that began off to one side, but then the noise grew as the stunned audience realised what it had just experienced and thunderous applause filled the carnival. They had seen and experienced everything they had expected—and more. The masochistically macabre spectacle had not disappointed and they would be talking about the pain artist for a long time to come. They would definitely recommend the show to their friends.

The pain artist sat quietly on his stool inside the cramped enclosure, a gentle smile gracing his lips as he stared at the curtain with unseeing eyes. He was still revelling in the pain. There was the pain he had caused himself in service to his art, but then there was also the other pain, the hidden pain, the pain that made it all worth it. The old lady with arthritis in the first row would discover her joints didn't bother her nearly as much as they had before. The blond boy would forget all about his night terrors and would not wet his bed again, would outgrow his shame to be everything he could be. The man with the slipped disc in the second row who had guffawed at his pain would notice his back did not hurt very much lately. The young man who had felt the artist's suffering for brief moments would finally let go of the deep emotional pain he had held on to for so many years. He would come to realise that there was more joy in life than he had expected or dared hope for.

This was the pain the artist craved the most. It would sustain him at least through part of the night. Then his real agony would set in, as the absence of pain would penetrate every fibre of his body—of his very being—leaving him writhing in the pale remnants of his art.

~ * ~ * ~

E. Florian Gludovacz has been a writer, musician, and artist since his teens. He was born in Austria and grew up living in different parts of Europe (Germany, France, the UK, and Austria). He currently resides in rural Southern California with his wife and their mixed Great Pyrenean Mountain Dog.

Carnival Chaos

DJ Tyrer

Holding tight to the straining lead that held Spot in check, Sergeant Axel hefted his axe and glanced at Constable Wheelwright as they prepared to enter the large circus tent from which a crowd of men, women, and children, human, elf, dwarf, orc, and troll, were fleeing in panic.

"It swallowed her!" someone cried as they ran past.

"Sounds bad," Axel muttered as he remembered their conversation from the day before, as clear as if they'd just spoken. Sometimes, he really hated to be right...

~ * ~

"The Carnival has come to town," Sergeant Axel said, tossing paperwork onto the desk.

"Carnival? Oh, I love carnivals," Constable Wheelwright said, clapping his hands, "circuses, sideshows, too. So much to see, wonderful games—"

Axel shook his head as he interrupted his subordinate, saying, "Not *a* carnival—*the* Carnival: *The Carcharic Carnival.* And, that means trouble."

"Does it? I don't know that word," the human had said.

"No, I mean, the Carnival brings trouble with it," the dwarf replied.

The brindled hound that bore the misname of Spot whined as if agreeing with his assessment.

"Never heard of it."

Axel shook his head again. "You're probably too young. It's only appeared twice since I've been in the Watch."

"Appeared? What do you mean appeared?" Wheelwright asked.

That was the crux of it, of course, the reason it brought trouble.

"It never rolls in like a regular one in wagons," Axel said. "No, it's like one of those peculiar little magic shops that appears out of nowhere and causes chaos. One day, the common's empty; the next, it's there; then, *poof,* it's gone again."

He shook his head a third time. "The savants say it travels to other worlds, but I wouldn't know about that. All I know is that it always brings trouble. *Always.*"

~ * ~

And, it had…

The Chief had put him and Wheelwright on the Carnival beat and, of course, all hell had broken out on their shift. Given the nature of the Carcharic Carnival, it was entirely possible Hell literally *had* broken out. They'd find out soon enough.

Pushing past the last of the fleeing patrons, they entered the tent. He made sure to keep a tight hold on Spot's leash—the dog was sometimes too brave in the face of unknown danger and he didn't want him rushing in and getting hurt.

Something shrieked from the darkness within, somewhere between a roar of anger and a howl of anguish. Its exact emotions were less of interest to Axel than the fact it sounded huge. The leash in his hand slackened; Spot was no longer straining to charge in. That was a bad sign.

"What could it be?" Wheelwright asked in a small voice. "A terrible lizard, do you think?"

"I hope not!"

There was another shrieking roar and Spot began straining in the opposite direction.

"Fine, boy, go stand guard outside. But, don't expect any sausages for dinner."

He let the dog run out of the tent as he and the constable entered its heart.

"I think," Wheelwright said, "Spot has more sense than us."

Axel shrugged. "He doesn't care about reputation. Come on."

The tent was large, like the largest of circus tents, and in the centre of its ring was a large vat of water. The dark interior was silent now.

"Maybe it's gone to sleep?" Wheelwright said, looking at the vat with hope.

"I don't think so," the dwarf said. "Look."

There was a trail of sloshed water leading from the vat and into the stands.

"Well, someone did scream a woman had been eaten."

"I guess that's where it happened," Axel said, cautiously looking about in case whatever left the trail was still there, although if it were, it was far smaller than it had sounded.

Then, he heard the awful shriek from somewhere beyond the confines of the tent.

"Oh, Khazaldak! It's got out—we have to stop it before we have a full-scale rampage on our hands."

They ran outside and Axel spotted the head of a patron peeking out from a barrel, eyes wide with fright.

"Which way did it go?"

"Follow the screams," the man replied, ducking out of sight.

It wasn't bad advice; there was a lot of screaming from the far side of the carnival.

They ran past cages with a variety of strange and alien-looking animals. Axel hated to see them confined, but it was the one that was loose he needed to concentrate on right now.

"There!" Wheelwright exclaimed.

He looked where the constable was pointing and saw a serpentine tail disappearing behind a sideshow tent. A strange little man with no head and his face upon his chest came running from it, crying out in a language Axel didn't understand, although he didn't need to know the words to understand the terror.

They rounded the tent and saw it.

"I think it *is* a terrible lizard," Wheelwright said.

It might have been. It was certainly terrible, and also quite, quite strange. If Axel had been asked at a later date to describe it for the Watch sketch-artist, he would have said the peculiar beast was a little like a dragon and a lot like a fish with the glittering scales that covered its long neck and belly, and had six clawed feet that reminded him of a bear's. Its head was something like a lion's and it had the flowing mane of a horse. The beast's sides were covered with a carapace similar to that of a turtle and along its back were rows of sharp scales like the blades of axes. It was one of the strangest sights he'd ever seen, and he'd taken the night patrol in the Westside slums many times.

"Actually," a voice said from behind them, "it's a tarasque."

Axel glanced round and saw a man with four legs and holding a mop peering out from a nearby tent, clearly one of the carnies.

"The Mistress found it on a distant world and just had to add it to her menagerie, but it does have a terrible habit of trying to eat people. In fact, I think it's got someone stuck in its throat at the moment, which is why it's in such an awful temper."

It was true. Now he looked, Axel could see a pair of feet sticking out of the beast's jaws, kicking feebly. No wonder it was upset. The woman probably even more so.

Just then, its tail caught the lock of a nearby cage and broke it off, releasing the beast confined within.

"Well, that's done it," the carny said, "that's a psyboar. They can psychically sense fear…so, I'm out of here." Dropping his mop, he ran as fast as his four uncoordinated legs could carry him.

"Show no fear," Axel told the constable, but Wheelwright turned and ran after the carny.

"Great!"

The psyboar, a creature much like an extremely large wild boar with tusks of shining steel and a pulsing brain extruding from its cranium, chose to celebrate its freedom by charging in his direction.

"Oh, Khazaldak!" He really wished he wasn't feeling fear.

No matter where he ran, no matter what ruse he attempted in order to evade it, the psyboar remained in pursuit, its psychic power allowing it to follow him even when he vanished from its sight inside a tent or under a cart.

Normally, Axel was proud to be a dwarf, but there were times when he envied humans and elves their longer legs, and this was one of them. He had plenty of stamina for long-distance running, but speed was lacking. The psyboar was going to catch him any moment now.

Then, he saw a popcorn stand and ran straight for it.

Please, let the psyboar be hungry! he thought as he toppled the stand, spilling popcorn across the ground.

"Hey!" a man in a striped shirt shouted. He was probably the employee who ran the popcorn stand, but he turned and fled when he saw the psyboar barrel up.

Axel had to halt and lean against a barrel organ to regain his breath.

Thankfully, the psyboar didn't follow after him, but paused to eat the scattered popcorn.

"Wheelwright! Get your rear end over here now or I'll have

you drummed off the Watch."

A nervous-looking constable popped his head out from under a nearby gaily painted caravan.

"Help me with this tent," Axel said. Together they got the canvas down and tossed it over the distracted psyboar. With the help of a couple of the braver carnies, they tied ropes round it to restrain it and attached them to the caravan so it couldn't get away.

"Someone can put it back in its cage later," Axel said. "We've got to deal with that tarry-thing."

"Tarasque," Wheelwright said.

"Yes, that, too. Come on."

The tarasque had left a trail of destruction and dampness as it crashed through tents and sideshows, still shrieking as it tried to either swallow or spit out the poor woman caught in its throat.

"There it is," Axel said, feeling weary before their struggle had even begun.

They paused and looked at it. With its carapace and axe-blade scales, it looked as if it would be impervious to their weapons.

What were they supposed to do?

"Right," Axel said, considering the problem before them. "One, we need to restrain this beast, so it is no longer a threat. Two, we need to free the woman from its throat. Three, it would be really good if we didn't get swallowed ourselves in the process."

Wheelwright nodded. "Quite."

"So," the dwarf said, "how do we achieve all that?"

"Er…"

"My thought exactly," Axel said. "We need to know its weakness."

"I don't think it has one, what with all those scales and things."

"Well, we know it likes water. Maybe we can tempt it into a pool and trap it?"

"It has lots of legs," Wheelwright said.

"An accurate observation, but I don't see how that helps us."

"Well, you know how Constable Tallfellow is always tripping over his own feet and he only has two of them. If he had six, he'd surely fall flat on his face."

"Trip it up? It's a possibility, I suppose."

Axel looked about. There was another big tent nearby with a high central pole.

"I'll get the lay of the land," he told the constable and ran over to it and began to climb a mooring rope before shinning up to the top of the pole. Although dwarves usually spent most of their lives underground, their use of ladders to climb the shafts connecting the different levels of their mine homes meant they tended to be surprisingly good climbers.

From his vantage point, he could see a vat of molasses used for making toffee treats. If they could lure the tarasque into it, the sticky morass might just trap it.

"Right," he said, having slid back down a rope to where the constable was waiting, "we need some bait."

"But, it's already chewing on someone."

"It's angry. It'll go for anyone." He looked at Wheelwright.

"Sir?"

"Thank you for volunteering, Wheelwright. Be a good fellow and put yourself between it and the vat of molasses, over there."

"Me?!"

"I'll put you in for a commendation."

"It doesn't sound worth much."

"Believe me, it isn't. But, you're a constable of the Watch and you'll do your duty."

"Yes, sir." The constable sagged, but didn't run away.

"Now, get going."

Wheelwright ran in front of the tarasque and taunted it, causing it to bellow and charge after him. He led it towards the vat. When it saw the vat, it made a growling sound and lunged into it with a great splash.

Trapped in the sticky, viscous liquid, it began to thrash about as the constable ran for cover.

"Well done," Axel called.

There was a crash and the side of the vat exploded out in a torrent of black molasses and the tarasque was free. But, Axel was relieved to see, the creature's legs were stuck together, causing it to stumble about awkwardly, barely able to move.

It wasn't perfectly restrained, but it would do.

But, how to get the woman free from its maw?

Axel smiled to himself and gave a whistle.

Spot came bounding up. Away from the sound of the awful creature, the dog had recovered his spirit and, seeing it barely able to move, showed no fear before it.

"Bite it," Axel commanded, pointing at the tail of the tarasque.

Spot did as he commanded and lunged at the beast, sinking his teeth deep into its serpentine tail which, unlike the rest of it, was not particularly armoured.

The tarasque let out a howl of pain, its jaws opening wide, and the woman came out with a *plop!*

"Help her up," Axel ordered Wheelwright, but the constable didn't come running.

Looking around, he saw the man was coated in molasses, too, and stuck to the side of a tent.

"Never mind." The dwarf went over to the woman, his boots making slurping noises with each step through the spilled molasses and helped her up. "This way, ma'am."

He called for Spot to follow him and led the woman away to safety.

"Don't worry, Wheelwright, I'll send someone to help free you. I'll make sure the Chief knows how helpful you were."

"Thanks!"

As he handed the woman over to a cleric for healing, he looked down at Spot and smiled.

"Sausages for you, after all, I think."

Spot barked happily.

"But, first, I need to find some of the carnies and get that tarasque locked up."

He shook his head. As soon as he found the woman the carny had called Mistress, he was going to give her a piece of his mind. They might not be breaking any laws he was aware of in keeping the animals in cages, but it wasn't fair to the fantastic beasts and, if today was anything to go by, it certainly wasn't safe. "Leave them in the wild well away from people," he said. "Best for them all."

Behind him, the tarasque yowled mournfully, its feet still stuck together.

"Serves you right, trying to swallow folk," he shouted back at it. "Come on, Spot, let's get things sorted, eh?"

Spot barked his agreement and followed close at the sergeant's heels.

~ * ~ * ~

DJ Tyrer is the person behind *Atlantean Publishing* and has been widely published in anthologies and magazines around the world, such as *Insurgence: A Fae Rebellion* (Corrugated Sky), *Tales of the Black Arts* (Hazardous Press), *Troubadours and Space Princesses* (Hamlein Publications), and *Borne in the Blood*, *The Dragon's Hoard 2* and *Crunchy With Ketchup* (WolfSinger Publications), and issues of *Fantasia Divinity*, *Broadswords and Blasters*, *BFS Horizons*, *The Fifth Di...*, and *Tales from the Magician's Skull*. DJ also has a novella available in paperback and on the Kindle, *The Yellow House* (Dunhams Manor).

You can find DJ on the internet at:

DJ Tyrer - Writer, Poet and Editor (djtyrer.blogspot.co.uk/) on Facebook at (www.facebook.com/DJTyrerwriter/) and at The Atlantean Publishing (atlanteanpublishing.wordpress.com/)

All is Not as it Seems

Emily A. Grigsby

As soon as the Ring Master's last word left her lips, she raised her arms and flung two pellets to the ground producing thick green and purple smoke. After the fog lifted, Isla could see faint sporadic glowing lights among the darkness ahead. The Ring Master was nowhere to be found. The crowd around Isla pushed onward. She grabbed the hand of her best friend, and they flowed along with the herd.

"Five cents, have your money ready! Nickle, pennies, don't matter. Five cents!" the ticket booth was manned by an enormously fat blob on a very small stool. "Ah, 'ello there darlins! It be ten cents for the two a ya."

Isla and Leena reached into their skirt pockets and paid the creature a nickle each. His arms resembled tentacles and he suctioned the coins off the counter.

"Thank ya kindly dears." He gave them a big, mostly toothless smile. "Oh, afore I forget. At the far end a the attractions, ya see," he pointed one of his several tentacles down the dark path. "It ain't for youngins, see. Even your grown folk dun't like it much. Aright, next! Five cents, five cents please!"

Isla and Leena saw floating heads in clear jars. Different species from around the galaxy they had never seen before. From large jars containing monstrous heads, to tiny jars containing those of distant animals. Each was more gruesome than the last. Isla began to question why they wanted to come so badly.

Vrooosh! Both girls jumped as flames started to roar around them. Two three-headed fire-breathing dragons were spitting a scorching red-orange fire all around them. The beasts were dull colors of blue and yellow, some of their scales missing. One of the heads started coughing violently mid-blast. Isla ran over to a bucket of collected rainwater, dipped in the long ladle and brought it back to the hacking dragon head. She held it up as far as she could reach, her skinny arm struggled to keep it that high. All the heads looked at her with skepticism, but he did finally slowly accept the dipper and had a long drink.

"What did you do that for?" Leena whispered as they continued.

Isla shrugged, "He was coughing."

They stopped in front of a small navy-blue and white striped tent. The sign read:

~ MADAM ASTRA ~

~ FORTUNES ~ CHARMS ~ ENCHANTMENTS ~
~ MEDIUM ~ ASTROLOGY ~ SPIRITS ~

~ GENUINE HEALING CRYSTALS FOR SALE ~

* INQUIRE WITHIN *

The girls exchanged glances. Leena flung open the flap, it was even darker in the tent than it was outside. There were several short candles barely lighting creepy trinkets and knickknacks. Little skulls, necklaces, dead flowers, a large red ceramic vase with a big crack zigzagging down the side.

"Welcome!" a voice wheezed from the darkness. "Sit, sit."

Isla and Leena sat shoulder to shoulder on the short, stout bench stuffed into the cramped space. A lantern was lit by a little creature, smaller than half the size of the girls. She was covered in light brown fur and had a long snout. She wore a long, patterned dress and a matching headscarf. Her hands had long painted nails and rings on almost every finger, her bracelets and necklaces looked oversized on her petite frame. She sat on the opposite side of a small table covered in a scarlet tablecloth.

"I am Madam Astra. What can I do for you two ladies this fine evening?" Her long snout drew upwards in a crooked smile. Her teeth were small but looked extremely sharp.

"We'd…we'd like our fortune read…," Leena squeaked. Even though Madam Astra was only half the girls' size, they were still frightened by her. "Please." Leena quickly added.

"Ah that's more like it! One cent each please, girls. Payment before services not after," she held out her tiny hand, the pennies almost covered her entire palm.

"Right! Now," Madam Astra pulled her blueish-white crystal ball from below the table and placed it gently in front of her. She rubbed her paws on the sides, humming softly. She stopped suddenly and abruptly looked up wide-eyed at Isla.

"You…" Madam Astra began. "You are…you are destined for great things, heroic things. Do not resist your urges. When you feel driven to act, do it without question. You will help many by one small brave act, many in need. Their lives will be forever changed. We…we…"

Madam Astra was trembling now, she had not taken her eyes off Isla. "Get out! Shoo! The both of you!"

"But you didn't do mine yet!" Leena protested. Madam Astra reached in her dress, pulled out the girls' coins and pressed them into Leena's hand. After pushing the girls out of her tent, Madam Astra erected her "*MADAM ASTRA OUT ~ COME BACK LATER*" sign and pulled her tent flap shut.

The girls stood in confusion staring at the little navy-blue and white striped tent.

"That was weird," Isla said finally. "Let's keep going."

Next to the fortune teller's tent was a row of strangely shaped mirrors. Isla and Leena stood in front of each one, laughing at their appearances. First, they were tall and skinny, then short and fat. Each mirror made the girls giggle amongst themselves. A tall torso and short base, a tall base and short torso. A fat face, skinny body and fat legs. A skinny face, fat body and skinny legs. Those were fun! The girls almost forgot how bizarre this place was.

Then, Isla heard moaning and groaning. Just faintly. She started walking towards the noise. Leena followed at a distance. The sounds brought Isla to a tent. The flap was wide open, so Isla entered. Leena peered in from outside. Isla saw a tall, slender woman sobbing next to a long, slender man laying on a bed. They both had smooth dark green skin, wide hands, a wide mouth, and bulging eyes. The one on the bed was making the wailing sounds, he was also choking up blood into a bucket. The seated one wiped his mouth, held his hand in hers, and continued to cry.

"I tried to tell her it was too wide. I'm sorry, my love," the bedridden one croaked hoarsely.

"Shhh, don't speak now," her voice was shaky but calming. "Nothing is your fault, I love you."

"Eh! What are you two doing?!" A very tall, slender dark green skinned creature burst into the tent. "Git! No guests! Git!"

The girls ran. As they went they could still hear coughing, moaning, and crying.

"What happened?" Leena asked as she huffed and puffed.

"I don't know, but I don't think it was anything good." They slowed and took a moment to catch their breath.

They looked up, they had run right up to the big, looming black canopy the ticket taker warned them about. They both stiffened when they heard growling.

"Boo!" Both girls jumped. "Hahahaha scaredy!"

"Oh, shut up, Chester! You too, Rory!" The boys high fived as they continued to laugh.

All four of them stood still when they heard a different kind of growl. It was deep, full, and made the ground tremor beneath their feet. They turned slowly toward the large, menacing black. There were no signs, no warnings, no descriptions of what was inside.

"Go, go check it out Rory," Chester said softly.

"No way, you go check it out," Rory countered. "Or you go, Leena!" Rory shoved his sister in the direction of the entrance.

"Stop it, Rory! I'm going to tell mom!" Leena snapped.

Before Rory had a chance to respond, there was another low deep growl that shook the ground. Followed by what sounded like mewing, squealing; a sound they couldn't quite place.

Isla started slowly for the entrance.

"Isla! No!" Leena quietly protested.

"Come on, Isla, this isn't funny," Chester whispered loudly.

Isla felt as if she was being pulled inside. Each step she took was a combination of her own free-will and an invisible tugging. She slipped inside the tent's flap without opening it. Pitch blackness surrounded her. She heard the growl again. Waiting for her eyes to adjust, she took very slow, very cautious steps forward. She accidentally knocked something over. Two large glowing eyes appeared suddenly, making Isla stop in her tracks. She eased her arms down to the ground and groped around until she felt something long and cold. A flashlight! What luck! She shined the light at the ground first, then gradually raised it until she saw the creature.

A great black mass, long black fur, pointed ears, and the two large glowing green eyes. Surprisingly, it did not growl now. Instead, it made a whimpering sound and lowered its big head. Isla came closer, squinting to make out the object the creature was now licking. Could it be…babies? Isla inched closer, yes, little black blobs nursing. Well, little compared to their mama anyways. Each one looked a good deal larger than Isla herself.

She heard a loud rattling sound. Isla moved the flashlight around until she found the source. Large, thick metal chains cuffed around two of the mama's legs.

"She mistreats us," a familiar raspy voice spoke from the darkness just beyond the black creature. "All of us. She forces us to perform. She keeps us sick. This beautiful Wisteria was stolen from the planet Hulara. She calls her The Beast, but I call her Duama. Which means "black" or "darkness" in my native tongue. Stolen from her family, from her home, and imprisoned here. As soon as she's able she will be forced to perform as a terrorizing monster no doubt. The rest of us were deceived. We were promised lives of travel, excitement, leisure. We were given a good sum upfront with the assurance of much more to come. None of us realized it truly was too good to be true." Madam Astra stepped into the light of Isla's flashlight. "Your fortune said you are the one. The one who will save us all. Save us from her and her evil devices."

"Who is "her"?" Isla inquired.

"The Ring Master," Madam Astra informed her. "She is a smooth talker, a talented charmer, and a master deceiver. Please, you must save us from her."

Isla thought back to the heads, the coughing dragon head, and the dying slender being upon the bed.

"How do I stop her?" Madam Astra smiled and pointed to a large key upon the wall. Isla started at once. Rushing over to the key, jumping up to reach it. She hesitated. *What if this creature…Duama… really is dangerous? Should I really free her onto the city?*

Duama looked at Isla with her large eyes, then lowered her head to lick her whelps. The babies mewled softly as they tried to stand and move around. Isla saw they, too, were chained. The key was heavy, but Isla managed to shove it in the keyhole and used all her strength to turn it. With one final grunt the shackle burst open. Isla then got to work on the kits. Adrenaline have kept her going, because her body was exhausted.

"Duama! Go now before she realizes you are free!" Madam Astra exclaimed. Duama jumped to her feet, then paused looking at her babies. "I'll watch over your precious little ones, now go!"

Duama leapt out of the opening, Isla close behind. Isla heard both screaming and cheering as she ran. Screaming from the guests and cheering from the carnies. She passed Leena, Chester, and Rory. Before Isla knew it, Duama had the Ring Master flat on the ground, baring her teeth just inches from the Ring Master's face.

The Ring Master was put in chains and marched onto the carnival's ship.

"A thousand thanks to you, brave one," Madam Astra gently placed her little hand on top of Isla's.

"What happens now?" Isla asked.

"We will return her to her planet for her crimes against the universe. I've also heard rumors that she is a wanted criminal on several planets for her various offenses."

Madam Astra moved aside, allowing the three headed dragon to approach Isla. It bowed low, then informed her they would be returning home to rest and receive medical attention. All of them were ill in varying degrees. They thanked her and headed towards their transport.

"Miss Isla, how can I ever repay you?" It was the long, slender dark green skinned woman from the tent. Her wide hands out-stretched, her wide mouth in an even wider smile, and her bulging eyes watery. "My husband," her voice cracked. "My husband didn't make it. We are sword swallowers. We have perfect mouths and throats for it. The Ring Master always forced us to swallow more, bigger, wider, longer. We all knew someday one of us would pay the price." She sniffed and drew a shaky breath. Then she collected herself and smiled again. "I am with child. If it's a girl I am going to name her Isla. Isla Jude, Jude after my husband." She gave Isla a big, hearty hug and the group of sword swallowers went on their way.

"Isla?" Leena approached her cautiously. "Isla, what in the world happened?"

Isla smiled, "I just followed my fortune." Duama lunged over, Leena stepped back several paces. First Isla stroked all the lovely cubs. Madam Astra placed them all very comfortably in two wheel-barrows lined with several blankets. The strong men pushed the wheelbarrows and the cubs toward the transport. Isla noticed the men were indeed muscular, but also unusually skinny. Sometimes having to pause to stretch and rub their muscles. *Hopefully now they will have time to rest and recuperate*, she thought.

Duama rubbed up against Isla, almost making her fall backwards. Then she licked her face with her wide, slimy tongue. Isla laughed.

"It was so nice to meet you, Duama. I hope you have the most fulfilling life raising your babies back in your own home." Isla was just able to rub Duama's underbelly when standing on her tip toes.

The other members of the carnival filed into the ships. Clowns with bright make-up, marked with tear tracks. Large four-legged animals with short fur, very long tails, and hard hooves. At least some of them had hooves, others limped around due to a broken hoof or even a broken leg.

Isla heard chanting. "We're going home! We're going home!" A group of short, skinny, white skinned critters jumped, cart-wheeled, and skipped in this seeming parade of freedom. They did back flips and walked on their hands. Others made a ladder of themselves, the one at the very top juggling small yellow balls. They were a wonder to watch.

The ticket man tipped his hat with one of his many tentacles as he crawled passed Isla. At the very end of the pack came a group of long-legged short-bodied winged beings with feathers covering their body and a stubby beak. Isla noticed the tip of one of the wings was cut at an angle on all of them.

Madam Astra stood on the ramp connecting Isla's world with distant space; she bowed her head before ordering the ramp closed.

Isla waited for the ships to leave then joined Leena. Leena looked frazzled. Isla took her hand and told her everything as they walked home.

~ * ~ * ~

Emily Grisby is a stay-at-home wife and homeschooling mom of three from Ohio. She has always enjoyed fantasy and sci-fi literature and films. She is a born-again Christian, and her faith is very important to her.

Death of a Clown

Tim Newton Anderson

"Gimpy died," Paul said. "They're burying him tonight in some big hoohaw. Sounds cool."

"He must have been like a hundred," I said. "My dad said he was in the circus when he was a kid in the last century."

"Make that even older," Paul said. "My granddad remembers him. The same funny, scary, weird clown."

"Unless it's like a family thing," I said. "The next generation steps into those big shoes."

"Perhaps that's how he died," Paul said. "Tripped over them big shoes, or crashed the clown car. Can't be all different people. though. There's some kind of trade union thing going on with clowns. They all have to have different faces. My dad told me. They paint them on eggs."

He laughed. If I was honest, I was relieved the clown was dead. I loved going to the circus when it came to town to see the animals and acrobats, but the clowns gave me the ick. Even the freaks they had in the sideshows were less scary. You could see they were just people who were a bit strange, or had been made up to look that way. But you never knew where you were with a clown. Anything could be going on behind all that makeup, and they seemed to be able to do anything they wanted without any of the adults questioning it. That whole fake bucket of water throwing. Even though as a twelve-year-old who had seen it a dozen times, I always dreaded that one day it would really be water rather than confetti. Or worse.

"Never worked out why he was called Gimpy," I said. "I asked my dad and he mumbled something about wearing a mask."

"My dad reckoned in the old days Gimpy meant you had a limp," Paul said. "Not that I ever saw it. Anyways, I just want to see the funeral. It'll be so sick."

"Surely they won't let just anyone go," I said. "We'll need an invite or something. And it's a school night so no chance if it's on late."

"That's the whole point," Paul said. "It's at midnight. Everyone will be asleep and we just sneak out. The circus folk will all be concentrating on the ceremony so we can find somewhere hidden to see it from. Up a tree or something. Or under a tent."

My cousin Paul was the same age as me—12—but a lot more adventurous. I'm not sure why. We've both lived here all of our lives and our fathers are brothers with the Great Witcherley look of ginger hair and beards. I bet mine will start sprouting in a couple of years. Paul already had some ginger fuzz on his chin.

Paul spent his life exploring and getting into one scrape after another while I did my exploring in a book. Even breaking his leg last year didn't stop him for long, although it slowed him down a bit. For me, the circus was about the only interesting thing that happened in the village, and despite the clowns, I looked forward to it all year.

My dad says Wishlock's Circus must spend the winter somewhere round here, or they would never pitch up at our quiet village in the fens. The seats in the big top are never more than half full, although everyone hereabouts goes, and you see the same faces in the same places at every one of the week's performances. Its arrival at the end of October is the last bit of brightness before winter sets in. The final performance features some of the villagers in the traditional Mummer's Play to celebrate Halloween. Some kind of pagan hang on with St George and the dragon and a man dressed as a woman. Oh, and the quack doctor who brings St George back to life. It finishes off the show and then the kids are sent to bed while the adults go down to the pub and get drunk.

Paul had lots of theories about where they came from and where they went. I was supposed to be the one with an imagination because of all that reading, but he could invent a tale at the drop of a hat. Aliens, that was his favourite. Come down for the season in a flying saucer, or though some inter-dimensional rift.

"When they come home at closing time, they'll be too sozzled to notice us sneaking out," Paul said. "They're lucky to wake up the next morning, never mind at midnight."

I wasn't sure about it but didn't want Paul to think I was scared. If I ducked out of going he would tell everyone at school and they already thought I was some kind of geek because I read books for fun.

"Okay," I said. "Throw a pebble up at my window—a little one or even drunks would wake up—and I'll climb down to meet you."

By making him come to me it at least kept the possibility open he would chicken out.

But he didn't.

Being Halloween, teatime kept being interrupted by knocks on the door from young kids trick or treating. News of Gimpy's death had obviously spread as most of them were dressed as scary clowns. With the Great Witchingham red hair gene, it felt like we were being invaded by a fast-food chain. Somehow their size made them even more terrifying and I let my mom and dad answer the door after the first couple of times. I was glad I was reckoned too old to go door to door as I would probably have had to wear clown makeup myself. The thought of wearing that greasepaint mask was actually more frightening than meeting a clown. Imagine seeing that in a mirror.

We went to the circus that evening with our families. You would think in a little village like this, the circus would be small too. In fact the big top could accommodate the whole village three times over—even with the new houses on the edge—and there was what the Americans call a midway by the side with fairground rides including a big wheel and a ghost train, and tents with unusual people in them. That's what I think they should be called, anyway. When my granddad was a kid they would have called them freaks. A mermaid, a fortune teller, and a creature that was either a bear or a Russian. That was different about Wishlock's Circus, too. It had animals, despite activists shutting down most shows with them in. Lions and tigers and an elephant as well as horses. They looked proper wild, too, not like the sad specimens I saw when we visited a small zoo a couple of years ago. I knew the sideshows were just people in costumes and make-up or some kind of puppets, but they looked pretty real. Perhaps Paul was right and they were aliens.

I'd seen the show before, of course. I have been going to the annual visit for as long as I can remember and we came to every show during the week. It was different tonight, though. No Gimpy the clown, for one thing. And, like I said, on Halloween the village people are allowed to put on their Mummer's Play in the big top. I asked my dad where they did it before the circus started visiting each year, and he just shrugged. Apparently his parents and grandparents had staged it at the circus as well.

Before that were all the circus' own acts: the lady on the trapeze with fake wings on her back and her partner who was also supposed to be able to fly; the acrobats in their skimpy outfits that all the adults looked at real close; the strong man lifting two people at a time with one arm; and the Ringmaster with his piercing stare and sinister moustache. No clowns, though. It wasn't really that I was glad Gimpy was dead, but I sort of was, because it meant his fellow clowns didn't perform out of respect.

The Ringmaster did the same spiel every time.

"Welcome one and all to Wishlock's Circus," he bellowed from the centre of the ring. He carried a long whip in his right hand and as he spoke he would twirl it around his head and body like that ribbon gymnastics thing at the Olympics. It was a bit hypnotic, but perhaps that was the idea. Make us relaxed and not look at things too closely.

"You are all privileged to have our amazing show in your midst. We have entertained Kings and Presidents, Sultans and billionaires. We have travelled across the globe to bring you the best acts from this world and beyond. And tonight you will have the great honour of performing your own historic play in this magical ring. Sit back, people of Great Witcherley, and prepare for the marvels we offer up to you."

The rest of the show was as wonderful as usual. I'd seen it a couple of dozen times, but still got caught up in its magic. I suppose it's like a conjuror, you know it's a trick but don't want to know how it's done—you don't want to look behind the curtain like in the Wizard of Oz. The ringmaster would produce flowers from thin air and hand them to whoever was this year's Carnival Queen. The couple on the trapeze really did look like they could fly. The acrobats must have been double jointed or something and seemed to bend and twist their bodies into impossible shapes.

But even though I had a thing about clowns, I had to admit to missing them. In a strange way they are more important to the circus than the Ringmaster. He seemed in charge, but the clowns showed even he was not respected by them when they would knock off his top hat and pin a 'kick me' sign on his back so they could playfully boot him with those big shoes. Their act mocked all of the other performers as they made a pantomime of acrobatics and played on the trapeze—almost falling but managing to leap to the other swing as miraculously as the real artists. One would dress up as a lion and pretend to be scared of another clown with a whip and chair before jumping on him as soon as his back was turned. Nothing and no-one were safe, and the laughter of the crowd made them immune from a telling off. Perhaps that's why Paul liked them so much. He would have loved to have the same immunity from the rules and have everyone laugh along with him.

My Dad and Paul's were both in the Mummer's play and they had disappeared during the lion tamer's act to get into costume. Half a dozen other men also left—uncles and cousins of Paul and me. No women—equality hadn't been able to change the tradition. After the lion cage was pulled out of the arena there was a fanfare and the village troupe bounced in.

Dad told me the play was some kind of fertility thing about the seasons and crops. Saint George had a fight with a dragon—a man in a kind of dragon shaped skirt costume—and won. Then the Devil came in, all in red with a long tail and a big fork thing. The dame—Busty Betsy (another man) —pleaded with George not to fight him, but was ignored, and in the tussle George was stabbed with that fork and collapsed on the ground. Then Betsy ran around wailing before the Quack Doctor came in. He pulled open his medicine bag and carefully lifted out a golden cup which he filled with some red stuff from a bottle and gave it to George who immediately sprang to his feet and restarted the fight with the devil. This time he won.

Perhaps it's not the makeup that worries me about clowns, because all of the Mummers had painted faces that made it hard to work out who was who. The fact all the men in the village had a similar look didn't help, of course. I knew my dad was the Quack Doctor, and Paul's father was Saint George, because we had seen their costumes. I couldn't work out which of my relatives played the other parts, though, even after seeing it every year, like, forever. Tonight was different, though. After the troupe took their bows, the Quack Doctor walked over to where Paul and I were sitting and gave my friend a drink from the gold cup thing. Paul looked as surprised as I was, and no-one else was offered the goblet.

"What was that about?" I asked afterwards. "It's not your

birthday for weeks."

"No idea," Paul said. "My dad didn't say anything about it beforehand."

"What did it taste like?" I asked. Knowing how much our families liked a drink, I assumed it would be wine, or some red soft drink if they knew they were giving it to a kid.

"It didn't really taste of anything," Paul said. He had that face on he got when he was doing something risky or bad, so I knew he was lying. "Probably just coloured water."

Part of me was relieved my Dad had picked Paul and not me. I would hate to be singled out in front of the whole village. But part of me was also jealous. Why *was* Paul chosen over me? It was as if he had been given a present I wouldn't like, but which should have been mine. To tell the truth I was always a bit jealous of Paul. All the kids at school said he was more fun than me. He was better at sports, could banter with the teachers and parents without getting told off, caught the bigger fish in the river. He was my best friend, but I sometimes felt like I was being dragged along in his orbit, rather than existing in my own right. Tonight's plan was typical Paul.

After the show we bought some candy floss and rock for the young kids at a kiosk before walking back home. There would be a fight in their brains between the sugar and the exhaustion, and I hoped the tiredness would win. I still wasn't sure about going to see Gimpy's funeral, but I wanted it to be my choice, rather than being forced to stay home to look after my brother and sister as they bounced off the walls.

I was fully dressed and waiting when there was the rattle of gravel on my window. Paul was in my back garden with a rucksack on his back. My mum and dad weren't back from the pub, but I was confident they would just stagger up to bed rather than checking on me.

I wasn't the climber Paul was, but it was an easy slide down the drainpipe next to my window. Paul had waited at the bottom to catch me if I slipped, but I made a show of jumping clear at the bottom as if I was one of the circus acrobats.

"Shh!" Paul said. "Keep it down till we get clear of the houses."

I grinned and mimed pulling a zip across my mouth. I let Paul lead the way down our back path and into the narrow lane behind the row of houses. A couple of minutes walking and we were past the end of the village and into the woods. The cleared field the circus used was just on the other side. It was a bit spooky in the wood at night—it was dense and overcast so the light of the full moon had to elbow its way in between the tree branches. A lot of the leaves had fallen as a crunchy red carpet hiding rabbit holes and tree roots, but there was still ivy wrapping the thicker limbs which kept us in shadow. Luckily the deer that lived here had made clear paths which we could follow without risking a tumble. We didn't dare risk using a torch in case the circus folk spotted us and sent us back home.

When we got to the edge of the wood we crawled forward through the un-cleared wild flowers at the edge of the circus field. Like I said, there was a full moon, but the scene by the big top told us no-one would be looking anywhere else.

The top itself was closed and the shutters were down on the sideshow attractions, but there was a big show going on in the clearing at the centre of the field. A giant bonfire had been built with a dozen smaller fires circling it, their flickering flames lighting the scene and dancing on the forms of the circus folk. That was sort of what we expected, but we hadn't reckoned on all the adults of the village being there as well, behind the performers in a second circle of onlookers. The actors in the Mummers Play were still in costume. And it wasn't just the people from the circus—the animals were there, lying quietly next to the performers. All of them were waiting for something. Something momentous.

At first I thought it was a bit of an anti-climax when the clown car appeared. Perhaps they were going to put on some kind of tribute to Gimpy they missed out on doing earlier in the evening when they didn't appear in the ring. But there was no riotous tumbling from the tiny vehicle when it stopped next to the unlit fire. The clowns looked solemn as they climbed out—heaven knows how they managed it, packed in as they must have been. I had a strange thought that it must be like Dr Who's Tardis as not only did six clowns climb out of a space Paul and I would find cramped, but they also slid out a full size coffin, and hoisted it on their shoulders.

It was a couple of hundred yards to where the crowd was standing, but the scene was so magnetic I could see everything as clearly as if I was in the front row. The coffin had been draped in

Gimpy's clown suit with its baggy pants and ruffled shirt. Those giant shoes were on the top, weighing the clothes down. Sometimes silence is louder than noise—like when you've done something wrong and there's a pause before your parents shout at you. This silence was so thick it felt like I was smothered in it. It was solid enough I don't think I could have moved, even if I wanted to. Even Paul wasn't doing his usual fidgeting.

Then the slow clap started, keeping time with the solemn steps of the funeral parade. Everyone clapped, and stamped one foot, as the clowns walked through the crowd to the unlit bonfire and carefully leant the coffin against it. One of them gently opened the coffin lid, and I could see Gimpy was inside. He was wearing an ordinary suit, but full clown makeup and his curly red wig.

I was so absorbed in what was happening I didn't hear the people creep up behind us and grab Paul and me by the shoulders. I tried to cry out as I was lifted up, but there was a hand over my mouth as well as an arm crushing my chest and we were taken, struggling, down towards the crowd. Part of me was bricking it, but part was quite calm. All our parents and neighbours were there. We would get told off, sure, but nothing bad could happen, surely. Could it?

The crowd parted as we were carried in. Still silent. I looked down at the arm holding me and saw it was in clown costume. It was like in my nightmares. A look left and I saw Paul was also being manhandled by a clown. The fear was so strong I stopped struggling and just shivered quietly, tears running down my face.

I could see Gimpy in his coffin really clearly now. There was a clown colleague on the left and on the right of him. The clowns who had carried us placed us gently on our feet right in front of the coffin. The set down may have been gentle, but they still held us so tight I could hardly breath, even if the situation itself hadn't been tightening my chest. They still had their hands on our mouths, too, although I was too scared to try and speak. I looked over to where my Dad was in his Quack Doctor get up but he didn't make eye contact—just stared at that coffin. I noticed he still had that goblet thing in his hands, and the gold colour was shining in the flames from the fires. The flames were red and gold, just like the cup and its contents.

The Ringmaster stepped out of the performer's circle and

walked towards the coffin. He took off his hat—in respect I guess —and held it under his left arm.

"Earlier this evening we witnessed the sacred tradition of your village," he said. "Now we witness a hallowed ritual of our own. Performers may come and go, but everywhere in the universe where the circus exists, the time-honoured continuity must be preserved. The mortal who inhabited the make-up and costume of Gimpy for many seasons may no longer be with us, but the eternal clown will rise again."

When he reached the coffin he did something so shocking it will haunt my nightmares as long as I live. He stretched his hand out to Gimpy's face, and he lifted the skin right off, exposing the clown's bare skull beneath. He lifted it up above his head as if it was some kind of trophy or something. I don't know which was worse, the limp skin with that horrible make up on it, or the dead white of Gimpy's skull. I had seen dead people, but only in a hospital and only for a short while before I was taken out of the room to get a drink in the canteen. This was not the peaceful sleep I had seen on relatives, it was just sick and wrong. Even a clown didn't deserve to be treated like that.

My dad stepped forward too, raising the goblet. I was frozen in fear as he moved towards me.

Then he stepped to my left and lifted the goblet to Paul's mouth again, the clown having moved his arm out of the way. I thought Paul would try and shout, or scream, or turn his head away, but he just put his lips to the cup and drank.

And then the second thing happened that has stalked my sleep and poisoned my dreams. The Ringmaster took Gimpy's face and placed it over Paul's like a shroud over the head of a corpse. There was a sharp intake of breath from everyone in the crowd, as if this was the finale of some spectacular and dangerous trick. I stared at Paul and could see his eyes staring back out of Gimpy's face. And as I looked his eyes changed from the sky-blue colour everyone in the village shared to a sickly green that seemed to glow like the hands of an alarm clock. He should have been horrified like I was, but he looked almost triumphant. Everyone knelt, and the clown holding me forced me to my knees too. The ring master took a length of wood with a cloth tied round it and handed it to Paul. Paul pushed it into the fire nearest to him to set it alight, and then threw it at the bonfire where Gimpy's coffin rested. It must have had petrol on it or something because there was a flash of flame as it roared to life and I felt its heat burning my face.

I guess I passed out then, because the next thing I remember is waking up in my bed, and everyone in the house acting like it was just another day. I tried to talk to them, but somehow the words stuck in my throat every time I tried to ask anything about what happened. Like I'd been hypnotised not to mention it.

As soon as I was allowed out I ran over to Paul's but of course he wasn't there. I tried to ask his mom and brother about him, but again my mouth just couldn't form the words. Instead, I just had some boring chat about going back to school on Monday, and had I done my homework?

At the field where the circus had been there was just flattened grass and bare earth where people had walked, plus a few ruts where the wagon wheels had dug in the mud when they arrived in the rain a week ago. They had taken everything with them including their litter. And Paul. The grass had been flattened in strange shapes like a message in a language I would never understand.

The last thing I remember before I passed out on that night was his face. Or rather Gimpy's face. The only part of Paul still there was his smile underneath that greasepaint. A smile of wild happiness and freedom. The clown had let go of his arms and he took a bow before those kneeling in front of him. There was a new king of the circus.

The circus came back again next year, and Paul was in it. Except everyone called him Gimpy, as if he had always had that name, and last year's nightmare was just that—a dream. And of course he didn't acknowledge me, and I was unable to talk about it with this strange compulsion of silence on me. I was sure he winked at me once, though. With the scary smile of a clown.

~ * ~ * ~

Tim Newton Anderson is a former daily newspaper journalist and PR manager who started writing fiction four years ago. Since then he has placed nearly 60 stories in a wide variety of genres and publications. His blog is at http://atjentertainments.wordpress.com and he has an Amazon Author page as Tim Newton Anderson.

Professor Vlkoslag's Traveling Medicine Show

Carol Hightshoe

"Step right up folks! Professor Vlkoslag's Traveling Medicine Show will be opening tonight, bringing wonders and marvels beyond your wildest dreams." I tip my top hat to a couple of ladies walking down the street here in Las Vegas, New Mexico. A brief gust of wind sends a swirl of dust and brittle leaves across the camp. The scent of damp canvas, oiled leather, and woodsmoke lingers in the air. In the distance, a dog barks, and the faint sound of a hammer striking metal rings from a blacksmith's forge. The town is waking up from winter's grip, but it hasn't quite shaken it off.

Despite the chill of the day, there is the promise of spring in the air as the scent of blossoms, faint but unmistakable, drifts on the breeze from somewhere beyond the town. "We have entertainments to delight and beguile, patent medicines to cure most every ailment and talismans to protect from every danger," My voice rings out with well-practiced charm, blending with the murmur of the passersby. I glance over at the roustabouts as they work to get everything set up and ready. The rhythmic *thud-thud-thud* of mallets driving stakes into the ground mixes with the occasional *clang* of metal as the stage is assembled. The coarse paper of the handbills scratches slightly against my fingers reminding me it's time for me to get started. The faint but sharp aroma of medicinal herbs—camphor, sassafras, and licorice root—drifts from my wagon as I set out to meet the locals. Time for me to see what we have to work with in this town.

Crunch. The sound catches my attention as I step away from my wagon. I lift my boot and see what looks like a cross between a spider and a scorpion. *A wind scorpion,* I think. With care I reach down and scoop up the remains. "You will be the star of the show," I whisper, turning back to my enclosed wagon. I pause for a moment taking in the sight of my traveling home. Like the other wagons used by our troupe my wagon has seen better days—once a grand, crimson showpiece, now faded and chipped from too many miles on dusty roads. The gold lettering still boldly proclaims *Professor Vlkoslag's Traveling Medicine Show* though the edges are peeling, and the flourishes could use a fresh coat of paint. The fold-down steps at the back creak when I step on them, but they hold, just like always. She's a little shabby, a little theatrical—but so am I, and she still gets the job done.

I place the wind scorpion on the table and with deliberate precision draw the chalk lines forming an intricate web to contain the magic I will be using. Softly muttering the words of the spell, I take the silver pin from my hat and stab the vein in my wrist, allowing several drops of blood to fall on the arachnid. Neither a true spider nor a true scorpion, wind scorpions are extremely common in arid regions like the American Southwest. But my version will only be seen by those who visit the show tonight and only for a very limited time.

~ * ~

With the magically revived wind scorpion secure in its display case, I pick up the handbills and head back out. Being on the Santa Fe Trail, and with the railroad stopping here, this is a prosperous town. However, it could also be a lawless town. When we arrived, I picked a spot closer to what had been the original settlement and hence the slightly more civilized area, but still accessible to the rougher types who call the other side of the tracks home.

My first stop is the hotel. The lobby is tidy but well-worn, with polished wooden floors reflecting the afternoon light filtering through lace curtains. A brass bell sits on the counter, its surface dulled by years of use, while a ledger book lies open next to it; the pages ink-stained, yet carefully kept. A faint scent of polished wood and old parchment lingers in the air, mixed with a touch of lavender from a vase on the counter.

"May I help you?" a pleasant voice calls from a back room after I tap the bell and its clear, gentle chime fades.

"I was hoping I could leave some of my flyers here." My handbills, slightly crumpled from the journey, rest on the counter, their bold lettering and swirling illustrations promising wonders and cures. I offer her my best smile as I pull several tickets from my pocket. "For you," I say handing her the tickets. "Free admission for you and your family as a way of saying thank you for allowing me to advertise in your beautiful hotel."

The lady smiles and pushes a stray lock of red hair behind her ear. "Certainly, sir," she replies, her voice soft as a springtime breeze. She takes the tickets then hands a few of them back. "I only need three," she says.

I raise my hand. The sharp tang of herbal tinctures, a ghost of camphor and licorice wafts from my coat. There is also a musty odor of sulfur still clinging to the fabric—residue from the magic I worked a short time ago. "My dear lady, you are free to give the extra tickets to your staff or perhaps you may choose to visit more than once."

"Thank you, mister…"

"Professor. Professor Vlkoslag." I tip my hat and bow slightly. "The first show will be tonight. I hope we see you there."

She laughs lightly as I head out to the street.

~ * ~

When I get back to the wagons, the sun hangs high, beating down on the camp and casting sharp shadows beneath the canvas and wagons. The air is thick with dust kicked up by the workers as they move back and forth, driving stakes into the ground. The rhythmic thud of mallets blends with the creak of wagon wheels and the occasional clatter of wooden crates being unloaded. Despite the coming spring there is still a chill in the air—a reminder winter is not over yet.

"Well, Professor?" Madame Roma, our fortune teller, calls as she steps out from behind her wagon, pulling her shawl tighter around her shoulders. The faint jingle of her bangles follows the motion as she folds her arms, her sharp gaze watching me with a knowing expression.

I scan the work being done. The stage is almost finished. "We will set up the tents for both burlesque shows and the magic show," I say, stepping forward, my boots pressing into the softening earth. "However, I want the menagerie front and center as people come in. I have the star attraction ready for display.

"Also, finish setting up the stage," I continue, tugging my coat closed against the chill. "We should look like we'll be offering a play. This town seems a bit bereft of entertainment." I let the thought settle for a moment before allowing myself a slow smile. "Tents and stage only. Have everything else, other than the menagerie, packed back up and loaded. I suspect we won't have to worry about holding actual performances tonight. And, if everything goes as expected, we will need to load and leave quickly."

Madame Roma nods slowly, tapping a ringed finger against her lips as she considers my words. Then, with a rustle of fabric, she turns to set things in motion.

I take a deep breath, the air crisp and tinged with the scent of woodsmoke, trampled grass, and the lingering chill of winter reluctantly giving way to spring. If everything plays out the way I expect, we'll be long gone before this town wakes in the morning.

"Of course, Professor." Madame Roma's dark eyes brighten, and she smiles. "The main performance will be a production worthy of San Fransico or Denver." She nods then spins around, her long black hair swirling around her like her colorful skirts as she hurries to deliver my instructions to the company.

I have no doubts everything will be ready in time.

~ * ~

"Step right up, folks!" I call, my breath barely visible, though the air still carries a crisp edge. A few townsfolk pull their coats a little tighter, while others seem eager to shake off the last grip of winter and welcome the night's entertainments. Overhead, the sky deepens from pale blue to dusky violet, streaked with the last golden rays of daylight.

Beyond the rope fence, nothing more than a few lengths of fraying cord strung between battered sawhorses, the crowd stirs. Boots shuffle on the cool, firm ground, still holding a hint of frost in the shaded places. The scent of damp wood and old hay drifts from our wagons, mixing with the aroma of oil lanterns being lit one by one, their flames flickering in the breeze.

I pull the rope aside, the coarse fibers rough under my fingers, though the motion is more for show than security.

"In addition to the menagerie we have on display, tonight's main attraction will be a play! A play that has been performed before the crowned heads of Europe! Kings and Queens have been amazed by the skill of our actors!" I sweep my arm toward the stage, the wooden boards newly cleaned but still wearing the scars of past performances. The wagons, forming a crescent moon around it, cast long shadows across the field, their paint dulled from miles on the road but still bold enough to catch the last slivers of the fading light.

A ripple of interest moves through the crowd. A young boy tugs on his father's sleeve, eyes wide with curiosity, while a few ladies exchange amused glances.

"For the gentlemen who prefer the simpler pleasures, we offer exotic dancers from far and distant lands." I turn toward the smaller canvas tent on the left. The wind stirs its edges, making the entrance flap sway slightly, as though beckoning. From inside, comes the whisper of perfume—spiced, rich, and just enough to tempt.

"But don't be dismayed, oh ye of the fairer sex! We also offer a similar show for the ladies." I gesture toward the opposite tent, its canvas slightly faded, but still bold, standing against the twilight sky. A few women in the crowd exchange glances, some intrigued, others pretending not to be. Just as perfume floated from the first tent; musk comes from the second tent.

"For the young at heart, Madame Roma will be performing various magics and sleight of hand tricks." I spot her lingering near her tent, the silver of her bangles catching the last light of day. "Tomorrow, she will be available to read your fortune in her cards."

A quiet moment stretches between us and the crowd, the air thick with anticipation. I glance over the gathered faces, reading their curiosity, their skepticism, their hunger for something beyond their quiet lives. Some already appear hooked; others only need one last push. I give them a slow, knowing smile and start to gesture them in...

"They're coming..." Madame Roma's voice is barely a whisper, yet it weaves through the gathered spectators like a creeping fog.

"They're coming," she repeats. This time, the unease is palpable.

Behind her, her assistant moves in slow, measured steps, her eyes glassy, unblinking, as if caught in a trance. The wicker basket she carries creaks softly, its contents shifting inside with a soft metallic sound.

A murmur spreads through the crowd. Low whispers, uncertain and nervous, coil around me like tendrils of smoke. I also hear a few scoffs, a chuckle or two—the skeptics always make themselves known.

"Madame Roma? Are you alright?" I step closer. As I do, a strange, silvery glow shimmers around her like mist catching moonlight. A few gasps ripple through the spectators, and I don't miss the way some take a step back, clutching their coats a little tighter.

"Please, excuse me, folks," I say, keeping my voice steady, controlled. "It seems the spirits of the other world are unruly this evening. I must attend to her."

Madame Roma's assistant moves forward, her hands cold as ice as she helps me guide Madame Roma to a stool. The wind shifts again, and then—

A sharp, glassy scratching sound.

It comes from behind me. From the insect menagerie.

The whispering voices halt as one by one, the crowd turns toward the source of the sound. Tiny legs skitter against glass. More than one. More than a dozen.

A shifting mass of beetles, spiders, scorpions—all clawing, clicking, and moving in restless, unnatural motion.

A woman gasps, clutching her husband's arm, and a boy presses closer, his mouth open slightly in morbid fascination.

Leaning toward Madame Roma, I let my voice drop to a loud stage whisper, just enough for people to strain their ears toward me. "Who or what is coming?"

"The scorpions," she breathes, her entire body trembling. Her head jerks to one side, then the other, as if scanning for unseen horrors. "The flying vampire scorpions."

A boy in the crowd yelps, his voice breaking with excitement. I can feel the energy shifting, thickening, turning from quiet murmurs to a growing wave of alarm.

"They are only a myth," I say in a hoarse whisper, clutching my top hat in mock fear, letting my hand tremble just a little—just enough.

"No. No. No," Madame Roma insists. She lurches to her feet, pushing me away with unexpected force, her voice rising. "I warned you when you caught that one."

She points, and all eyes turn toward the magically revived wind scorpion.

The glow from the lanterns shimmers off its exoskeleton, too large, too sleek, its legs twitching against the glass.

"That's just a wind scorpion," I say with a practiced laugh, but the crowd isn't so easily convinced.

"Don't look like no wind scorpion I ever seen," someone mutters.

"How so, my friend?" I ask, keeping my tone light, but the tension is thick enough to choke on.

"Well, ain't never seen a wind scorpion get that big. They's usually smaller than my hand, and that one, well…it's 'bout twice as big."

The murmuring deepens, shifting like a tide rolling in.

"So he's bigger than average. Just means he takes his medicine and drinks his tonics." I gesture grandly toward my array of bottles, letting the lamplight gleam off their glass.

"But what about them wings?" Another voice, sharper now.

Wind scorpions don't have wings. Everyone here knows it.

The crowd leans in, a collective motion, the kind that signals danger or discovery.

"See? I told you it wasn't just a wind scorpion," Madame Roma warns, her voice trembling with just the right edge of terror.

"So it's a mutation of some sort." I walk over to the terrarium, my boots thudding against the ground. The glass feels cool beneath my palm as I rest my hand on it.

"I tell you, my friends, flying vampire scorpions are just a myth." I grin, tilting my head just so, letting the firelight glint in my eyes. "They're as much a myth as actual vampires are."

A collective gasp.

A shudder moves through the crowd, almost like a wave of wind sweeping across dry grass.

"Vampires?" someone repeats, their voice just above a whisper.

I hold up a hand, palm out in a placating gesture. "Now, friends, don't tell me you believe those old legends and stories. I can see you are all much more intelligent than to believe in fairy tales." I pause just long enough to let them think.

I can see their minds grinding against their own fears, their own doubts. The trick to a good performance isn't in the illusion—it's in the hesitation.

"Yes, fairy tales and legends," I say, my voice carrying over the hushed crowd. "Surely you don't believe the Almighty Himself would be so cruel as to curse a man with immortality."

"That don't sound like a curse," someone heckles from the back.

I chuckle, a slow, measured sound, and step forward. "Think about it, friend. All those you love, growing old and dying while you continue on." My voice drops, and the crowd leans in. "Yes, there may be challenges that make it interesting and fun for a while, but after you've done everything you wanted to do, traveled to all the places you wanted to see—you would grow bored."

Laughter ripples through the audience, sharp and uncertain, like the crackling of dry leaves in the wind.

"That might be you. I doubt it would be everyone," a young-looking cowboy calls out. His voice is smooth but carries the cold steel edge of confidence. I take note of the way people give him space, their eyes flicking toward the low-slung holster at his hip.

I keep my expression friendly but thoughtful. "Perhaps. But there is more to the curse of the vampire." My voice softens as I let my gaze sweep across the gathered faces, some intrigued, others wary. "To survive, he must drink the blood of others. According to the stories, there are those who are made into slaves just so he can occasionally feed on them." I pause, letting the words sink in like the weight of an unseen shadow.

The crowd grows still, the night pressing in.

"Keeping them alive only to serve his needs." I lift my hands slowly, fingers splayed, as though conjuring something from the air. "There are those he passes the curse onto, and others he drains completely dry, leaving only a withering husk that blows away on the wind."

I flutter my hands like butterfly wings. A thick mist rises, swirling around my fingers before settling to the ground in ghostly tendrils.

The crowd gasps, their attention fully mine.

"And…" I pause, stretching the silence. I can feel them holding their breath, waiting, their pulses quickening. "Many of the legends say the vampire is able to control those he has bitten so they will unknowingly perform any acts he desires."

I let my gaze settle on a young blonde woman in a shabby dress. I smile slowly as I see the shudder ripple through her shoulders, her arms pulling tight across her chest.

"So how did flying vampire scorpions come into being?" The

voice belongs to a boy, his eyes wide with curiosity, shining in the dim light. He has no fear—only wonder.

I glance at Madame Roma. She gives me a small, almost imperceptible nod, her fingers tightening around a cross made of two silver nails.

"According to the legends, my good lad," I say, "a vampire once visited the American West and was bitten by a wind scorpion." I let the words settle, then gesture to the terrarium, where the massive scorpion twitches inside. "Now, if you've ever seen the mandibles on a wind scorpion, you know they would hurt."

The boy follows my gaze, his breath hitching.

"Hey, he ain't got them big pincer jaws—he's got fangs!" the boy cries, his voice high with excitement.

I blink and tilt my head as if seeing the creature for the first time. "Fangs?" My voice drops, barely above a whisper. The hush deepens. "You say he has fangs?"

The audience is mesmerized. Now is the time.

I stumble, knocking into the terrarium.

Glass shatters against the ground.

"Watch out!" I cry, throwing myself back with theatrical panic as the wind scorpion unfurls his wings.

The crowd screams as the creature launches itself into the air, its wings a blur of movement.

Madame Roma shrieks, her voice cutting through the chaos like a blade. She raises the silver cross, her other hand trembling. Her voice spills forth in a rapid torrent of words in her native tongue.

My hand darts to my pocket. I find the silver pin, snap it in two.

The creature bursts into sudden, brilliant flames, its body blackening and curling as fire consumes it.

It never touches Madame Roma.

"She destroyed the vampire scorpion!" someone shouts, breathless with awe.

"She said *they* were coming," another voice cries out. "Will there be more?"

Madame Roma smooths her skirt, recovering her composure with practiced ease.

"Yes." Her voice heavy is with foreboding. "There will be more."

A ripple of uneasy murmurs sweeps through the crowd.

"Can you protect us?"

I hold up my hands in a calming gesture, but before I can answer, Madame Roma steps forward.

"I have more silver crosses," she says smoothly. Her dark eyes gleam in the lantern light. "I can bless them, and they will protect you from the flying vampire scorpions."

A moment of hesitation—then the dam breaks.

People surge forward, their fingers digging into pockets, pulling out bills and coins, frantic to be first.

"They are not cheap," Madame Roma warns, her voice even and firm. "It takes much out of me to bless them."

"Please! How much?"

She tilts her head, as if considering. "I understand your fear. I will offer them for only five dollars each."

Hands wave money in the air, trembling with urgency.

I survey the crowd, my mind quick with numbers. At least a hundred people here—ten who aren't buying—but Madame Roma has two hundred crosses ready.

"Friends, please form an orderly line," I say, lifting my hands again. "Madame Roma should have enough for everyone."

Mist eddies around her as she kneels, its soft tendrils curling around her skirts.

Her assistant places the woven basket beside her, and she reaches inside, pulling out a silver cross. She presses it to her lips, whispers softly, and sets it aside, the pile slowly growing.

I glance toward the roustabouts. They catch my eye and nod. Under the cover of mist, they move swiftly, pulling down ropes, folding canvas, packing what needs to be packed. By the time the last of the crowd has their talismans, we will be nearly ready to vanish into the night.

~ * ~

"All I have is three dollars," a soft voice filled with sadness murmurs.

I recognize her immediately. It's the same shy young woman I smiled at earlier. She clutches her shawl tightly around her shoulders, her golden hair catching the glow of the lanterns as the wind tugs a few strands loose.

Madame Roma, still finishing up with the last of the stragglers, turns toward her. The boy—the curious one who asked about the scorpions—stands nearby, watching everything with keen, wide eyes, his hands stuffed into his too-short sleeves.

Madame Roma smiles, a gesture both warm and knowing. She steps forward, taking the girl's hand gently in her own, then tilts her head as if appraising her like a jeweler studying fine gold.

"You have beautiful golden hair," she says, her voice smooth as honey. She holds up a silver cross. "Two dollars and a lock of your hair."

The young woman hesitates, then nods once. Madame Roma moves with practiced ease, producing a small pair of shears from within her shawl. The metallic snip is nearly lost beneath the murmur of the dwindling crowd. A single golden curl drifts free, catching the lantern light before Madame Roma tucks it into her pocket.

She continues in the same fashion, bartering locks of hair in exchange for talismans. Each time, her fingers move lightly, almost reverently, as she places the strands into the folds of her skirts, as if gathering something far more valuable than mere hair.

All except the boy.

For him, she does something different.

She smiles broadly and offers him the cross she herself used when the creature attacked. It glints brightly in the dimming light.

The boy shakes his head. His small hands curl into determined fists.

"I want to learn," he says.

Madame Roma's smile falters, just for a moment. A flicker of something—respect? Amusement? A hint of concern? —crosses her face.

"What about your parents?" I ask, stepping forward.

The boy doesn't look away, his gaze steady, fierce with the kind of stubbornness only a child who has seen too much too soon can possess.

"My Ma died last year. My Pa ran off several years ago. It's just me." His voice is matter-of-fact, neither seeking pity nor offering excuses.

The wind shifts, a cool gust curls around us, rustling the fabric of my coat. The mist is starting to fade, thinning at the edges, revealing the last of the audience lingering near the wagons.

I study him for a long moment. His eyes are sharp, filled with questions he's too young to have to ask.

"Very well." I lift my top hat and place it on his head, the oversized brim dipping low over his forehead. The weight of it makes him straighten his spine, as if he already feels the role settling onto his small shoulders.

"What's your name, lad?"

"William," he says, his voice steady.

I nod approvingly and gesture toward the menagerie, where the roustabouts are already securing the cases.

"Welcome to the troupe, William. Why don't you help secure the menagerie?"

William's face brightens, and without hesitation, he rushes toward the wagons, slipping between the workers with the ease of someone eager to prove himself.

I watch as he climbs up beside the men, his small hands already at work tightening straps and checking locks. The last wisps of mist coil around his feet before finally vanishing into the night.

~ * ~

Other than William, no one lingers.

The last few shadows slip away into the night, the hurried shuffle of boots fading down the dirt road. The air is thick with lingering fear, as if the very earth itself has absorbed the panic of the townsfolk. Doors slam shut in the distance, shutters rattle as they are drawn tight. Even the saloon, which would normally be alive with late-night revelry, is silent.

The field where my traveling medicine show once stood is now empty. The outlines of trampled grass and scattered footprints the only signs of the crowd which gathered here as the day was ending. The lanterns cast flickering shadows, their glow barely reaching the mist still clinging to the edges of the wagons.

People are fearful of the unknown, and when what was previously unknown suddenly takes shape before them, they scramble for protection. Whether their talismans work or not doesn't matter. What matters is that they believe.

By morning, the people of Las Vegas, New Mexico will wake to find *Professor Vlkoslag's Traveling Medicine Show* gone—a mere ghost in their memory. They will reach for their precious silver charms, only to find polished lead, cold and dull in the rising sun.

As for me?

I have a new apprentice to train. Young William, who now stands by the wagons, his small hands steady despite the night's chaos. He is watching, learning, already fitting into the rhythm of the troupe. His sharp eyes gleam with the hunger of one eager to understand the craft.

Madame Roma? She will have new assistants. Those who gave up pieces of themselves tonight—their hair now tucked safely away in her keeping—will feel an odd pull in the days to come. When she calls, they will follow.

Yet, even as the last tent pole is packed away, even as the wheels of the wagons begin their slow, familiar creak toward the next town, a sound reaches me.

A faint, fluttering whisper.

Not the wind. Not the fabric of the tents being folded. Something else.

I freeze, my ears straining.

A sound like dry wings skimming the surface of the night.

I glance toward the black sky, ink-dark and endless, the stars cold and watching.

Had my magic created only one flying vampire scorpion?

Or had it created more?

~ * ~ * ~

A native Texan, **Carol** found her way back to Texas after a five-year detour in The Nederlands and over thirty years in Colorado. Both detours were courtesy of her husband Tim and the US Air Force.

An avid reader at a young age, her strong desire to write came from her love of (her husband calls it her obsession with) Star Trek. It was this early love of Star Trek that led her to the Science Fiction and Fantasy genres. Now retired, she spends most of her time writing and publishing other authors as the editor and publisher of WolfSinger Publications and the online magazine The Lorelei Signal.

She has been published in various anthologies and magazines including *Creature Fantastic*, *PanGaia Magazine*, *Stories of Strength*, *Baen's Universe*, *Tales of the Talisman* and *Kepler's Dozen*. Her books include: *Call of Chaos*, *Chaos Embraced*, *The Road into Chaos*, and *Chaos Challenged*.

Drink Your Lemonade

A.J. Malachite

This time the circus had returned to Earth.

The drinks vendor remembered it all—nothing had changed. There was even still the damp, heavy, hot summer-in-the-south air, the same dusty soil and long-parched grass, the same faded blue sky that itself seemed to long for cooler temperatures. The ingredients that had been delivered earlier that day felt so familiar in his hands —the lemons and limes with their thick peels and sharp smells, the bags of sugar, the ice in rough cubes. It took him a moment to remember the right tools for making lemonade—the peeler, the fruit juicer, was this plant called rosemary or mint? —but he did and began his prep for the day.

The heat was sticky and oppressive, and he wished it was a different season. That he was making hot chocolate or apple cider instead. He longed for the drinks of the ice planets, the mountain planets, even some of the underwater worlds, that warmed chilled bones with a cozy embrace or a fiery shock.

After he had made enough lemonade to keep him stocked through the early crowds, he peered around the counter of his stall to catch the eye of his friend, the sweet treats vendor. She was waiting for him, as usual, and he had to laugh at how she looked as a human. The disguises circus management provided made them appear incongruous to the inhabitants of whatever world they were visiting at the moment. His friend made a face at him—he knew what that face looked like in her true form, and it came across completely wrong on human features, tragic rather than sarcastic. He laughed at her again and stuck his tongue out at her.

In unison, the two popped back into their own respective stalls and waited for the circus to open. He could hear the ringmaster over a megaphone at the gates, doing the traditional welcome speech.

Across the way, the psychic emerged from their den. They looked like an ancient woman wrapped in stereotypical shawls but were actually a teenager in their species despite being over two hundred Earth years old. They set out their sandwich board and turned on the tiny fog machine hidden in the entrance to their tent. It hissed plaintively and the humidity of the air around them swallowed the water vapor easily, the efforts of the poor machine barely visible. The psychic sighed, turned it back off, and disappeared into their tent.

Further down the row of brightly painted stalls and striped tents, the smell of popcorn and sausage-on-a-stick came wafting on the weak breeze. The sweet smell of funnel cake drifted from next door, mixed with the headiness of the strange, gooey squares the sweets vendor always sold. They were from her home planet, and they were popular everywhere the circus went. The sweets vendor gave them freely to children and charged the adults for them. They were made from a plant that contained a hormone that caused universal happiness in almost every species.

To no one's surprise, a group of rowdy trapeze artists and contortionists in their own human disguises charged the sweet stall at the last minute, begging her for the squares, claiming they couldn't possibly perform without them, teasing her and showering her in compliments. As they pleaded and bargained and she pretended to scold them, one of the acrobats caught the drinks vendor's eye.

Everyone in the circus had seen him in his true form before— disguises weren't necessary on worlds that knew other life-bearing solar systems existed—but there was always something different about seeing someone on their home planet. He stood, a little self-conscious, as the acrobat's gaze took in his strong hands, muscled arms, the tattoos from a dozen different worlds made with a dozen different kinds of ink and tools, some of which shifted and changed into different designs over time, and the way his human clothes hugged his skin. The acrobat, one he knew well and could recognize in any disguise, raised an eyebrow at him, a show of interest. The drinks vendor leaned over the counter on his elbows, twining his fingers together, a small smile crossing his face. The acrobat grinned too, wide and anticipatory. The moment was broken when the acrobat's closest friend shoved a paper cone of oozing purple squares into his hands. The group ran back towards their dressing rooms, laughing and yelling and popping squares into their mouths as they went. The drinks vendor watched them go, still smiling. The acrobat would be visiting his tent at sunrise.

Then the crowds came in, and he was swept up in the bustle. He sold lemonade and promised adults harder stuff would be available after nightfall. At times he was almost struck dumb by the alien familiarity of it all.

He remembered his last week on this planet clearly. His parents, mean and hurtful, stingy with money and love but generous with discipline and his father's belt. His older sister, itching to run away to a friend's house in another state. An impending visit of his grandparents, who were worse than his parents. Uncomfortable clothes, painful shoes, sitting still and being quiet in church pews and at school desks and at the dinner table.

And then, the circus came. It came, and on a whim, his parents took the family as a summer treat. He remembered the ringmaster, with his lavish clothes and thick makeup—which the drink vendor's father sneered at. He remembered the welcome speech, the promise of things worlds beyond, and the sentence '*You will never be the same.*'

He remembered the strong man, the acrobats performance, the knife thrower, the woman who swung from the tent ceiling by her hair, the dancers and clowns, the sword- and fire- swallowers, the animals that had looked to him like elephants, donkeys, and lions but of course were actually animals from across the universe, the freak show his mother refused to let them watch (that he knew now was simply species from other planets letting their disguises slip a little) and the psychic's tent his father had loudly wished someone would burn down.

He remembered the sausage-on-a-stick, which fizzed and snapped on his tongue in a distinctly not-Earth way. He remembered the cotton candy, which had made him see colors—he still couldn't fully explain what that meant, despite having since gotten high off the actual proper dose of the ingredient that just lightly graced the cotton candy. And most of all, he remembered the lemonade.

It had been toward the end of the night. They were returning to the arcade so they could purchase a turn in a photobooth to take family pictures, which was the worst possible reason to return to the arcade. It was still hot, even after dark, and his sister had successfully pleaded for ice cream. He had asked for a much cheaper lemonade and was silently handed the cash for the smallest size.

He had rushed up to the stall, already happier than he could remember being in his life. This circus was slightly off in a way that made the adults uneasy, but he loved it. Every tent, every sideshow, every performance showed him things he had never seen before, that shouldn't be possible, and no one could find wires or pulleys or smoke and mirrors to explain any of it. He was dreading going home. The circus made him feel like how his small child self imagined being drunk felt, rich and alive and whirling from moment to moment like the rickety thrill rides he had earlier been denied.

The vendor had handed him the lemonade with a solemn look on his tattooed face. His child self hadn't understood why until he took his first sip.

The lemonade didn't taste like lemonade. Well, it did. But it was something more than that. It started like lemonade, and then it changed. It curled down his throat like it had a mind of its own, tasting of smoke and metal, of leather and incense, of chocolate and some unnameable savory spice. In that first swallow was a promise—of touch, of boldness, of worlds and worlds and worlds, of the feel of other people's hands in his, of adrenaline rush, of highs and highs and highs, of swinging from a trapeze, of a knife's edge brushing by his ear on its way to a target, of cheers and laughter, of stars and starlight and nighttime and bright lights, of ink scratching its way into his skin, of *himself* and *himself* and *himself*.

Now, as the drinks vendor he had been for twenty-odd years, he watched others take their first sip of lemonade, the intoxicant in his recipe swirling in their mouths and binding with neurochemicals to give each person a taste of whatever it was they wanted most. Just as abstract as his own experience had been, just as ineffable, but always as profound.

A child chugged her lemonade in one gulp and begged for more. A woman smirked into her cup as she walked away, lost in thought. An old man lit up and seemed years younger. His wife, when he persuaded her to try it, drank and then looked at him with fury and hatred. A young teenager hugged his drink to his chest and fought back tears, wandering away from his knot of friends alone into the crowd. The drinks vendor watched them all, wishing he could taste what they were tasting and wondering why so many people—no matter the species—seemed to crave their own destruction.

After that first sip of lemonade—he had been what, ten? eleven? —he had snuck out of his family's house the very next night. His parents had complained about the circus and its unconventional-looking workers and the way it beckoned and lured. They weren't going back, they said. They didn't trust it. He hadn't been able to bear the thought of never seeing the circus again, so he left after everyone had fallen asleep. It was after dark, but not too late, given his family slept early on nights before Sunday church. The circus was open until sunrise, the ringmaster had proclaimed the day before. He still had plenty of time before he had to be back in bed.

He had snuck into the circus by creeping around the back. An acrobat exiting the dressing rooms had raised an eyebrow at him but didn't stop him. He had rushed past the trailers and backstage tents and found his way onto the main thoroughfare.

Dizzy with possibility, he had pleaded his way onto the thrill rides he had so desperately wanted to ride the day before. He was handed a paper cone full of gooey purple treats that he ate gleefully and was filled with blinding happiness for the entire stage show. He had nervously entered the psychic's tent, explained to the old woman inside he had no money but was just curious, and spoke with her about nothing and everything for an hour or maybe more. He had visited the freak show, delighted and fascinated, knowing deep down there was something *beyond* to what he was seeing.

Time was marked for him by the thinning of the crowds. He soon was the only child in the circus, the adults becoming drunken and bawdy. He hadn't minded, though. He had watched them struggle with the arcade games and had revisited his favorite sideshows, which seemed darker and more thrilling now so late in the night. They attempted more dangerous tricks, defied more dangerous laws of physics, and some of the performers seemed to have less fabric to their costumes than they had before.

Deliriously happy, he had stumbled on tired legs to the lemonade stall, where he was hit with the realization it was almost over. That he would be back at his family's house soon, and inevitably, the circus would leave and might not ever return. And, too sleep deprived and young to do anything else, he had plopped down in the feet-flattened grass ten paces from the drinks vendor and started to cry.

The vendor with tattoos on his face had approached him, crouching next to him and holding out his hand.

"You don't have to stay here," the vendor had said, kindly, solemnly. "You can come with us. Please, come with us."

His child self had looked up into the face of the man above him. He had blinked tears out of his eyes. The vendor had repeated his plea. And his child self had taken the outstretched hand, and stood, and walked with the vendor—who would become his mentor, who would teach him to make drinks both familiar and alien, and how to live in a circus that bounced between planets and worlds—to find circus management. To sign his name in the roster —a new name he had chosen, shedding his old like a too-tight snakeskin. He had slept in a hammock in a trailer all through the next day, while the circus packed itself up and left as quickly as possible to avoid search parties looking for him. He had never once regretted taking the vendor's hand, even over a decade later when the vendor had vanished one day on a cold and snowy planet, taking one of the acrobats along. Leaving him to manage the drinks stall on his own.

Now, as an adult back on earth for the first time, he prepared more lemonade for the late crowds. The families were beginning to leave, the children tired and limp like sacks of potatoes in strollers or their parents' arms. The sun had gone down, but it wasn't yet time for the night to truly begin. He longed for it, for when everyone who stayed was too drunk or high on lack of sleep to notice when the circus became more lax in its disguises, when the worlds beyond began to bleed through around them. When every possible thrill the universe could offer threw off the layers of costuming that hid them and begged for attention, ripe for the taking. An invitation, a beckoning, a friendly but still dangerous siren's call.

And then he saw her. Small, too clean for a child, her hair pulled back in painfully tight pigtails. She clutched a few dollar bills in her hand and waited patiently, too patiently for a child, on the other side of the counter. Waited to order lemonade.

He recognized her. Oh, he recognized her. He knew that sundress, the way the rough fabric scratched and bit into the wearer's skin. He knew those shoes, cheap but made to not look it, and the way they pinched the back of the heel. He knew that face, those hands, the hair kept stringy and unhealthy-looking by a childhood of stress and helplessness.

It was his own face, his own hated sundress, his own hands

holding the cash his mother had given him for lemonade twenty-odd years ago.

Somehow, he had known, hadn't he? From the day he realized the circus' travels sometimes took them back and forth in time by necessity, because of how journeys across galaxies worked, he had sort of known. Somehow, he had to have known.

He took the cash, poured the lemonade, and solemnly handed it to the girl he once had been. She sipped it, and her entire body changed. She stopped hunching into herself and unfolded, emboldened and seeking the world and everything in it. She looked into the cup with wonder and unfiltered desire, and then wandered away from the counter lost in reverie.

The drinks vendor returned to the next batch of lemonade. He looked around his small vendor's stall. He would have to rearrange a bit and have some extra supplies delivered. He tried to remember where the circus had gone right after Earth all those years ago but couldn't. He would ask the ringmaster later, after the acrobat's visit. He dusted off his hands and, on a scrap of scavenged paper, began to make a list of what he would need for his newly imminent apprentice.

~ * ~ * ~

A.J. Malachite is a trans man who writes queer horror and dark science fiction/fantasy. He has worked in front of house management for live performance for eight years. In both his writing and his career in the theatre industry, he strives to promote storytelling as a means of individual and community healing. "Drink Your Lemonade" is dedicated to his fifteen-year-old self.

You can find him at ajmalachite.weebly.com.

Farnham and Foyle Traveling Carnival

Stephen W. Chappell

"Slow down, Larry! Are you trying to get us killed?"

Larry tapped on the brakes as they rounded a curve. Visibility had plummeted so much in the past few minutes the light from the streetlamps barely reached the pavement. He gripped the wheel tighter and hoped the conditions would soon improve.

The visit to Ellen's parents had been terrible, and the thickening fog added to their misery. Between their passive-aggressiveness toward Ellen and their outright aggression toward Larry, their stress levels were through the roof. It was clear her parents barely tolerated him, and more and more, the feeling was mutual. One day soon, he thought, he would end up dropping her off and waiting at the local watering hole. Which, now that he thought about it, didn't sound like such a bad idea.

She fiddled with the radio. "Fog is so thick, even the radio is blocked," Ellen complained.

Larry smirked. "I don't think it works like that."

"Really, Larry?" She pierced him with an icy glare, and he braced himself for the onslaught. "Do you even know how it works, Larry? Do you know how anything works? Because you certainly don't know anything *about* work." His lack of employment was just the tip of the iceberg. Her rant continued with a long list of additional grievances that included his lengthening to-do list, their mounting debt, the unmowed lawn, and the neighborhood cat that wouldn't stay out of their garden.

If I only knew then, he thought, even as he chided himself for thinking it. Her rant was the stress talking; all he had to do was weather the storm.

Ahead, the soft glow of streetlights appeared, struggling their way through the fog. They were joined by spotlights which swept through the mist as if trying to wipe it away. Further on, the electric glow of pink, orange, yellow, and blue neon sliced through the fog, dancing with an enticing rhythm.

"Are you even listening to me?"

"What's that up ahead?" he asked, ignoring her.

Structures materialized out of the mists. The eerie metal frame of a Ferris wheel slowly traced a haunting path. Brightly lit machines whirled and twirled in eerie, hypnotic patterns, and pole-mounted lights shone down on red-and-white striped awnings. Larry slowed the car as they approached the entrance, an arched gateway with pulsing lights. Bright blue letters splashed across a striped sign.

"Farnham and Foyle Traveling Carnival," Larry read.

"I don't remember seeing that on the way to my parents," Ellen said. "Did you make a wrong turn?"

Larry shook his head as he brought the car to a stop. It had been thirty or more years since he had been to a carnival. He had snuck into the beer garden with Anne Marie Llewellyn. He didn't remember getting thrown out, but witnesses had assured him it was epic. Epic or no, it was also the last time he had spoken to Anne Marie, and that was decidedly *not* epic.

Or so he thought at the time. He loved Ellen, stress rants and all, and wouldn't trade her for anything.

"Maybe we should stop and ask for directions."

He made a face. "We don't need to do that. When we're out of the boondocks, we'll have some signal again." He held up his phone for emphasis. "I'll bring up directions. I'm sure I didn't miss a turn, though."

"Well, you've already stopped. And I do have to pee."

He grimaced. "Alright, then. But we have to be quick. This fog is going to get worse before it gets better."

~ *~

The welcoming music of the carnival organ embraced them as they stepped out of the car. It led them through the parking lot to a ticket booth situated beneath the archway. Beyond the entrance, rides swooshed and riders screamed, promising thrills for those who ventured within. The smells of popcorn and other carnival treats tantalized their olfactory senses and set their stomachs grumbling.

"Do I need a ticket?" Larry asked, raising his voice to be heard over the din.

"No, sir," the weasel-faced kid in the booth said. "Tickets are only for the rides."

Larry chuckled and ran a hand through his graying hair. "I think I'll pass."

"Where's the restroom?" Ellen asked with some urgency. The kid pointed to a row of portable toilets. Ellen scrunched up her face in mild disgust, then made a beeline for them. Larry followed, arriving just as she hurried into an open stall.

A hunched-over old man with scraggly hair and a long, salt-and-pepper beard shuffled past while he waited. Larry thought he must be a mechanic, as he wore a drab, dark blue uniform and an oil-stained cap with a patch depicting some kind of wheel. When Larry noticed the man's pronounced limp, he unconsciously rubbed his own leg, aching with the memory of a childhood accident.

Though the brim of his hat and the dim lighting conspired to hide the man's features, when the man's sad gaze fell on him, Larry shuddered as if someone had walked over his grave.

"Don't do it," the man said in a gravelly voice. "Leave now, before you can't." He raised a shaky finger at him, then slumped and continued on his way.

"Wait, what do you mean?"

Ellen chose that moment to emerge from her stall. "What's that?" she asked.

The man rounded the corner but took a long look back at them before wandering out of sight.

Larry shrugged as the man disappeared. "Nothing, Ellen. I was …the guy down there…he was kind of strange."

"Uh-huh." Her features softened as she looked at him. "I'm sorry for being cross. You know how my parents stress me out."

He did. "It's okay. They stress me out, too."

She reached up and gave him a quick kiss. "Thank you for putting up with me." She looked past him at the row of food and game stalls. "Maybe if we stay a little while, the fog will clear. Want to get a snack?"

He bought her a box of popcorn, then moved on to some games of chance. He failed utterly at the ring toss but managed to win a prize at a water pistol game. She was not amused when he chose a happy-looking pink hippo as his reward.

"But I got it for you."

She snatched it from him and bonked him in the head with it. "Let's go ride the Tilt-A-Whirl."

"Tilt-A-Whirl it is." Larry returned to the booth for tickets while she headed off to stand in line for the ride.

~ * ~

With a string of tickets in hand, Larry turned away from the booth only to be accosted by the old mechanic.

"There's still time!" The man's face held the wild, wide-eyed look of one gripped in madness.

Larry staggered back, looking around wildly. "Where did you come from?"

The man backed away, wagging a finger. "If you don't leave soon, you never will." He took another step back, seemingly to avoid a large group of teenagers. By the time they cleared, the man was gone.

"I just saw that guy again," Larry said when he caught up to his wife.

"Oh, weird. Who do you think he is?"

Larry shrugged. "No idea. He looked familiar, though, now that I think about it. He keeps telling me to leave while I still can."

She made a face at him. "Well, we're not leaving before we try this." She led him away from the ride.

"What about the Tilt-A-Whirl?"

"This is better."

They passed through throngs of people, between a few game stands, and down an alleyway behind a row of stalls.

"How did you even find this?"

At the end of the alley, Ellen led him to a large, well-lit stand with a red-and-white awning. A carnival barker in a striped vest stood behind the counter. Behind him hung a large, multi-colored wheel waiting to be spun.

"Step right up and spin the Wheel of Time!" the man barked. "See history like you've never seen it before! See the sights before they were sights!"

The wheel was laid out like a giant prize wheel. But instead of dollar amounts, it listed dozens of dates and events. Larry picked out the entries for Wembley, July 13, 1985; New York City, December

31, 1999; Berlin, November 9, 1989; and Cape Kennedy, July 16, 1969. Other entries were marked with "Your Wedding Day," and other personal events. Some slots were marked with dates in the future but gave no clue as to what the event might be.

Larry looked at it in disbelief. "What is this? They stick you in a booth and show you a video? How cheesy is that?"

Ellen shook her head adamantly. "No, it's real. I met a kid in the Tilt-A-Whirl line while you were getting tickets. He said he saw the three wise men."

"No way."

"Yes! The kid told me they came just like it says, bearing gifts."

Larry shook his head. "I don't believe it."

"Wait and see."

A blond girl in her teens walked up to the counter and handed the man a bill. "Is it safe?"

"Just follow the rules," the barker said, smoothly moving the bill into his apron. "There's only two: don't interfere, and don't be late!" He handed her a paper. "Sign on the dotted line, sweetheart." She did and stepped up to the wheel. "Put all your personal effects in here, please." He held open a bag to her.

"Will I get everything back?" she asked sharply.

"Yes, ma'am. Don't want to pollute the timestream." He shook the bag. "Purse, phone, money, anything with a date on it." She placed the items in the bag, and he handed her a receipt. "Now spin the wheel and embark on the trip of a lifetime!"

The girl smirked as she reached up and yanked the wheel. It spun around and around, lights flashing and speakers blaring with sound effects.

Larry pursed his lips and folded his arms. "It's a scam."

"Just you watch."

The wheel slowed to a stop. "Woodstock!" the barker yelled.

There was a bright flash, and the girl was gone.

Larry's mouth dropped open. "What?"

Another flash, and the girl reappeared. But she had changed. Now, a flowered wreath adorned her disheveled hair, and dark sunglasses hid her eyes. She took a step and stumbled. "Far out," she said.

The barker handed her the bag with her things. "Take a trip through time! Experience moments in history like never before!"

Ellen looked at him with bright eyes. "Let's do it, Larry!"

"You believe that? They just handed her some props."

"Who did, Larry? And when? She was gone for, like, one second. I'm telling you, it's real."

"Maybe, maybe not." He looked again at the wheel. "Even if it is, look at some of those entries. Gettysburg, July, eighteen sixty-three? Why would anyone want to go there?"

The barker must have heard him. "We don't judge, sir. Follow the rules, and your safety is guaranteed."

Larry looked skeptical. "What about that one?" He pointed to a space on the wheel marked only with a lone question mark.

The barker smiled. "Why, that's the mystery space! Nobody knows where, nobody knows when. Guaranteed to be an important moment in your own life!"

Larry thought about important moments in his own life. Were there any he would want to revisit?

"I'm going to go," Ellen announced. "Hold my stuff." She gave Larry a quick peck and handed her purse to him.

"Sign on the dotted line, ma'am," the barker said as she handed him a bill.

She signed with a flourish and pushed the paper across the counter. "Here goes nothing." She reached up and spun the wheel.

~ * ~

Larry watched the wheel, mesmerized, until someone bumped into his back. He was not surprised when he turned to find himself face-to-face with the crazy mechanic again. He felt he should know this person—the weathered, bearded face was so familiar—but he was at a loss to put a name to him.

"This is your last chance, Larry. Don't do it. Don't spin the wheel!"

"What? Why? Who are you?" Larry demanded. "How do you know my name?" He looked the man in the eye and gasped. The eyes looking back at him were so close to his own it was as if he were looking in a mirror.

"Don't you dare spin it!"

A woman stepped between him and the old man, breaking the spell.

Just a trick of the light, Larry thought. *Those are* not *my eyes.*

"Come on," the newcomer said. She wore a nondescript gray suit with a gold nametag on her lapel that read, "Ms. Epping, Security." She placed a hand on the mechanic's shoulder. "I've told you before not to bother our patrons." She turned an apologetic face to Larry. "My apologies, sir. He gets a bit confused sometimes."

"Sure," Larry said, offering a limp wave as she led the old mechanic away. He turned towards the booth just in time to see the wheel slowing to a stop.

"Sweet sixteen!" the barker announced. Beside the wheel, Ellen flashed out of existence.

~ * ~

When she flashed back to the carnival, Ellen had on gloves, an apron, and a sun hat, as if she had been gardening. In one hand she held a plate with a slice of cake. It took a moment for her eyes to adjust; she had been in the bright afternoon sun for hours now. Shielding her eyes, she spotted Larry and made her way over to him.

"Here, I brought this back for you," she said, handing him the cake. "That was intense."

Larry looked at her quizzically. "What happened?"

"I was there, Larry," she said, her eyes bright with excitement. "I was there at my sweet sixteen party! I watched from my neighbor's yard. I don't know how they did it, but I had all this gardening stuff on when I got there. I sat in their yard pulling weeds, and I watched the whole party, Larry. It was fantastic! I forgot how much fun we had."

Larry smiled. "That's great!"

Her expression turned somber. "I could have stopped it." She wrung her hands nervously.

He reached out a hand to her arm. "Stopped what? I thought it was fantastic?"

She sighed. She had never told Larry about what had happened and wasn't sure she wanted to tell him now.

Her best friend, Donna McGill, had brought her brother to the party for some reason. Ellen kind of liked him, so when he suggested a walk into the woods behind the house, she didn't object. When he wanted to take their make-out session too far, that was when she objected. His efforts were ended with a well-placed knee, but it also ended her friendship with Donna. The memory of it left her distrustful and kept her from dating until Larry came along in her senior year of college.

She had a chance to stop it. The path into the woods went right past the neighbor's garden. But painful as it was, she knew she couldn't interfere. She might save herself some trauma, but then she might not ever meet Larry. That wasn't a trade-off she was willing to make.

She didn't tell him any of that, though. That encounter used to have power over her, but not anymore. She was done with letting it control her. She would not let it be the reason he passed up this opportunity.

"Nothing, Larry. The trip was fantastic," she said at last. "It was great to remember how much fun we had that day." She smiled at him brightly, forcing the memory of Donna McGill's brother out of her mind. "Now it's your turn."

~ * ~

"I don't know, Ellen." Larry turned away. "There isn't much in my past I want to see all over again. For my sixteenth birthday, all I did was sit around playing video games."

Ellen pulled a bill from her purse and shoved it into his hand. "Come on, Larry. Look at all the things on the wheel! Who wouldn't want to go to those places?"

"The Cretaceous?" he said, incredulous.

"See the dinosaurs!" she said.

"Or get eaten," he said wryly. "What's that paper you signed?"

She wrinkled her face, annoyed. "It's a waiver. Says they're not responsible for any consequences if you break the rules. And your safety is guaranteed, remember? Now, come on, Larry. It was awesome!" She looked slyly at the plate. "You might even get cake."

He opened his mouth as if to continue arguing but then shut it again. The mechanic kept telling him not to go, but was he really going to trust some crazy old dude that he just met over his wife? With a shrug, he handed Ellen his phone and wallet, then approached the barker.

"What have I got to lose?" he muttered.

The wheel spun, the lights lit, and the sound effects played. Finally, it stopped, and Larry grimaced.

"Mystery!" the barker said. "Lucky, lucky! That's our first one today!"

"Great," Larry said.

There was a flash, and Larry was gone.

~ * ~

Ellen waited for the second flash. "What's going on?" One minute passed, then another, and still no flash. She ran up to the barker. "What happened? Where's my husband?"

"Couldn't say," the barker said. "We almost never lose people."

"But you said it's safe!"

"Yes, ma'am, as long as you follow the rules."

Panic took hold of her. "And what if you don't?"

The barker shook his head. "Couldn't say, ma'am, but there are consequences."

Her eyes flew wide.

"Don't worry, ma'am. Security will look into it. I'm sure they'll take care of your husband."

She flinched at a hand on her shoulder.

"Ellen?"

The old mechanic stood beside her, watery eyes threatening to overflow onto his cheeks.

"Who are you?" She searched his face until recognition dawned. "Larry?" She reached up and touched his beard, took in every inch of his old, weathered visage. "What happened to you?"

The aged Larry looked away. "I tried to stop him. I told him not to spin the wheel. There are rules, though. They warned me not to break them again."

Ellen looked to the Wheel of Time, then back at Larry. She put a hand to her mouth. "Oh, Larry, what did you do?"

~ * ~

Blackness surrounded him, but only for a moment. As if someone were turning a dimmer, the space he had arrived in gradually got brighter. He was outdoors, standing on the corner of Carlton Drive and Gibson Lane. It was an intersection he knew well, one he passed by it every day as he walked to school. Around him, kids wandered through the neighborhood with varying degrees of enthusiasm. The crossing guard stood a block away, helping children to cross busy Washington Street. Gone were the smells of popcorn and fried things; he was well and truly somewhere else.

*Some*when *else too*, he corrected himself.

A beep drew his attention. On his wrist was an eighties-style wristwatch, black with blocky, red numerals. But rather than showing the time, they were counting down. "0:29:42." *Only half an hour*, he thought. *What a ripoff.*

He jerked his head up at the sharp whistle of the crossing guard. Cars stopped as the woman held up a sign and walked into the road. She waved, and a group of children crossed to the far side of the street.

This is an important moment in my life? He looked around, trying to figure out *when* he was and what he was supposed to see. There were nothing but zombie-like kids walking on Gibson. He had a clear view up Carlton towards Washington and didn't see anything noteworthy. When he turned to look the other way on Carlton, though, the dam of memory burst open and flooded into him.

Halfway down the block, he, or rather the young Larry Pilgrim, stood in front of a house. The baseball cap on his head was his favorite, and the money in his hand had been hard-earned on his paper route. He was handing it to a skinny upper-classman in exchange for a sheaf of papers.

Larry had forgotten about this exchange, the first of many such dealings that helped him cheat his way through high school. Today was the day of a big exam in history class, he remembered. It was his least favorite subject and the worst of his grades. He was on the cusp of flunking and needed a good grade to have a shot at passing. The upper-classman, Jimmy Bobbetti, had hacked the teacher's email, stolen the answers, and offered them for sale. Larry didn't think twice about taking him up on the offer.

Larry had memorized just enough to pass the exam—a few more transactions like that "earned" him a passing mark for the year.

As he watched his younger self approaching, he was embarrassed and ashamed. He had never told Ellen about it; in fact, he had done his best to bury those memories after muddling his way through community college and landing his first job. He had told himself getting the diploma was all that mattered. Now, he hung his head in shame.

What could he have accomplished if he had been forced to

apply himself in the tough classes? How would his life have changed if he hadn't learned that, where there was a will to skate, there was a way around the hard things in life? Would he be employed *now* if he had learned a better work ethic *then*? With Young Larry approaching, he wondered if he had an opportunity to find out.

Don't interfere. The rule flashed through his mind like a blinking neon sign, giving him pause. How *would* it change his life? What if he never married Ellen? What if he never even met her? Was he willing to risk losing her?

No, he thought, *I don't believe that. How can changing something like this change my life so dramatically that I don't end up with Ellen?*

The more he thought about it, the more convinced he became. This would be a change that made life better for both of them. He would have a job, and she would be happy. Hell, her parents might even like him. Wouldn't he trade anything to be able to give her a better life? *Hell, yes,* he thought, *I have to try.*

Young Larry was just crossing Gibson, his face buried in his ill-gotten papers. Larry bided his time, waiting for the perfect moment. His younger self came closer, absorbed with history, not realizing his own was about to change.

Larry stuck out his foot.

Young Larry flew to the sidewalk in spectacular fashion. Limbs sprawled, books flew, and the papers scattered all around. "Shit!" He bounced back up and reached for his bag while the elder Larry collected the papers.

"I'm sorry, son. I didn't see you there."

Young Larry stood and brushed himself off. "Yeah, okay. Just give me my papers, mister. I need to study."

Larry made a show of looking over the papers. "Oh? Are they important?"

"Yes, they're a, uh, a study guide." Young Larry reached for the papers, but the elder Larry pulled them away.

"They look more like an answer key," he said with a note of disapproval.

Young Larry's face twisted with rage. "They're mine, you jerk. Give them to me!" He reached again for the papers. "If you don't give them to me, there's going to be trouble."

Larry backed up a step. "You better get a move on or you're going to be late for school."

Young Larry threw back his head and started yelling. "Help! This man is trying to molest me!"

"What? No, I'm not!" Up at the corner, Larry saw the crossing guard reach for the radio at her hip.

There was a sound like shattering glass, and Larry felt dizzy. *What have I done?*

"Help me!"

Not knowing what else to do, Larry ran.

~ * ~

The patrol car caught up to him one block away, at the corner of Carlton and Nolan. The car had been nearby, and Larry had never been a sprinter. It rounded the corner, lights flashing and siren blaring. An officer jumped out and pointed something at him. Larry thought it must be a Taser.

"Get in the car, Larry."

"Wait, what?" *How does she know my name?* He couldn't place her, but the officer looked familiar.

"Get in the car!"

Larry put his hands up and slunk towards the car. He climbed in when the officer opened the back door for him.

When the door slammed shut, the scene around him shattered as if it were a glass TV screen. Shards spun around his head like bits of broken glass. Each one played a video, a broken piece of his life. That one had his birthday party from when he was five years old. Another held his high school graduation. One shard showed him in a classroom—college, he thought, but not a room he recognized.

The shards continued their furious swirling. They spun and mixed and shattered further still. There was his first paycheck, but why was it so high? And what was the company that issued it? *What is happening here?* That shard showed a new car pulling into a small house that was nothing like the one he shared with Ellen. Another showed his wedding day, but it wasn't as he remembered: everything was different: the venue, the tuxedo. The bride.

Ellen!

He frantically searched the shards, grabbing at them as they flew past, but all of them evaded his grasp. They started to settle, to rearrange into a new pattern. Ellen was nowhere to be found.

"What happened?"

The last piece fell into place. It showed the intersection of Gibson and Carlton. It was cracked in the middle. One half showed Young Larry on his way to school, never bothered by his elder self. The other half showed the elder Larry snatching up the papers. Larry gulped as half of that shard shattered into dust, and the newer, changed shard fell into place.

There was a bright flash, and then everything went black.

~ * ~

Larry opened his eyes to see the officer smiling back at him through an opening in the patrol car's barrier. He recognized her now. It was the woman he had seen with the mechanic at the Wheel of Time. The security officer, Ms. Epping.

"Congratulations, Larry. You broke the timeline."

Larry shook his head, trying to clear the cobwebs. "What?"

Ms. Epping slapped the top of the seat. "Yep. The universe took a left turn at the corner of Gibson and Carlton."

A thick fog swirled outside the car, preventing any view of their surroundings. "What are you talking about?"

"*You broke the rules*, Larry." She turned to face forward and put the car in gear, driving forth in spite of the conditions outside. "There are consequences."

"What consequences?" He reached for the door handle, but there was none.

Ms. Epping chuckled. "Well, for starters, you're stuck here."

"Stuck? What do you mean, stuck?"

"Stuck in the here and now, Larry. See, you came from a universe that went straight at Gibson and Carlton. But your little intervention, you know, to set Young Larry on the straight and narrow, well, that sent the universe in another direction. And it took you along with it."

Larry wrinkled his face in confusion. "Well, how do I get back, then?"

"You can't, Larry. It's gone."

"Gone?" he shouted. "What about my life? What about Ellen?"

"Oh, you won't be seeing any more of her. You saw the shards, you know what happens. Young Larry Pilgrim, he knuckles down, gets into a good school, and so on and so on. But he doesn't meet Ellen. She didn't go to that nice new school. She went to that community college where you met her and found someone else." Larry's eyes started to water. "Aw, it's okay, Larry, don't worry. Young Larry finds somebody new, too."

Larry examined her reflection in the mirror. "Well, isn't that me? My life will be different now, too, right?"

"Oh no, Larry. It's not you. You lived the life of a cheat. Then you went back and broke the rules. Young Larry never did that. His future is bright. But it's his, Larry, not yours. For you, it wasn't such a good trade."

"I didn't want a *trade*," Larry moaned. "I wanted to make our lives better."

Ms. Epping nodded. "You did, Larry. Ellen and Young Larry are both better off. They're just not together. They never will be."

Larry banged on the partition. "No! That can't be it! You have to help me fix this!"

"It can't be fixed, Larry," she said sadly. "Now you're stuck in a reality where, frankly, you don't belong. But it's okay, we've got you covered."

Larry looked out the window nervously, trying to peer through the gloom.

Ellen!

The car turned and came to a stop. Ms. Epping got out and opened the back door. As Larry got out, she handed him a bundle. "This is for you. For your new job."

Larry looked at the bundle. It was a drab, dark blue uniform, complete with a cap. Sewn onto the front of the cap was a patch depicting the Wheel of Time.

"Come on out, Larry. Welcome to your new home."

A tear fell from his eye as he stepped out of the car. He looked up to read the sign above him. "Farnham and Foyle Traveling Carnival."

~ * ~ * ~

Steve Chappell is the chosen servant of four feline overlords who grudgingly tolerate his service. They live in the outskirts of the NJ pine barrens with his wife. He currently works as a systems engineer. His writing credits include stories published in *Dark Horses Magazine*, Hiraeth Publishing's *Flash Digest*, and in the anthology *Ruth and Ann's Guide to Time Travel*. Besides writing, he enjoys reading, photography, and hiking. He can be found online at www.facebook.com/stephen.chappell.author/.

Mirror Ball

Liam Hogan

The *SS Plymouth* has no windows. It has no mirrors, either. Instead, every surface of our colony ship is nano-printed, and every corridor, workspace, and sleep area has its cluster of dark-eyed lenses. So anything can display pretty much anything; the schematics of engineering hidden beneath a panel, the whiteboard of a teacher long since passed, or the disembodied heads of other kids my age, group-chatting as we play call and response games until each of us is reduced to fits of giggles.

The cameras cover the outside of the spaceship as well, a host of eyes on stalks, so the ship's AI can check for damage, flecks of ancient dust travelling scarily fast relative to us. The colonists use the externals to see where we are and where we're heading, even if there's nothing to see but distant stars.

In the zero-gravity heart of the massive ship, there's a dedicated viewing area. A hollow globe, twenty metres in diameter, popular when we have no classes and no duties, which is often enough, and whenever other age groups are not enjoying their turn, which is less so. There, the AI can project stitched-together images, so you can float in deep space, with no sign of the *Plymouth*. Or, if you're feeling homesick for somewhere you've never been, any of the countless full-panoramic views from Earth. Or the Earth itself, the day the *Plymouth* left, its surface geometrically mapped onto the inner curve of the sphere, a breathtaking view of the whole globe that no-one could ever *actually* see. One day, it'll display the planet we're speeding towards in equally stunning detail. But we'll have to get a *lot* closer first and it won't be us who sees it. Our children's children's children, perhaps?

Not Emily's, though. She was the one who turned the viewing room into a mirror ball. I suppose it was an accident. A chain of thought she ran with, and that then ran away with her.

We each get a brief period to choose what the sphere shows. Using it to spy on any one room or person on the ship, that would have been unthinkable. But to spy on them all? At the same time? I guess that was different. Certainly, the graphics AI didn't baulk as Emily ordered it to "Display all internal views", the curved screen splintering into a million shards. Flickers of movement and light, but you had to have your nose pressed against them to see what each one was.

We did exactly that, the rest of our age group, two dozen in total. We drifted to the outer wall, excited by Emily's imagination, impressed by her daring, squinting at the thumbnail views. Most were pretty boring—empty corridors—but, as we swam along, using the lightly magnetised gloves that paused our motion, every so often we caught a glimpse of somewhere we knew, someone we recognised.

Emily remained at the sphere's heart, where her commands would be followed, though the clock was ticking and the next kid was already working out what they would view when it was their turn.

"Remap to a 3D model of the *Plymouth*," Emily instructed, and the view swirled until we were looking at a scaled, real-time version of our vast spaceship, every wall and bulkhead ghostly glass, populated by a miniature crew, the graphics turning them into ants. This was even better, like a giant doll's house, except the dolls were real. The dolls were us.

"Centre on the viewing room, one to one scale."

Laughter as we found ourselves staring at our mirror images, just the other side of the curved screen. But there was a plaintive wail from Emily. She spun around, like a dervish, hair loose and floating. She could see us all, in duplicate. But where was *she*?

Like the view of space, minus the *Plymouth*, the graphics AI had edited her out. Uncertain, perhaps, how to cope with something at its very centre.

"Zoom in!" she demanded, and would no doubt have stamped her foot if there was anything to stamp it against. "Focus on me!"

No-one knows what exactly she saw. No one is willing to repeat the experiment, not even the adults. The AI probably wouldn't let us. From where we were, at the safety of the sphere's edge, it looked like a distorted fairground trick, mirrors reflected in mirrors, with Emily trapped between, front, and then back, then front, each version getting smaller as they marched off into the distance. But inside that view, at its heart, stretched to infinity, what Emily could see; what had *that* been like?

Like a butterfly, mounted and pinned and peered at through a magnifying glass?

Like a genii, trapped within a silvered bottle for all eternity?

Like a mote, floating in the precise centre of a giant's colossal eye?

Like a soul, alone in the echoing void, in the uncaring, vastness of space, aware of every facet of itself, every flaw exposed, nothing hidden, nothing left to the imagination…?

Whatever she saw, Emily's been in the med-bay ever since. When we visit our former classmate, out of guilt, out of duty, she doesn't acknowledge us as we chat inanely about the day's lessons, about the friendships and petty frustrations of ship life. She sits hunched on her cot, thin arms tucked around her knees, rocking back and forth. The med-bay walls are just themselves, plain and dull, not even her vital stats displayed. But she still won't look anywhere near them, her eyes squeezed shut. And the walls, the programmable panels, the potential mirrors, they surround her, as they do everywhere on the ship, so she is forced to retreat deeper into her solitary world, sight averted from anything and everything beyond.

We hear her voice though, growing slowly fainter, for those brave enough to visit more than once. Emily sits rocking and wasting away, muttering the same nonsense, over and over and over: *"Mirror, mirror, on the wall…"*

~ * ~ * ~

Liam Hogan is an award-winning short story writer, with stories in *Best of British Science Fiction* and in *Best of British Fantasy* (NewCon Press). He volunteers at the creative writing charities Ministry of Stories, and Spark Young Writers. Host of the live literary event Liars' League for twelve years, he's now escaped London, but remains a Liar.

Visit him online at: happyendingnotguaranteed.blogspot.co.uk

Section Two
Visit the Menagerie

Step right up! Gather close, my curious wanderer, my seeker of the strange and the wondrous! I see you there, eyes wide, heart thundering like the beating of a drum. You have come searching for marvels, for beasts beyond imagining, for creatures that whisper in the dark and prowl at the edges of your waking dreams.

Well, you have come to the right place!

Here, in the shifting shadows, a menagerie unlike any other awaits. Beasts of legend, nightmares spun from the fabric of forgotten fears, creatures not bound by bars of steel, but by secrets too dangerous to speak aloud. Some with fangs like daggers, others with voices like lullabies—each waiting, watching, eager for their moment under the flickering glow of the carnival lights.

But beware!

Not all cages are made of iron, and not every creature longs to be tamed. Some were caught, while others…simply followed us home. And you, dear guest, are about to witness wonders beyond reckoning, terrors that will slither into your thoughts long after the show has ended.

So keep your hands inside the ring, and—whatever you do—do not look too deeply into their eyes.

Let the show begin!

Buck Fever

Jordan Hirsch

The stillness of the woods in the evening is incomparable to that of the morning's quietude. At dawn, you tiptoe through the trees so as to not be the one responsible for waking the world. How audacious, to crack a twig, robbing the birds and field mice of just a few more minutes of dreaming.

When the sun goes down, however, the silence is for your benefit alone. As the creatures tuck themselves in for the night, it's hard to say what else is out there to hear you as you make your way back to your truck, resisting the urge to run and willing the forest floor to dampen each step.

It was this latter trek I was readying myself for, the sun sitting plump on the horizon line, when I saw it. Antlers spanning years of growth and rural legend—a buck of at least 14 points stepped from behind a brush pile off to my left. Slightly obscured by impending twilight, he was only 60 yards away. An easy shot, any hunter worth their snuff around these parts would say.

Sitting on the overturned red bucket that had supported three generations of Dennyson backsides, my right knee began to bounce up and down like it does before I throw up. This was only the year's second shotgun season, but my Facebook feed had been filled with downed deer all week, and this one was a monster.

A deep breath, and I slowly, silently, slid off safety off and lifted the gun to my eye. He was even bigger through the scope. I smiled to myself. Of course he was.

I sighted carefully; the buck was broadside, offering me a shot that was basically target practice.

Another long inhale, exhale, and then a branch shifted off to my right as I pulled the trigger, making us both jump.

I got him; I had to have gotten him. But, he ran off deeper into the woods, so I jumped up and followed, unable to wait, ears pounding.

Two bright red dots here, six there: the trail became easier and easier to track as I traced my prey's steps. Praying I'd find him before it got too dark, I pushed from my mind any memory of blood trails ending without a deer at the end. It happened to everyone, but it wouldn't to me—not this time.

I scaled a fallen log, squeezed between two trees into a small clearing, and stopped.

He was there, and he was down.

Resting my gun against a tree trunk I reached for my phone to text my brother (I wasn't going to be able to get him to the truck myself). Suddenly the deer shifted, and I froze.

He was down, but he was still alive, and I needed to put him out of his misery as fast as I could, not wanting him to suffer longer than needed.

I didn't even have time to put my phone away.

An unearthly groan echoed from the other side of the clearing, like an ancient oak being torn up by its roots, paralyzing me where I stood.

Striding forward, slow and deliberate, was something I'd never seen before. Tall like a man, but not one—it was no yeti, no bigfoot, it was nothing I knew. The light was fading, but my sight had never been more acute—I saw every inch of it as it came toward me, all woody and splintered and creaking like a walking tree trunk.

My knees almost gave out when it stopped at the deer laying between us.

As it knelt—if you could call it that—it made the low groan again, producing an ache in my chest. Moisture pricked behind my eyes as the creature stroked the deer's neck. It appeared to be whispering to the buck, but the sound was more like the whistling of a sharp wind through a weeping willow.

I was frozen, unable to run, unable to do anything but watch.

And then the beast plunged its twiggy hand deep into the deer's side, and I fought to stifle a scream. As it rummaged around, I watched in horror and waited for the beast to wrench out its dinner, taking advantage of my fresh kill.

It didn't last long, and the creature rested a hand on the deer's neck one final time, then stood.

The deer—the monster buck that could have fed our family all year and whose antlers would have gone on my wall—rose with it then, no worse for wear, no hole in its side. Even in the growing dimness, I could see he was unharmed where the creature's hand had entered him. The deer shook his head, its prize of a rack proud and tall, and ran off, not giving me another thought.

The creature, however, looked right at me then; how, I don't know, as it didn't have eyes.

It held my gaze for a few seconds, and right before I broke it to look away—to look anywhere else—it held out its hand and dropped the metal pieces of the buckshot it'd taken from the deer's body, letting them fall one by one to the forest floor.

It didn't say a word, didn't utter a sound to break the absolute silence of the woods after those metal shards hit the ground.

I took this as a warning, and I believe that's exactly how I was intended to take it. I turned and ran, as fast as I could in the coming darkness, not caring how much noise I made. What other creature could be out there that I'd need to avoid?

I didn't realize until I reached the tree line, impossibly fishing my keys out of my pocket in the last 10 yards to the truck with shaking hands, that I'd left my gun behind.

I never went back for it.

With that demon—that terrifying angel—protecting the creatures of those woods, I saw no reason to. It had made sure I knew my place.

And with every hunter's story I hear where a blood trail came up empty, where they knew they'd made the shot but could never find anything, I wonder if maybe their aim was truer than they thought.

Maybe something else just got there first.

~ * ~ * ~

Jordan Hirsch writes speculative fiction and poetry while occupying the ancestral and current homelands of the Dakota people, Mni Sota Makoce. Her debut poetry chapbook *Both Worlds* is out with Bottlecap Press, and a collection of her short fiction is forthcoming with Red Bird Chapbooks. You can find more of Jordan's work on her website: jordanrhirsch.wordpress.com.

Cat's Collar

Rose Strickman

It was a dark, drizzly morning when Andrew first met the black cat.

It was his first day on his solo mail route. He fizzed with nervousness and excitement as he parked his truck outside the garden gate. He collected the wad of letters for the addressee, climbed out and began crunching up the drive. Unlike most of her well-heeled neighbors, Emmeline Stokes didn't have her postbox attached to her gate, but up by her house. Andrew was thus forced to walk all the way to her front porch, through her extensive garden.

Emmeline's garden was a lush landscape of leafy trees and smooth lawns. Her flowerbeds glowed with colors, pink, white, red, blue and yellow, all blurred by the rain. Birds called from the trees and bushes. Andrew made his way through this soft painting of a place, toward the beautiful old mansion, its shingle roof glistening in the rain.

There came a soft mew at his feet.

Andrew looked down, startled, to see a small cat crouched in a flowerbed, fur black as night. The cat looked up at him with reflective eyes. Rather odd-colored eyes. Andrew had never seen a cat with eyes that shade of orange. The cat crouched down, tail snaking.

It was wearing a collar, Andrew realized, an ornate band with an identity tag hanging off it. This must be Emmeline's cat.

"Good kitty." Cats weren't as potentially dangerous as dogs, the other postal officers had told Andrew, but it was still better to leave them alone. He therefore edged around the feline, proceeding further up the drive. The cat's eyes followed him, ears pricked, gaze alert.

"Lial!"

Andrew jumped at the sudden shout. Standing on the porch, as though she'd just appeared out of nowhere, was Emmeline Stokes. The old woman stood tall and ramrod-straight, her iron-gray hair drawn back from her severe face. A face that showed the remnants of great beauty and was still very handsome. She was wearing a dark, elegant dress and a shawl pinned with a jeweled brooch. Dark gems glimmered in her ears and on her fingers.

"Sorry, Miss Stokes!" Andrew blurted out, then felt like an idiot.

She paid him no mind. "Lial, come here!" The cat flattened its ears and let out a growl but rose from the flowerbed to trot up the porch steps, its identity tag jingling slightly. Emmeline crouched down, surprisingly limber for such an old woman, and gathered her cat into her arms. She straightened, cradling Lial, and eyed Andrew.

"Like my cat, do you?" She stroked Lial's head.

"He's very cute," Andrew said after a moment. "I've got your mail here, Miss Stokes." He strode up to the porch, holding out her letters.

Emmeline made no move to take them. She continued petting Lial, an odd little smile on her lips as she regarded Andrew. Her restless fingers dislodged Lial's collar slightly, bringing his identity tag further into the light. Only it didn't quite look like a normal pet tag…

"You wouldn't think Lial was so cute if you knew the truth," Emmeline said abruptly. A playful, malevolent spark danced in her eyes. "Oh, no."

"Really?" Andrew shifted around, already wondering how he could get away. "Why not?"

Emmeline threw her head back and laughed, long and loud, echoing through the rainy garden. In her arms, Lial crouched down further, ears pinned back, his purr closer to a growl.

"I like you," Emmeline gasped at last. "Oh, I do like you!" She watched Andrew a moment longer, the dangerously amused spark still dancing in her eyes. She didn't seem so handsome anymore. "If I told you the truth about Lial, young man," she said at last, "you wouldn't believe me."

"Oh, really?" Sweat ran down Andrew's neck. When he'd first gotten this route, he'd wondered how he, the most junior delivery-man, had received a route in such a wealthy, high-class neighborhood. Now he was starting to understand why none of the other delivery officers wanted it. "Well, I'll just leave your mail here in the box, how about that?"

Emmeline and Lial stood back while Andrew climbed the stairs. The steps rang hollow under his feet. He deposited Emmeline's letters in the postbox nailed to her porch pillar. Standing on the porch, he got a further glimpse of Lial's tag. It seemed weirder than ever—but Andrew had no time to think on it. He could feel Emmeline's predatory gaze on him, and he was desperate to escape.

He finally got her mail into the box and turned back. "Well," he said into the awkward silence, "nice to meet you, Miss Stokes. Have a good day." He started back down the steps.

"I'm older than I look, young man." Emmeline's voice rang out, sly and malicious. "Oh, yes. Much older." Her manicured hand scratched at Lial's ears. "Want to know how I'm so well-preserved?"

"Have a good day," Andrew said firmly, and headed back down the drive.

Emmeline's laughter followed him, like the cawing of soulless crows, all the way back to his truck.

It was only when he'd safely shut himself into the driver's cab and was moving on to the next house that Andrew suddenly realized what had bothered him so much about Lial's identity tag.

It hadn't been an identity tag at all. It had been a silver star inside a circle.

A pentagram.

~ * ~

"So, Andy! How do you like your new route?" Padma grinned over at Andrew.

"Oh, it's fabulous," Andrew sighed. It was the end of his first solo day and he was back in the post office, exhausted and in no mood for his fellow postal workers' ribbing. "Lots of big houses with hidden postboxes and large dogs."

"Just wait," Roberto called from the other side of the sorting room. "Everyone gets bitten eventually."

"Thanks, Roberto." Andrew slumped down into a seat and sighed. "That—that Emmeline Stokes, though. She seemed a bit ...weird."

"That's one way to put it!" Roberto rolled his eyes. "You know what they say about her, right? That she's been in this town literally forever?"

"You mean, all her life?"

"No. *Forever.* As in, before anyone else here was even born."

"That's not possible," Andrew protested.

"That's what people say," Padma put in. "No one can remember a time when she wasn't in that house, not even the folks at the Fair Creek Retirement Center. The city council keeps trying to get her to move, but they can't budge her."

"Why would they want her to move?" Andrew asked, his curiosity roused.

"Well, they say she hasn't paid taxes for at least fifty years," Padma said. "And apparently half the city government really, really hates her. She's always getting out of taxes and never pays attention to laws or regulations. She thinks she's above the law, and the rumor is she's got some really dodgy graft schemes going—not that anyone can pin anything on her. And…" Padma trailed off.

"What?"

"There was an incident." Roberto spoke now, voice low. "Apparently Emmeline Stokes got into a fight with the mayor a couple of years ago. And then the mayor's kid turned up drowned dead in the river."

Andrew's skin crawled. "An accident?"

"Yeah—officially. But it seemed plenty suspicious, you know? It's not like the river was flooding or anything. There shouldn't have been any accidents."

"Did they ever find proof it was…?" Andrew found he didn't want to say the word *murder*.

"No." Roberto shook his head. "But it's a hell of a coincidence, isn't it? And there've been a lot of other things, nasty things, happening to people Emmeline Stokes doesn't like."

"And even besides that," Padma jumped back in, "she's a total Wall Street wolf, apparently, and does some super dodgy stuff with investments. She's ruined people. The city council's terrified of her, and so are her neighbors."

Andrew remembered the predatory edge in Emmeline's ghastly smile, and thought her neighbors were right to be afraid. And he anticipated tomorrow's route with no small amount of trepidation.

~ * ~

Sure enough, Andrew's visits to Emmeline Stokes's house soon became a daily torment.

No matter how quietly he tried to park, or how early he tried to arrive, she was always there, sitting or standing on her porch, holding that cat, a cruel smile playing on her lips while she considered how to toy with him today. Sometimes she asked him intrusive questions: "Where is your family, young man? Are you married yet? Have a girlfriend?" Other times she made sly, oblique references to her own life, hinting at a history of degeneracy and license, but never giving him any details. He was welcome to ask for more, she always implied, that malevolent spark dancing in her eyes.

Andrew never did. He got through his daily drop-offs with minimal interaction and maximal efficiency, making noises in response to Emmeline's questions and depositing her mail before retreating down the drive back to his truck. It did no good. She could see how angry and helpless she made him, and she reveled in her power.

Andrew wanted to report her to his supervisor, but Emmeline was careful never to say anything too explicit or aggressive. She never swore at him, never touched him or invited him into her house. She merely stood on her porch and made airy, malicious conversation, playing with him as a cat would a mouse. Only her cat was a lot nicer than she was.

Indeed, as time went on, Andrew began to develop a certain fellow feeling for Lial. The black cat seemed as unhappy with Emmeline as he was. Every time Andrew saw Lial in Emmeline's arms, the cat was curled up, ears back, back stiff, whiskers drooping miserably.

Other times, Lial snuck off into the garden and was there to greet Andrew on his way to the house, rubbing and purring against his leg. Andrew always said hello, scratching his ears, defiant of whether Emmeline could see him or not. If she objected to him petting her cat, let her say so. She certainly wasn't shy about saying everything else.

"Hi there," Andrew said. "How's my favorite boy?" Lial half-closed his orange eyes and rubbed harder against Andrew's pantleg.

"Lial!" Emmeline called from her porch, an evil old crow.

Lial stopped purring, stopped rubbing. He gave Andrew a long look. His expression, if he'd been human, might almost have been pleading. Begging Andrew for help.

Then the cat unwound itself from Andrew. Head and tail down, he headed toward the porch, toward his mistress, the pentagram on his collar gleaming against his night-dark fur.

~ * ~

Some three months after Andrew started his route, on a glorious summer day, he pulled up yet again outside Emmeline Stokes's mansion. He sat in his truck a moment, reluctance and resentment like stones inside him. Then he let out a vicious curse before going to grab her mail. The cab door slammed behind him as he headed up her drive.

It was a bright summer's morning. Birds sang in the trees and sunlight danced over the colorful flower beds. Andrew took a deep breath of the summer air, inhaling the scent of dew and green growth, trying to take strength from the beauty of the morning.

He didn't know how much longer he could stand this.

A soft mew sounded at his feet. Lial was crouched down in his usual flowerbed, peering up at Andrew.

"Hey there, boy." Andrew bent over to scratch Lial on the ears. The cat purred, angling his head to better enjoy Andrew's caress.

"How is she today?" Andrew deliberately did not look at the porch. He knew Emmeline was there, watching them. He would not give her the satisfaction of seeing him glance over in fear.

Lial stared into his eyes. "*Rrrawful,*" he mewed.

Andrew jerked his hand back. The hairs on the back of his neck stood up.

"Lial!" Emmeline's voice rang out from the porch. Lial put his ears back and growled but trotted off toward the porch as usual. Andrew watched him go, heart still pounding.

Emmeline gathered Lial into her arms and watched as Andrew approached and climbed the steps. "What were you and Lial talking about, young man?" she asked.

"Nothing." Andrew deposited the letters and bills into the box. "He's a cat."

"Oh, is he?" Emmeline stroked Lial's head, slow and possessive. Lial tensed up, a trilling growl sounding.

Andrew gritted his teeth. For no reason he could discern, this was the absolute last straw. Something inside him snapped.

"Yeah." He glared at Emmeline, rage and disgust making his jaw clench. "He's a goddamn cat! What else could he be? Why can't you just be fucking honest for once? What the hell are you getting at, Miss Emmeline Stokes?"

Emmeline fell still, and for a second Andrew tensed, fearing—he didn't know what. But then Emmeline smiled, like the rictus of a skull, and he realized he'd fallen right into her trap.

"All right," the old woman purred, as smug as any feline, "I'll tell you what the hell I'm getting at." She sat on her porch swing in a swish of skirts, settling Lial in her lap. The cat crouched, more tense than ever.

"A long time ago," Emmeline said, "when this city was just a dab of a town on the edge of wilderness, a girl of poor family discovered a certain book. It was very old, even at the time, and from its pages the girl learned—certain things. How to summon the inhabitants of the infernal regions, and how to bind them."

The hairs stood on the back of Andrew's neck again. "You mean she sold her soul to the Devil or something?"

"Certainly not." Emmeline's claw-like hands never ceased stroking and scratching Lial. Scratching under his collar. "It is perfectly possible to bind a demon to your service without selling it anything at all, if you know the right procedure. The right...tools." She tugged on Lial's collar, jerking the silver pentagram further into the light. Lial let out a protesting mewl.

"Pentagrams," Emmeline murmured. "A silver pentagram can bind a demon forever, if the caster's will is strong enough. And I assure you, this girl's will was more than strong enough. She summoned a demon, bound it with silver and with salt and with ash. She forced it to give her everything she wanted. Wealth, health, status, and extreme longevity. Though, alas, even a demon can't stop the aging process altogether. Merely slow it down." The old woman's lips drew back in an even wider grin.

"He's trapped forever, this demon," she continued in gloating tones. "Bound by silver and by a mortal's will, he's trapped in this house forever."

The porch pillar bumped into Andrew's back. He hadn't even realized he was backing away. Sweat broke out under his shirt.

"Oh, don't look like that, young man." Mischief lit Emmeline's eyes as her tone lightened. "It's just a story."

At this, Lial suddenly jerked away, snaking out from under Emmeline's hands. He jumped down to the porch floor and ran to the far end, tail twitching, glaring at both humans.

"Just a story." Andrew's agreement sounded weak and unconvincing even to his own ears. He took a step down the porch stairs. "Well, have a good day, Miss Stokes. See you tomorrow."

"Tomorrow!" Emmeline's laughter rang with evil triumph, following Andrew back down the drive to his truck.

~ * ~

For the rest of that day, while he completed his route, Andrew was distracted and disturbed. Emmeline's story was nonsense—of course it was. No one could really summon a demon from the depths of Hell, bind it with a silver pentagram and force it to give magical gifts…could they? But he couldn't rid his mind of the gloating look in Emmeline's eyes, her malevolent laughter. Of Lial's eyes, the rage in them. How the cat had seemed to *speak*. The gleam of the pentagram around his neck.

The next day was warm and fair. Andrew headed up Emmeline's drive with even more reluctance than usual, his every footstep heavy, her mail weighing like a stone in his hand. Emmeline was going to be dreadful today, he knew already, eager to gloat over yesterday's victory.

To his surprise, however, the porch was empty. Emmeline was not waiting for him. Andrew let out a sigh of relief and hope. Having finally provoked a response from Andrew, would she now leave him alone?

There came a small commotion at his feet. Thrashing branches, accompanied by desperate mews.

Andrew peered down. There, under a hydrangea bush, was Lial. The cat's collar had somehow gotten tangled in the bush's boughs and he couldn't get free. Lial twisted and turned, mewling, and looked up at Andrew in desperate pleading.

Andrew cast another glance at the still-empty porch before crouching down. He regarded the trapped cat. Lial stared back, whiskers twitching.

"If I let you free," Andrew murmured, "what will you do?"

Lial writhed again, making the bush's leaves rustle and sway. The pentagram on his collar shone brighter than ever. A silver pentagram, to bind a demon's might and make it a mortal's slave.

Slowly, Andrew reached for Lial's collar. The cat went still, watching Andrew with urgent orange intensity.

The collar was rough under Andrew's fingers. He found the

silver buckle, the metal stinging his skin like electricity. But still he unlatched it and pulled the band free.

The collar fell to the ground. For a moment, Lial stood frozen, as though he couldn't believe he was actually free. His tail snaked through the bush's roots. His throat looked almost obscenely bare.

Then the cat—*smiled*. A human smile, on a cat's face. Or not so human.

"Mrrrthank fffhhhyou," he purred to Andrew.

Then he streaked away, disappearing into the shrubbery, back toward the house.

Eventually, Andrew found he could move again. He scooped up the collar and dangling pentagram, careful not to touch the metal with his bare skin. He stowed them both away in his shirt pocket and rose to his feet. He strode briskly to Emmeline's postbox, deposited her mail, and turned to head back to his truck.

He saw neither Emmeline nor Lial. A deep silence hung over house and garden alike.

~ * ~

The next morning, Andrew entered the post office to a buzz of excitement.

"Hey, Andy! Did you hear?" Padma came bustling over.

"Hear what?" Andrew tapped at his phone, clocking himself in on the app.

"Take a look!" Padma thrust her own phone into his hand, the screen displaying a news article.

Local Eccentric Found Dead, the headline read, accompanied by a picture of Emmeline's house. They could not display an image of Emmeline's body, the caption noted. The corpse was just too graphic.

Blood running cold, Andrew scanned the rest of the article. Emmeline Stokes, 97 (perhaps), had been found dead in her bed, ripped apart by what seemed to be the teeth and claws of an animal, possibly a large cat. The police were mystified. There was no sign Emmeline had been keeping a large animal in her house, and local zoos and wildlife centers reported no missing big cats that might have escaped to maul an old woman in her bed. The police suspected foul play. The article commented on the many people ruined by Emmeline's predatory investment practices, and the enemies she'd made in local government.

"Awful, isn't it?" Padma took back her phone. "She was on your route, right?"

"Yeah," Andrew said through numb lips.

"Well, I hope you didn't run into any attack-lions while you're out there. Crazy to think she might've had enemies who actually wanted her dead," Padma said with a chuckle. "Do you think it was one of the city councilmembers?" She laughed aloud at the idea.

Andrew laughed too, weak and mechanical. He knew it was not one of Emmeline's enemies on the city council who had done this. It was an enemy in her own home.

He thought of Lial, of the inhuman hatred in the cat's glowing eyes. He thought of just how sharp a cat's claws were. He thought of a demon, imprisoned and enslaved for over two hundred years, and the hatred and rage such a creature could store up over that time...

The back of Andrew's neck prickled.

Slowly, he turned to the office window, knowing already what he would see.

Crouched on the windowsill was a small black cat with bright orange eyes, its throat free of any collar. Any pentagram.

They stared at one another, man and cat. Then, for the first time, Andrew acknowledged the creature's true name.

"*Belial*," he whispered.

On the windowsill, the demon Belial smiled.

~ * ~ * ~

Rose Strickman is a speculative fiction author living in Seattle, Washington. Her work has appeared over 60 times, in anthologies such as *Sword and Sorceress 32*, *Sun Rising* and *The Dragon's Hoard 3*, as well as several e-zines. Her novella, *Island of the Drowned*, was published as a standalone Tiny Terrors title from Graveside Press. She has also self-published several novellas on Amazon. Please see her Amazon author's page at www.amazon.com/author/rosestrickman or follow her on Bluesky @rosestrickman.bsky.social.

Celestial Ritual

Josh Schlossberg

Aldra paused under the archway leading into the vast basalt amphitheater, hundreds of guests—mostly kin—sprawled across the black stone pews. High above, jagged volcanic crags spurted lava into a roiling sky of deep purple clouds, blurry treble suns glowing pinkly through.

In the midground, on the edge of a low cliff, a tiny wormlike figure stood on a boulder in the midst of a bubbling lava pool beneath gushing falls. Yagru, her mate. Fond warmth flushed through Aldra's heart followed by a jolt of gut-twisting anxiety at what she was about to do.

The priestess, grasping the sparkling tantalum band in both claws, towered over Yagru, her scales a drab green to his ashen grey. A rattle of her tail, and a choir of atonal voices piped up from somewhere deep within the rock caverns.

All eyes on Aldra, she took a bracing breath and glided down the aisle. Joyful hisses and flicking tongues from those gathered, including her eldest sister, Gormi, sleek wings folded against a massive milk-white bulk. And, as Aldra reached the front row, a corpulent giant, scales brilliant blue as the heart of a flame. Aldra's mother. Nested amongst the fat coils of the older female, her latest young husband, a grub whispering in her ear as she threw back her wedged head in laughter.

A pang of jealousy from Aldra at the elder's stunning beauty, outshining her own even on this special day. But, as she slipped past with a practiced smile, Aldra remembered she was lovely, too, any lingering doubts dispelled by the piercing gaze of every male. Because, as of late, her scales glowed a radiant orange like cactus blooms, belly proudly plumped with hundreds of fertilized eggs, thanks to Yagru.

Naturally, like all Naga females, Aldra hadn't always been this appealing. Indeed, the change had only come over the last six sun cycles, as for the prior four-hundred-twenty she'd been vine-thin, scales a dull olive, wings mere buds. Only when the orange broke through the green and her wings branched out did the opposite sex even look her way. Along with her female rivals, several of whom eyed her from the back pews.

Indeed, Aldra was growing more fertile every cycle, her orange destined to burnish to a deep red, followed by gold, then pale like Gormi—who, for the first time in their lives, seemed to see her as almost equal—laying more eggs each clutch. Until finally, in another seven-hundred cycles or so, she'd turn bright blue like her mother, stuffed with eggs until she burst apart like fireworks, rejoining the universe in one ultimate glory. But Aldra had a long time before that, and, in the meantime, she intended to enjoy every moment of her newfound splendor.

She slid up the winding path, smooth from the passage of countless brides before her. When she reached the cliff face—a sweltering, sulfurous heat wafting from the lava pool at the foot of the falls—Yagru met her with a simpleton's smile. Reminding her of the awkward night of her four-hundred-twenty-sixth cycle when they first mated.

That early clutch was only eight eggs. The second, a cycle later, twenty-three. The third, thirty-eight. Now, this one distending her belly would be as many as all those put together. Solemnly, she found her spot next to the priestess, lava mist tickling her scales.

The tantalum band glittered as the red primary sun broke the cloud cover. But Yagru wasn't paying attention, gaze drawn overhead by a swarm of fat buzzing blowflies. Aldra shook her head in pity and not a little shame. Was this even her beloved anymore?

When they'd first been introduced at worship, Aldra was lured in by his genius, his talent for improvising heart-rending verse on the Planetary Lights as easily as he could cipher a twelve-digit sum, finally a match for her own sharp and inquisitive mind. Indeed, he was famous across the Craters as both an engineer and philosopher, having discovered a more efficient way to harness magma to warm Naga nests while uncovering new layers of consciousness through experimental research.

Yagru snapped absentmindedly at the flies, making it hard to believe how, during their courtship, Aldra had been honored to join him on strolls around the pits and ledges, his reputation radiating over her like heat from a sunbaked rock. Lecturing around the

Craters, Yagru had accumulated overflowing storehouses of Viath tusks, ranking him as one of the wealthiest Naga. Then, as her orange ripened, the stage had been shared equally.

But as it stood now, drool stringing from slack jaws, Yagru could barely do simple addition and subtraction anymore, and the clawful of tusks he earned were doled out in pity; it was an open secret Aldra supported them both from her screenshows on scale care. Standing on the black crag above her kin, she alone was the prize to behold, a majestic river coursing past a stagnant puddle.

Still, after all, no tragedy had befallen Yagru, just mere biology, like the seasonal frosting of the Northern Wastes. Indeed, the Naga had long ago made peace with its males peaking early only to quickly fall apart. At a mere two-hundred-forty cycles, little over half Aldra's age, Yagru, flecks of flies on his lips, was *supposed* to be a shadow of his former self.

The priestess shook her rattle, the hidden choir fell silent, and the audience watched with rapt with expectation. Every one of Aldra's children—both female and male—laid proud eyes upon her, as the more revered Aldra became, the higher their own standing.

"The Great Lamia blesses this ceremony." The priestess' hiss echoed around the amphitheater. She handed Aldra the band, which, despite the scorching lava all around, was ice cold, its razor-sharp inner edge gleaming.

"Give this ring," the priestess' golden eyes fell on Aldra, "as a reminder of the vow you both have taken."

Mouth dry, Aldra slipped the band over Yagru's throat. Only then did his bleary eyes focus on hers. And from their insensate depths, black pupils dilated like two divers coming up for air.

"Now," the priestess stepped back with a respectful bow, "you may take the groom."

Aldra reached out and grasped the frigid band in both claws. All that was left was to twist the metal so it slit Yagru's throat and then lap up the blood as he lay dying. Tough as the moment would be, she pictured the night's celebration to come, the glut of feasting and dancing, the dozens of young males parading their wit and acumen before her in hopes of being the next to bask in her glow, however briefly.

Her trembling claws clicked against the band. Down below, Aldra's mother had risen to her full colossal height, hood spread in wrath at the delay. Though not a word passed between the two, the younger knew what the elder was thinking: she should be ecstatic to shed this dead skin of a mate to make way for the new.

Yagru's eyes dull as so much domestic stock, Aldra turned the band a single degree. A trickle of black blood flowed down his throat, though not a whimper came from Yagru.

The priestess flicked her tongue in encouragement while an agitated rattle lofted up from the attendees. What was happening to Aldra? Was it that fear of success—feeling unworthy of this crowning achievement—Gormi had warned her to guard against?

Or was it something else entirely? That, no matter the changes her mate had undergone, was there not still a taste of the fresh ripe Yagru somewhere within the rotting husk? Had he not, even that morning, penned her new verse?

You are the sunrise,
the light and warmth from above
that keeps me from cold.

While nowhere near as lyrical as his earlier epics, it had a touching simplicity lacking in those other gaudy rhymes. A subtle beauty, like a shard of glass smoothed by aeons of sweeping tide. Much like the Yagru who stood before her.

Aldra's mother stormed off her pew to slither up the ramp. Aldra knew if she didn't complete the ceremony, her mother would do it for her.

Still, a faint light shone in Yagru's eyes, proving he knew what was about to happen, and welcomed it. And it was that very acceptance that made clear the lengths of his love. What if they had it all wrong, and the former Yagru, all fury and flash, had been the imposter, and this humble being her true mate?

Aldra shook her head violently. Enough! Shortly after hatching, each Naga was taught how emotion poisoned rational thought. It was time to do what she'd come for!

Veins bulging in her forearms, she grasped the band. Took a deep breath. And, in a single motion, slid it up and over Yagru's head to fling it in the lava pool, where it sunk.

Deafening hisses and rattles from below, Aldra grabbed her beloved Yagru, spread her wings wide, and leapt from the cliff. Rising above the furious, writhing crowd, she flapped north towards the Wastes, where no Naga could tell her who—or why—she must love.

~ * ~ * ~

Josh Schlossberg's short fiction has been published in numerous magazines and anthologies. He's the author of the collection, *Where the Shadows are Shown*, the eco folk horror novel, *Charwood*, the cosmic horror novella, *Malinae*, and overseer of Josh's Worst Nightmare (JoshsWorstNightmare.com), where he surveys the dark landscape of eco-horror fiction.

Chronovore

Pat O'Malley

Listen. Do you hear that? Time is passing us by.

Most people believe when the present turns into the past it disappears into the ether, like footprints near the tide. If only that were true. No, the terrible truth is yesterday is gone because the chronovores ate it.

From the dawn of time, when the first seconds of the universe ticked into the next, the chronovores were there, hungry and waiting. Swarms of floating, sharp-toothed mouths, gobbling up wasted moments and what-ifs. They have many names, Langoliers, Clockroaches, Hounds of Tindalos but all of those trace back to what they are; "those that eat time."

Exact descriptions of them are impossible. To say the creatures have bodies would be inaccurate. From what is known, portions of their "bodies" exist outside of standard dimensions.

Time as we know it is like a tube. Inside, a current flows in one direction left to right. These time-eaters live outside the tube inhabiting the *angles* of time.

Disturbingly, the flow of time is meaningless to them. The creatures can come and go from any point in the tube they want. Most remain in the past as there's plenty of wasted time to feast on there.

Individuals or objects whose time has been devoured by these multi-dimensional predators are transmuted into various states of their history. Records indicate Earth's pre-historic dinosaurs had their time eaten by chronovores, transforming them into the buried fossils they were destined to become.

Few sentient species know these creatures exist. Hidden on the far edges of the Milky Way there is a planet known as Zilxik. A marble of teal seas and crystal mountains. This is the home-world of the Zilxikians; one of the most technologically advanced races in the cosmos.

They are aware of the chronovores.

For centuries, these silver-skinned humanoids have stealthily launched probes across the galaxy gathering data on a never-ending search for greater cosmic awareness.

It is through this research the silver people have learned of and have begun collecting blasphemous and forbidden knowledge from the darkest corners of space. Written by long-dead races that pre-date even the Zilxik, these sinister tomes speak of nightmarish creatures like the chronovores, their hunger, and their ability to crawl across the centuries.

These stories are fascinating. Close examination of such an organism's temporal biology could reveal secrets of the fabric of time. Unlocking the nature of spacetime was one puzzle the bold scientific minds of Zilxik were eager to solve.

Further reading of these texts reveal how to cage such preda-tors, which leads to today. In the dimly lit corridors of a floating crystal pyramid on Zilxik, a group of astronomers, scientists, and mathematicians are gathered around a large hologram. Countless flowing corners and angles twist and shift like a kaleidoscope. Cloaked in robes tailored from star clusters, the Zilxikians stare with golden eyes at the pulsating shape.

This is the Tesseract cage, years of careful design and calcula-tions come to fruition. It is a shape whose existence blips between the here and now. In a few seconds, the Zilxik plan to lure a chronovore from whatever point in spacetime it lurks into the float-ing construct here in the present.

Once it has materialized within the tesseract, the cage will spring colossally heavy dwarf star chains across the target. Naturally, portions of the clockroach and tesseract will continue to flicker in and out of dimensions. Though by occupying the same space at the same time, the tesseract will lock the chronovore in quantum entanglement.

Immobilized, the mysterious organism will be ready for study and reveal its secrets.

The danger is clear and present but the Zilxik built their culture under the belief that any pursuit of knowledge as great as this is worth the risk. They are unafraid of the unsettling stories they have read about the chronovores. The Zilxik were not present in any of them. Had they been, the narrative in the ancient records would have gone differently.

These time-eaters are no different from any other interplanetary beasts that need to be caged. Primitive-thinking creatures such as these do not deserve the power they wield.

The silver people will make much better use of such an incredible ability. The entire history of the galaxy, from start to finish will open to them. It will be like reading a book and jumping in at any page.

Today, the Zilxik become the masters of spacetime.

A flat panel glowing with mysterious glyphs floats in front of each of the gathered figures. One by one, the Zilxik place the palm of their four-fingered hand on the floating panel in front of them until a loud hum echoes through the corridors of the pyramid.

The sound is a beacon they have meticulously composed. The high-pitched frequency replicates the abstract sound of time passing. If the pitch was slowed millions of decimals lower it would sound not unlike gears turning inside a clock.

They wait patiently.

Soon the malleable prism begins convulsing at an alarming speed. The shape folds and stretches itself into several complex and intersecting angles. From the point of origin, each line is pointed exactly at twelve degrees.

Lightning crackles around them. A great gust sweeps through the chamber. The Zilzikians shield their golden eyes as large plumes of smoke begin billowing in the chamber.

The view of the tesseract becomes clouded by the creeping smoke. Where is that smoke coming from? Before they can register what's happening, they all hear a steadily growing sound coming from the smoke.

The noise is difficult to identify. One moment it sounds like a growl then a moaning coming from far away. Whatever it is, it sounds alive.

The silver scientists are on high alert. There it is! In the smoke, they can make out the visuals of figures unknown to the tesseract having appeared twisting and flailing within the shape.

The chronovore is here! Activate the cage! Prepare to witness quantum entanglement!

Dozens of silver fingers hurriedly tap on the glyphs floating in front of them. The frequency of the luring beacon is replaced by a shrill buzzing sound. A crisscrossed webbing of lights springs on the cage and foreign presence, netting them together.

The gathered Zilxikians watch in awe as the glowing net constricts. A strobe light flickers through the thick wisps of smoke. Images of what's inside the amorphous prism change with each second. Even the Zilxik do not possess the words to describe what's caged within the tesseract.

The experiment is a success! The Zilxikians have lured and captured a chronovore from the edges of time. The secrets of spacetime are theirs!

Lightning crackles around them. The moaning sound from the tesseract amplifies sharply. The panels in front of each of the scientists begin flashing an alarming red.

They are unafraid. They have taken every precaution. Tighten the dwarf star chains! The neon webbing appears to struggle against several forces pushing against it.

The howling sound is becoming deafening, rattling the nerves of the Zilxikians. Something is wrong. Accelerate the Tesseract's shifting! Activate the reserve containment fields!

A waterfall of blue glyphs surrounds the struggling shapes. Back-up security comes online. Less than a minute later its system crashes.

Pale lights begin to flash in the chamber. Movement everywhere seems to slow down. A deafening moan rocks the pyramid. Awestruck, the Zilxikians watch as the tesseract turns inside-out. Then, like a supernova, the shape bursts.

Emergency! Quantum entanglement breached! The chronovore has escaped!

The silver androgynous figures remained at their panels desperate to bring the tesseract back online.

Lights flashing continuously. Swarms of eyes bubble in the air. A long, invisible tongue licks their face.

They scream. A sound like the vibration of a wet finger tracing the rim of a glass. Then silence.

In a blip, the pyramid hovering in the sky they all stood in was now a sunken ruin. The cracked triangular stone structure lay half-buried in the teal sand below the other floating pyramids. A once proud fortress brought to its inevitable end much faster than anticipated.

Inside things are worse.

Cobwebs and ruins. The chamber that once held the tesseract

now resembles a crypt. Be careful where you step. All across the rubble were many small oozing chrome puddles.

The ambitious minds who set out to become masters of space-time. Their bodies transmuted eons backward to the primordial amoebas their race descended from. Centuries of evolution undone in an instant.

It still wasn't enough. Those silver fools didn't just fail. They've doomed us all. Their experiment, the Tesseract did something to the monster they summoned.

Right now that chronovore is growing bigger. It remains in the here and now, biting away at our present. Think about it, hasn't time felt like it's been going faster lately?

~ * ~

Somewhere, lightyears away from Zilxik on the planet Earth, a young boy stares gloomily at a calendar hanging in his bedroom.

"Summer's over already?!"

~ * ~ * ~

Pat O'Malley lives with his wife in New York. He is best known for writing eccentric short stories and tall tales. Over the duration of his writing career Pat has become a fan favorite of those who enjoy the bizarre, weird, and tragically ludicrous. His bibliography boasts 20 short stories, most of which are included in his debut anthology *Fever Dreams*. Pat's stories have been featured in text and online publications such as *Down in the Dirt, Trembling with Fear, The Dark City Crime & Mystery Magazine* and more!

You can find him on Instagram @patomwrites where he occasionally posts snippets from his short stories.

Nibbles

Emily Gennis

Hey Mina,

How's it going? Wow, can you believe it's been ten years? Crazy! I feel like I just saw you. HAHAHA!

So what have you been up to? I heard you're living it up in Miami. Must be pretty nice living so close to the beach.

I heard a few other things too. You live alone. No husband. No kids. What's up with that, huh? You never struck me as the independent type.

Me, I'm good. Really good, actually. Had a steady job at an auto body shop. Bought my own place. Met a girl, Shelly. Not much to look at from the neck up, but sweet. Kind. Generous. Nothing like me. Or you.

All that's gone now, but it doesn't matter.

Speaking of which, I need a favor. I know, I know! We didn't exactly part on good terms. You're probably telling me where to shove my favors right now. But the thing is, the favor isn't really for me. It's for Rob.

I didn't see you at the funeral, Mina. What gives? You're too good to say one last goodbye to the guy you almost married?

To tell the truth I wasn't gonna go either. Sure, back in the day, the two of us were thick as thieves. Best friends even. But after what happened, I figured I'd never see Rob again. I couldn't believe it when his sister Tina called me and said he'd been asking for me at the end. Those were his last words, she told me. "Bring me Jonathan." Funny, in the old days he'd always called me Johnny. But a lot's changed since then.

I guess my sentimental side got the better of me. Maybe after all these years Rob finally wanted to patch things up between us but croaked before he had the chance. The least I could do was turn up to give him a decent send off.

Turns out I was right about never seeing him again. It was a closed casket funeral. When I asked Tina how he'd died, she just started crying. No, not crying. Wailing. Moaning. Crazy bitch sounded like a damn fire engine. Looked like one too with her face all red. Makeup smeared with snot and tears. Shame you weren't there to see it, Mina. You'd have died laughing.

As far as the rest of the funeral, you didn't miss much. Just a bunch of relatives who hadn't seen Rob in years yammering about what a nice guy he was. A sensitive soul. Kept to himself.

Reading between the lines, it sounded like our boy had turned himself into a shut-in. No job. No friends. Barely left the house except in the middle of the night. Shame how that happens to people.

The weirdest thing was nobody would tell me how he died. Every time I asked someone, they'd cringe. Shake their heads. Look away. At the time it drove me nuts.

Now that I know the truth, I don't blame them.

The whole thing gave me the creeps. I couldn't get out of there fast enough. I was halfway to the bus stop when Tina caught up with me. She was carrying this big ass plywood box. Big as the old TV that used to sit in the yard outside your dad's place. Just as busted looking too.

Whoever had put that box together must have been in a real hurry. It was crooked as hell. Splinters and nails sticking out all over the place. "Here," she said, snorting a blob of snot back up into her nose. "Rob wanted you to have this." She shoved it into my arms, turned around and headed back to the church.

I'll be honest with you, Mina. I thought about leaving that box sitting on the curb with the rest of the trash. Almost did too. But all of a sudden, I just got this feeling like whatever was in there was important. So I sat with that thing on my lap the whole way home, holding onto it like it had my own soul locked up inside. In a way, I guess it did.

When I got home, I knocked the empty cans of Bud off my kitchen table and set the box down. That's when I heard it. Real quiet, but insistent. Demanding even. Something in there was squeaking.

I grabbed a hammer and started yanking the nails out as fast as I could. It was like I couldn't breathe until I got it open. My hands started bleeding from scrapes and splinters, but I didn't care. I needed to see what was in that box. It was calling out to me.

Finally, the sides fell open and I saw what was inside. It was a clear plastic cage. The bottom was covered in wood shavings. There was a water bottle in one corner and a bowl of sunflower seeds next to it. And in the middle, slowly waddling along on his wheel, was a chubby, peach colored hamster.

The cage looked even crazier than the box had. At first I thought it was covered in random scratches. But after staring at it for a minute, I realized the scratches were words. SNUGGLE BALL. BUBBLE CHEEKS. BESTIST FRIEND. And carved deep into the roof of the cage was the word NIBBLES.

I sat down and stared at the hamster. At Nibbles, apparently. He had long white whiskers that stuck out on either side of his pink little nose, which never seemed to sit still. The tips of his ears were brown and there was a white patch on his belly. His paws looked just like teeny tiny hands, which he held together in front of his chest like he'd just asked a question and was politely waiting for the answer. In short, he looked like any other hamster I'd ever seen. But there was something hypnotic about the way he was looking at me with his beady black eyes. I shook myself and turned away.

Why in the hell had Rob left me his damn pet hamster? He knew I don't do pets, or anything else that needed taking care of. I rely on nobody and nobody relies on me. Shelly knew the score. If she needed to get her rocks off, I was her man. But if she needed a shoulder to cry on, she was on her own.

I ran my hand through my hair and winced as a splinter dragged through my thumb. I sucked on the cut and pulled the splinter out with my teeth. It throbbed and a fat drop of blood swelled and trickled down my wrist. I went to the bathroom to grab a wad of toilet paper. Screw Rob. I couldn't believe I ever thought of him as my best friend. He didn't even have the backbone to stand up for himself. The guy was better off dead.

Do you know what he said to me when he found out we'd slept together Mina? Nothing. Not a goddamn thing. He just stood there, staring at me with this puppy dog look on his face. I'd just banged his fiancé when she was too drunk to see straight and he didn't even call me a sleazy, worthless slimeball. Lord knows he should have.

I ran my thumb under the tap and pressed toilet paper against it until the bleeding slowed. Then I marched back into the kitchen, ready to chuck that cage into the dumpster outside, Nibbles and all.

I stopped in the doorway. Nibbles wasn't waddling on his wheel anymore. He was standing upright, scratching at the wall of the cage, wiggling his furry little tummy. His whiskers were twitching like crazy. He sure was a cutie, I had to give him that.

"What are you up to, little man? Trying to bust out?"

He stopped scratching and pressed his little paws/hands against the plastic wall, licking at it with his tiny pink tongue.

"What the heck are you doing, bro? You can't lick your way out of there!"

I laughed and knelt down so my face was level with his. Then I stopped laughing.

There was a smudge of blood on the outside of the cage. I must have brushed it with my thumb on the way to the bathroom. Nibbles kept on scratching and licking, almost like he was trying to lick the blood on the other side.

Sure, it was creepy. But the thing is, Mina, he was just so freaking cute! I couldn't help but feel sorry for the little guy. All alone in the world. He'd just lost the only friend he'd ever had. All he wanted was some love and affection. Maybe a cuddle. Just a little cuddle.

I opened the door on the roof of the cage. Nibbles started pacing back and forth. I reached my hand in slowly, trying not to scare him. For a second, his body went totally still.

Then he was on me, sinking his claws into my skin. I yanked my hand out of the cage and shook it to get him off, but he only clung on tighter. He bit into my thumb and I felt a chunk of flesh being torn away, his little tongue probing the wound.

Finally, I ripped him off with my free hand and threw him back into his cage. I did not want that little rat scurrying around in my house.

"What the hell?!" I kept yelling. "You little asshole!"

I examined my thumb. A bite shaped piece was missing. Blood streamed down my arm. I looked at Nibbles, crouched next to his water bottle, chewing and licking the blood from his fur.

Part of me wanted to run. To get as far away from Nibbles as I could.

But he seemed so happy. So satisfied. So grateful.

It was soothing to look at him. So I sat back down and watched him clean his paws and whiskers. I watched him waddle on his wheel, a little quicker than before. I watched him fill his cheeks with wood shavings and spit them out in a corner of the cage, making a little bed for himself. And I watched him curl up in a furry, peach colored ball and go to sleep.

I don't know how long I sat there staring at Nibbles. At some point the sun went down. My thumb stopped bleeding. I got a text from Shelly, *i'm so horny rn—can u come over?* None of this was as important as watching Nibbles' belly move up and down as he slept. But eventually, my eyes wouldn't stay open and I went upstairs to bed.

That night, I tossed and turned for hours. I'd drift off, then wake up covered in sweat, shaking like I'd had a nightmare I couldn't remember. Then, at around four in the morning, I finally fell deeply asleep. That's when I heard the voice. Soft. High pitched. Commanding.

"I am in need of alfalfa."

I jumped out of bed and grabbed my keys, not even bothering to put my shoes on. I got in my car and hit the gas, gunning it all the way to PetSmart. Nothing mattered to me at that moment. Nothing except alfalfa.

When I got there, I read the sign on the door that said the store opened at eight. Good, I thought. That was only three hours and forty minutes away. I sat down on the curb and waited.

There was only one other car in the parking lot, the driver leaning against it with his arms folded over his chest. He looked pale and gaunt and his eyes were bloodshot, like he hadn't had a decent night's sleep in weeks. As my eyes adjusted to the darkness, I realized he was staring at me.

"Sadie," he said in a scratchy, exhausted voice. "Labradoodle. She's on a raw food diet. We ran out last night."

I nodded. "Nibbles," I said. "Hamster. He needs alfalfa."

Neither of us spoke after that.

My memory of the next few days is hazy. I found myself watching Nibbles for hours at a time, mostly at night when he was most active. I'd stay up until dawn, watching him be his wonderful, adorable self. Then I'd drag my ass up to bed for an hour of sleep before heading off to work. After a while, I didn't bother going to bed at all, letting myself drift off to the soothing sound of him rustling around in his wood shavings.

But something was wrong. Nibbles was getting thinner. He stopped walking on his wheel. He stopped doing anything besides sleeping. I called the vet and they told me to bring him over right away.

I picked up his cage and grabbed my keys. But when I tried to go through the front door, I couldn't. My feet were stuck to the floor like they'd been nailed down. I set the cage down on the floor and immediately my feet got unstuck. I stepped out the door, then back inside. When I picked the cage back up again, my feet wouldn't budge.

I fell to my knees and sobbed. Nibbles was dying and there was nothing I could do to save him. It had only been a few days and already I couldn't imagine my life without him.

I looked up and saw him staring at me with those black beady eyes. All of a sudden, an idea popped into my head. I remembered the way he'd scratched at his cage, trying to get at the smudge of blood on the other side. The way he'd chewed on the chunk of my thumb he'd bit off. The way he'd licked the blood from his little paws/hands. Like he was enjoying it.

I opened his cage and slowly lowered my hand inside. This time, knowing what was about to happen, I had the sense to shut my eyes and clench my jaw. Immediately, Nibbles latched on and I felt his teeth sink into my flesh. At first he seemed frantic, biting and burying his face into the meat of my palm. But as he realized I wasn't pulling away, he got calmer. He took his time eating.

That night, he was back to his old self. Better even. He ran on his wheel. He played with all the toys I'd bought him. He waddled around, happily wiggling his stubby little tail. I was so relieved I didn't even care about the pain.

The next day, I bandaged up my hand as best I could and kept a glove on so the fellas at the shop wouldn't notice. I knew they wouldn't understand. Nobody would.

I tried to focus on work. I needed to replace the battery on a Toyota Sienna. It was the kind of thing I'd done a million times, which never took more than a few minutes. This time, it took me nearly all day. All I could think about was Nibbles. What was he doing when I was out? Did he miss me? Was he lonely? Was he hungry?

I was on autopilot when the owner came to pick up the Sienna. I didn't register a single word he said to me until I noticed the little girl standing next to him, crying into a teddy bear.

"Sorry about my daughter," he said. "Her gerbil died this morning." He knelt down and rubbed her arm. "Sweetie, why don't you go wait in the car while Daddy finishes up." She climbed into the back seat and fastened her seatbelt, then strapped the teddy bear into the seat next to her.

"Actually," the guy said, laughing a little as he scanned the invoice, "we euthanized it. Little rat bit my wife when she was cleaning its cage. We've got it in a zip lock bag in the freezer. Apparently, that's the humane way of doing it. As if it matters. Say, do y'all take Apple Pay?"

I pictured the gerbil suffocating next to a bag of frozen peas. My heart broke. What if someone did that to Nibbles? How could anyone be so cruel? A person who does a thing like that deserves to have the same done to them. Or worse.

As I was thinking all this, a funny thing happened. It was almost like I'd been asleep. And when I woke up, I was straddling the guy, pressing down on his windpipe, watching his eyeballs bulge out of his head. I didn't register what was happening until the fellas pulled me off him.

I was told to pack up my stuff and if I ever showed my face there again, they'd have me arrested. I don't know what they said to the guy to convince him not to call the cops there and then. But eventually, the Sienna drove off, tires screeching.

The next day, while I was putting together another tube maze for Nibbles, I heard on the news there'd been a major accident on the highway. A Toyota Sienna had suddenly stopped in the left lane and got plowed by the semi behind it. A man and his six-year-old daughter were killed. The cops were looking into what happened, but apparently the car battery had been installed incorrectly. People can be so careless.

Anyway, now that I didn't have a day job to worry about, I could devote all my time to Nibbles.

I got him a brand-new cage with built in ramps and tubes. I got him a bag of fancy food pellets that had probiotics in them. I got him special toys made from Himalayan cedar wood that were supposed to be good for his teeth.

But he didn't seem to have much interest in the new cage. Or the food pellets. Or the toys. He only wanted me. And I was happy to give him what he wanted.

Every night when he woke up, I'd let him out of his cage. He'd scurry all over me, tickling my face with his whiskers, snuggling into me with his soft, warm little body. I'd bite on a wooden spoon to stop myself from screaming. Then slowly, gently—he was always so gentle about it—he would start to eat. First, my right hand and fingers. Then he started working his way up my forearm. Then down my thigh.

Bills started piling up over the next few weeks. My power got shut off. I got a letter saying the house was being foreclosed. Shelly sent me one last text saying SCREW YOU in all caps. I barely noticed any of it.

I know it sounds crazy, Mina, but Nibbles made me happier than I'd ever been. We needed each other. We trusted each other. He was my best friend. Still is.

There's not much left of my right arm. Just bones, mostly. And my left leg is starting to look like Swiss cheese. Now I know why Rob's funeral was a closed casket.

About a week ago, my skin started to turn a little green. There's a smell coming off me like spoiled milk. I wasn't surprised when Nibbles stopped eating. I'm rotten, Mina. I can't feed him anymore.

In my whole life, I've never cried as much as I did when I realized I'd let my best friend down. I cried so much, I passed out right there on the kitchen floor, next to Nibbles' cage. It was four in the morning when I woke up and for a second time, he spoke to me in that squeaky voice of his.

"Take me to Mina."

I got up off the floor, picked up the cage and walked right out the door. My feet felt as light as air.

I spent the last of my money on a plane ticket to Miami. Nibbles told me where to find you. He told me to wait behind the hedge across the street from your house until you got home.

You look good, Mina, even with that short haircut. You look like you've got your life together. Just goes to show how much people can change.

That night when you came to me a week before your wedding, stinking of tequila, blubbering about how Rob was too good for a piece of trash like you, I wasn't surprised. The truth is, you were right. He was too good for both of us, because he wasn't afraid to really love somebody. To give his whole self over to it. To let it consume him.

You may have the expensive haircut. The fancy clothes. The big ass house. But if you've got no one to come home to, you've got nothing, Mina.

I used to be like you. But Nibbles changed me. He'll change you too. You'll see. You could never know how good it feels to love someone that much until it happens. It's the best feeling in the world.

Having a pet is a big responsibility, Mina. But you'll take good care of Nibbles. I know you will. And don't worry. After a while, it doesn't even hurt anymore.

I've left him on your doorstep, along with a nice big bag of alfalfa. That's his favorite brand, Mina. Don't get him the kind in the blue bag, he doesn't like it. His water needs to be changed every day with COLD water. If it's too warm he won't drink it. He likes belly rubs and cheek scratches. He likes to be fed as soon as the sun goes down.

I miss him already and it's only been a few hours. It's taken me that long to write this email with just one hand.

I'm sitting on a park bench and a couple of cops are giving me the stink eye. I know how I look. They'll tell me to move along soon. Where will I go? I guess it doesn't matter. Without Nibbles, I may as well be dead already.

I'd better wrap this up. It's getting dark out. The sunset was so beautiful. I wish my best friend was here to see it with me.

It's time, Mina. Nibbles is waiting for you. Go to him. He's hungry.

Johnny

~ * ~ * ~

Emily Gennis is a writer, amateur cook and professional cat lady. Her work often blends the genres of horror, humor and speculative fiction. She is particularly interested in how our relationships impact the ways we navigate the world around us. Her work is scheduled to appear in *Freedom Fiction Journal*. She lives in New York City.

Mirage

Moss Springmeyer

Violent pulling, almost tearing, stretching, stretching me out into a weirdly quiet, crystal-clear pool, surrounded by low greenery. Then separate sharp tugs making green dotted poles. Trees, I would learn to call them.

The shocking, irresistibly demanding need quieted and ceased to torment me. I was simultaneously called into being and creating my first oasis. I was not very skillful yet, so I wavered and shimmered.

Two beings I would learn to call men ran towards me, screaming, "Water, water at last!".

"Stupid! Look away, it's just a mirage!" another man urged.

Somehow, by instinct, I floated backward as the men ran toward me. I was curious about them. They made noises that seemed to be directed to each other. Their need became many separate, smaller, jangling feelings that no longer had any power over or for me.

I faded, receding into the distance, then vanishing. I would learn to call it waiting.

These beings were people. There were sometimes other beings with them, but those did not move me or feed me.

I began to attend to the noises they and others like them made near each other, at each other. I caught glimpses of images the noises called up in their minds, almost like miniature flashes of me, but of things I had never seen. Some of these fleeting images occurred again and again. I began to trace them back to the noises that preceded them. The people were sometimes using the noises to give each other images. This was "talking". Some images I could not understand, like the shiny wagon train with no mules to pull it. It belched dark clouds and could only run in one place, guided by shiny strips side by side that they called a "track".

I learned I was in a "place" and there were other, very different places. They called this place the Dragon's Breath Desert and called the faraway places of their raging need "oases" and "springs". Sometimes, they followed me till the oasis need vanished and the "heaven" need cried out. I'd learned about heaven in the images they made and talked to before lying down for the night. When the heaven need called, I did a heaven or an angel till that need ended, too.

When I took form as the crystal pool with the greenery, as one of their oases or springs, they called me a "mirage". Some of them referred to others like me they had seen, but that seemed like one of their "dreams", stunted versions of me rooted in each one separately. I think they cannot see each other's dreams, but they try to share images from before the Dragon's Breath Desert. One will call up an image he can see and that I can see, then he talks to another human who calls up an image, sometimes very similar, in their own mind. These images are usually just glimpses, but sometimes a need flares around them. Not raging like the oasis need, but strong in their way.

Bit by bit, I followed them towards the sunset. As they went that way, their oasis yearnings became more urgent. I became stronger. I could hold longer before I would fade. I added scraps from some of their image memories: boot prints in my sand, sage brush around me with an open path leading to the shining water. One of the scraps took me many becomings to build: A tree by the waterside that was much shorter than my pines, with many, many long thin branches dangling down, some touching the water. With each emergence, I became more complete and intricate.

At my edge towards the sunset, I saw another oasis, much more complete and alive than the humans' images. I felt the need that called it and began to take form as an oasis myself. But I noticed I was embodying as the other's oasis. Panic. I faded myself, then emerged as my own oasis. I could see the other oasis, but not feel it. Unlike the humans, it did not need. I was almost overwhelmed with astonishment, disorientation, excitement.

A foolish bubbling joy pervaded me. Half exhilarated, half terrified, into my oasis I called forth a wild peach bush. Its spiky branches jerked into being, each thorn twanging faintly in my mind as it sprang out. Then I deeply assented and the blossoms burst forth, pinky orange, thick and dense. The humans' needs had not yearned for it, but I called it forth.

The other's oasis was beautiful, with tall palm trees. Although I'd never seen a tree growing in the ground, I knew about palm trees from the little mirages humans created for themselves when they slept. But the humans' trees were mostly static, like rocks. For a moment, the other's palm trees swayed gracefully, lifting and waving the green branches at the top, bending and straightening towards the middle, with still bases amid lush grass and flowers.

I fluttered the leaves on my sage brush and the blossoms on my wild peach. I ruffled my pond surface.

The other sprouted ferns around the base of the palm trees.

I felt myself fading in patches as the wagon train and its humans' needs receded. But the other stayed bright. Maybe I could, too. I reached inside for brightness and I found it. I was glowing. I put a moon in my sky.

The other wavered, then shimmered. Some blooming lilies appeared in that pond.

I put a bucket beside my pond and then I was not.

~ * ~

All the time, it was like night. I could not happen. Weak needs strained towards me, but they did not reach me. Then a yearning called me forth. With a shimmer, I was: My oasis took shape on the desert about a mile from the wagon train. I added a palm tree. Doing that work made the rest of me fade, almost to the point of extinguishment, but once the palm tree was fully created, the rest of me brightened again. Joy.

Then I noticed the other's oasis almost beside me. The other blazed for a tiny second.

We approached each other, close so the humans would almost see one oasis with two ponds. But not quite, our oases were slightly different and there was a kind of ragged streak of patches of oasis and emptiness where we abutted. It bothered me, so I started to mend it, but then everything went dark. A long night again.

~ * ~

From time to time, human yearnings faintly tickled and itched, then another different, even more compelling yearning, distant at first. The other was yearning, as well as the humans, the combination so powerful I burst into being fully formed as a simple oasis, again about a mile from the wagon train. The other was simple this time too, with just few palm trees. Several humans turned away from the wagon train, limping and staggering towards us. We backed gently away, but stayed close enough to drink their need.

Very close to each other again, we took turns slowly mending the ragged streak: it was delightful, frightening, and exhausting. We were completely absorbed, so we did not notice the mule-pulled buckboard approaching the pedestrian humans following us. Six humans scrambled out of the buckboard, seized the humans who were following us, flung them into the buckboard, then returned to the wagon train, dragging us after them.

Our mending tore apart and the other disappeared. I too went dark.

~ * ~

I stretched and felt myself becoming. I was aware the other was, too. This time, there was no wagon train, just us. We were both pale, but there was a quiet delight in gazing at each other's oases. We could not hold it long.

~ * ~

A long wagon train came through and we were both fully formed with lots of detail. We learned to deflect the yearnings of just one or a few people. We waited, unformed, for the bigger wagon trains, drinking the energy of their yearning while creating simple oases for them and then unforming on purpose. We learned to pace ourselves, making images for each other that we could sustain and sustain.

We began with images we had harvested from the humans while they slept and sometimes while they read or sang or talked. Some of these were images of bigger versions of the wagons, like several or even many, put together and covered with a kind of shell of rock or wood, "cabins" or "houses". There were sometimes herds of these.

Many of the images were of bigger waters, some of them seemed alive with little, ever changing, hills and valleys. I had seen a hammered surface on a flat metal disk one family used for carrying things when they talked and ate and moved in a way they called "dancing". I learned to make my pond surface like that, it felt especially wonderful when I gave to it the colors of the light of the rising sun, glowing on the tiny peaks. The other would flash when I embodied this.

~ * ~

We'd drifted along with the big wagon trains, always in the direction of the sunset. We floated over a hill. This location was drastically different: It had houses and cabins grown tall and crowded together. Suddenly myriad needs screamed. Our patchwork seam strained, then the needs slashed at it with a thousand tiny cuts. We were severed. We strove to remake it, but some of the patches came loose and drifted away. I shuddered with horror as multiple needs pulled me a thousand ways at once. Instead of giving me energy, they began to tear away bits towards my edges. The bewildering chaos of screaming needs dragged us further and further apart and I saw little puffs of darkness as they tore scraps off us. I could not fight the savage dismemberment, but I was not fading, instead the scraps remained bright. What was left of the other flashed at me and I flashed back, then I lost sight of the other as they tore me into more and scraps…

~ * ~

At the western edge of the Dragon's Breath Desert, Sapphire Lake gathers water from the deep snows atop the towering Tormentoso range. In time, the railroad came there and a boomtown erupted. Respectable folk tried to name it "Lake Town", but the appellation that stuck was "Mirage City," for the opium in its dens was said to induce especially vivid and piercingly sweet waking dreams.

~ * ~ * ~

Moss Springmeyer explores the variety of realities, both natural and supernatural. Moss's "Fur-Break" concerning a resourceful, ageing werewolf is in the Spring 2024 issue of *Altered Reality* (p. 16) www.alteredrealitymag.com/spring-2024-issue/. Moss's "Mountain Mail Runner" will appear in *Academy of the Heart and Mind* (Autumn 2024). Moss's "Choirboy" probes the glory and cruelty of a very special gift in story block 2 of the Spring 2024 issue of *The Green Silk Journal* www.thegsj.com/current-issue-spring-.html.

Follow Moss on Instagram or subscribe (free) on SubStack.

Cheeseburger Please

Reggie Kwok

In Freedom MMO, Paige's human avatar with long blonde hair gazed at the various mounts she could purchase. The interface gave her a list and pictures of griffins with random usernames attached to them. She couldn't name the mount herself, but that didn't stop her from finding the coolest one. She stopped at a rainbow feathered griffin with yellow eyes called Diagonalnn-32. Paige instantly bought her, and the sunstones were deducted from her account.

The rainbow feathered griffin said in chat, "OnionDog, I've been waiting weeks to get into the game. Call me Diagonal. We're going to be the best of pals!"

How Freedom MMO incorporated talking mount chats was a mystery to Paige, but she hopped on the back of Diagonal and off they went to grind experience on slimes and other creatures. In this game, she was a level twenty-seven mage, but Diagonal was only level one. Through research, she had learned the griffin could also join her in combat. For Diagonal to gain experience, she would start in the newbie area, so the griffin could learn how to fight.

Paige didn't have access to Diagonal's skill tree. Instead, the griffin picked up skills on her own. It was as if another user was playing the griffin. No, it had to be an AI, right?

At a dungeon a few hours later, Paige and Diagonal were battling a goblin, who targeted the latter.

"I need healing!" Diagonal said.

Paige gave Diagonal a healing potion, and the griffin sighed. Diagonal whacked the goblin in the face with her talons, and the goblin evaporated.

Diagonal cheered, "Cheeseburger, cheeseburger, cheeseburger please!"

After completing the dungeon, Paige asked Diagonal, "Why do you like burgers so much?"

"Our burgers come from plants. One day, I will eat a meaty burger from cattle."

Surely, Diagonal was talking about in game burgers and not real-life ones. Maybe Diagonal was an omnivore. Perhaps Paige could go to the market and purchase some meat for Diagonal.

After a week of killing monsters and getting loot, Diagonal gave Paige a level forty Elemental Wand of Justice.

Paige and Diagonal spent an hour killing water slimes. With her new wand, Paige melted the slimes in one blast. After the session, they both gained one level.

"Say, do you want to meet in real-life?" Diagonal whispered.

"How are we going to do that?"

"Portals!"

Paige's computer screen lit up a bright pink. At first, she thought the computer had a glitch somehow. But the portal was not a glitch.

A blonde feathered griffin hurtled through the screen into real-life, knocking Paige backward on her chair and sending her black hair above her head.

At first, Paige thought the griffin would be as muscular as the mount in game, but instead Diagonal was as small as a housecat who had had one too many treats. How could the griffin fly with such small wings? She probably wasn't capable of flight or walking for thirty minutes straight. Diagonal looked like she hunted daily and succeeded.

Why did a griffin enter her life? Paige wanted an answer to this question to explain why a portal formed in her computer screen. Why didn't the wall break when the griffin collided with it?

Paige's mouth formed an O. "Holy Guacamole, you exist!"

Diagonal rolled onto all fours. "Of course! I can't believe that worked."

"Was that your first time?"

"Who knew portals were so much fun?"

"Wait. My mount was a user this whole time?" Paige gasped.

"Yes, I'm Diagonalnn-32. You are OnionDog, right? I teleported correctly, right?"

"Yes and yes. I'm Paige."

"Cool! Let's go get two cheeseburgers."

Paige had mentioned cheeseburgers as treats for special occasions, but she didn't know why Diagonal wanted cheeseburgers now out of all the times.

Then, she realized something important. Griffins weren't something the public knew about. If anyone were to find out Diagonal existed, Paige would be in huge trouble. Like, the FBI would come knocking on her door, and she didn't want anything bad to happen to Diagonal. Paige wanted to play videogames with her again.

Diagonal pawed her way out the door.

"Diagonal!" Page called. "You're lucky my parents aren't here. This is Earth we're talking about. Griffins are myth on Earth. If you get caught, you won't be going back home. You'll have humans dissecting you against your will. Do you want that?"

"Earth sounds more hostile than I thought." Diagonal rubbed the underside of her beak.

"Here's what we'll do. I'll hide you inside my backpack and head to the fast-food restaurant down the street. I'll bring you along for the ride. Throughout the whole walk, you must stay quiet, and don't leave the backpack. Got it?"

Diagonal nodded.

Paige's backpack was rather large and could fit all her homework and books in it at one time. Surely, it could fit a griffin as well, right?

Paige stacked the binders and books from her backpack on her desk. Then, she ushered the griffin into it. Paige could handle carrying it for a little while.

Paige left the house and went down the street to the Burger Joint.

Most of the customers waited in cars and ordered food through the drive thru. Paige didn't drive, so she needed to order takeout at the counter. The walk took a lot out of her, and she could also take a break before heading back home.

The furniture was mostly made of metal. Even the counter was metallic black. The inside could use some color. The digital menus were not enough. For a moment, no one was at the counter, until a man in a white and red uniform appeared to assist.

A claw poked out of the zipper hole. Paige ignored the claw and attempted to order from one of the screens.

Diagonal shoved her head out the bag and shouted, "Cheeseburger please!"

The cashier gasped. "Is that a griffin?"

"It's AI." Paige shoved the head back into the backpack.

Diagonal's head poked out again. "Where's my cheeseburger?"

Paige whispered, "You must wait. I'll order it on the screen, and they'll serve the food."

Diagonal locked eyes with the cashier. "Human, where's my food?"

The cashier pointed at the backpack. "You have a griffin in your backpack. No way that is AI."

Paige stared at Diagonal. "Initiate squawking sequence."

Diagonal remained silent.

"I said, initiate squawking sequence."

Diagonal nodded and chirped like a car alarm with a rooster's call in it.

The cashier covered his ears. "Make it stop!"

"Only if we get our cheeseburgers." Paige snapped her fingers. "Hurry."

The order came through so fast Diagonal didn't have to cry for long.

Paige took the bag and frowner at the cashier, "And remember," she said, "you didn't see a griffin in my bag at all."

"But I did—"

Paige stuffed the griffin and the food into her backpack. "No, you didn't!" She headed for the door.

~ * ~

Paige made it back to her room and set the backpack on her bed. When she unzipped the bag, Diagonal rolled out with crumbs on her beak. Digging through the backpack, Paige found the take-out bag rolled into a ball and the cardboard containers for the two cheeseburgers empty.

Diagonal had eaten both burgers!

The griffin burped. "I'm sorry, but I couldn't stop at one. Cattle burgers are the best."

"I was going to have one." Paige moaned, and her stomach growled. She would have to resort to eating a peanut butter sandwich.

"Look at it this way," the griffin said. "I gave you a wand, and you gave me burgers. It's the perfect exchange."

"I would love to head back home," Diagonal said. "But, the portal on your computer won't open until eight hours have passed."

"You can share my bed."

Diagonal curled up on Paige's pillow.

"I said share." Paige rested her head on Diagonal's stomach as she drifted off to sleep.

~ * ~

A rooster's call woke Paige. The rooster was Diagonal.

"Sorry, but I got to go now," Diagonal said. "My parents opened the portal and are wondering where I am. Want to come with me? It could save me a whole lot of trouble."

Paige had a whole life on Earth she didn't think would transition into another world. Heck, they barely even talked about Diagonal's world. Why would she want to go there if they hadn't discussed the pros and cons?

"I can't," Paige said. "My parents would be worried sick if I went."

"Could you at least log into the game to tell my parents what I did here? They would praise me for surviving in another world all by myself."

"Technically, you had me by your side."

"I hope I can fit into the portal." The screen lit up pink. "There's my ride. Talk to you on Freedom MMO!"

"See you online."

Diagonal jumped into the screen, and for a moment, she was stuck. Paige had to push to get her through, but once she did that, the log in screen for Freedom MMO popped up.

Paige could disconnect from the game in its entirety and ignore it for the rest of her life. But that would mean she wouldn't have a wand that could kill slimes in one shot. She wouldn't have to journey across lands to level up her character. She wouldn't have Diagonal.

A promise was a promise. She would log in to help Diagonal plead her case. Clearly, if the griffin could exist on Earth for eight hours on her own, Diagonal could live by herself. Though, what would happen to the griffin's waistline if no one controlled her portions while living alone? Surely, the griffin was fine.

When Paige logged onto the MMORPG, Diagonal was busy killing some slimes. Paige got her pal's attention, and the griffin spammed sad emojis in chat.

Diagonal begged, "Please tell my parents you are real. You aren't just an avatar but a real human. Say it!"

"I am a human from Earth," Paige typed out.

"See?" Diagonal paused in chat.

Why did Diagonal go silent? Maybe she was speaking to her parents about how real Paige was. Did she need more proof? What would the griffin need to prove Paige's existence?

The portal on the computer opened again. This time, Diagonal's head and right paw popped out.

"Give me your hand. They don't believe me."

"What do you mean by 'give me your hand?' I like my hand."

"I'm going to show them your hand. Just stick it through the portal."

Was Diagonal going to chop off her hand? She needed her hand to write, type, and play video games. How would she play Freedom MMO with only one hand?

"Are you going to chop my hand off?"

"No! If you want, hold onto my paw. That way, my parents know to trust you."

Paige nodded. "Okay, let's do this."

Paige held onto Diagonal's paw while the griffin's head phased through the portal. Then, her right hand went through the portal.

At first, Paige suspected a trick to get her into the griffin's world, but no, her hand stabilized through the entire process. Then, her hand came back to Earth, and Diagonal's paw waved.

In Freedom MMO, Diagonal waved. "They believe in your existence now. They want to know if they can try out your burgers."

Paige said no.

~ * ~ * ~

Reggie Kwok (he/him) holds a B.A. in English and a master's in education. He currently lives in Massachusetts, USA. His Twitter is @KwokReggie. His Bluesky is @reggiekwok.bsky.social. He has published short stories at *Samjoko Magazine*, *Underland Arcana*, *Scrawl Place*, *Androids and Dragons*, *Inner Worlds*, *Orion's Beau*, and has two forthcoming from *Zooscape* and *Madam, Don't Forget Your Sword*.

Wyrm and Drang

B. Morris Allen

Sure, I can breathe fire. It's surprising how seldom that comes in handy when you have to change into a two-ton dragon to do it. Melt a couple of your were-kin's barbecues and you don't get invited back much. It makes for a lot of awkward questions in the neighbourhood, and crackpot journalists hanging around looking for monsters.

The were-pups get all the attention, of course, and they complain a lot, but they bring it on themselves, really, with all that baying they do when the moon is full. They could learn something about secrecy from wyrms. They never do, though.

Anyway, we wyrms like to get together once a year to stretch our wings, mope around together, and generally socialize. Wyrms tend to be loners, but very few normal humans can appreciate or understand the drawbacks of being twenty meters long, or using a chainsaw to clip your nails.

The truth is, we have to get together. The wyrm's urge to reproduce doesn't come often, but when it does, there's no resisting it. Our little gatherings are less social occasions than meat markets. Nothing like the smell of a really sweaty underwing to get your juices flowing. Thankfully, we're also not that fertile. Without getting too technical, a lot of heat is required to get things moving.

We were meeting on Cascade Head this year, and I loved it. For one thing, the approach is easy, even at night—you can just swoop in over the ocean, and glide to a soft landing on the hillside. For another, the place is covered with fog most of the year, so the norms don't get freaked out and report giant bat sightings. But mostly, I just love the air—the soft moisture of it, the smell of salt and seaweed. My grandfather likes to say I'm part sea dragon, and he always asks me what kind—leafy or weedy. Honestly, I don't know what he's talking about, but I figure leafy has to be better.

Anyway, it was Cascade Head this year, and I was happy. I arrived early and wandered around for a while by myself. I like to go around by the cliff and bark at the seals. They take it in stride ever since the selkies had their own meeting at the Head a few years back. The puppies make noise, alright, but seals are in a class of their own.

I was just poking my neck over the edge when I heard a noise from back up the hill. It was a ways away, but dragon senses are acute. I whipped my neck back up to full periscope and looked around. I didn't see or hear anyone, but there was a funny smell. A hint of dog, maybe. The puppies know better than to interfere with the festivities, but there's always the occasional intrepid hiker to consider. I couldn't pin the smell down, but I decided to do a little site inspection.

I had just reached the northern edge of the clearing when I heard the subtle sound of wind sliding over scales. I turned back to see Fancy gliding in, pretty orange wings spread wide to display very fetching sub-aripal scale patterns.

"Hey, Nancy!" That's her human name. It's not talking we do in wyrmform, so much as sub-aetherial thought projection transference, but it works about the same. "Looking good, as always." Nancy's a scriptwriter for movies and such. We had mated a couple of times in the past, as wyrms, not humans. Human-wise, she's not my type.

She folded her wings and stuck out her neck for a friendly twine. "Hey Wolfgang." My mother was part wolf, and I guess when she named me, she was hoping it would breed true. My father was part wyrm, though, and his genes won out. I'd have asked him what he thought about the name, but he wasn't around much. "How's the book trade?"

"I *should* trade," I said to Nancy. "Losing ground to the online stores as always."

"You should get into another business. As always."

"What else could I carry in 'The Book Wyrm'?"

She just shook her head. Not a reader. "Any sign of others?"

"Not a thing. Thought I smelled something, though. Wolf, maybe. Coyote."

She extended her neck. "I don't smell anything. Probably just a dog."

"I guess." The smell was gone now, washed away by the salty ocean breeze.

"So, any particular plans for this…gathering, Wolfie?" She spread her wings a bit, as if the wind had made her lose her balance. She's a subtle one, Fancy is.

"You know. Just checking in with old friends. Have you seen Edgar lately?" You never want to commit too early at these meets. The drive to reproduce is strong, but when you only get one shot every few months, you want to make it count. Nancy's hot stuff, but I like a little romance too. Too much o' that dern readin', I guess. Plus, Jinghua Li had dropped a hint or two.

Luckily, at that moment, a whole flight of old friends swooshed in, and I didn't hear Fancy's response. The flame trickling out of her cute little upturned snout kind of gave it away, though. We trundled off to opposite extremes of the new group, and that was that.

Pretty soon, the arrivals came thick and fast, until upwards of forty of us were slithering around. Jimmy Djukic had brought along a couple of barrels of absinthe, and after that it got a bit wild. When Jinghua and her sister flew in, I lost track of the rest of the party.

Afterward, we all joined in on the Cleanse, which is always fun. The thing to realize, without getting too graphic, is that wyrms are big. Really big. Unfortunately, so is the drang—the sperm. And, well, sometimes some of them escape. Let me tell you, those suckers are destructive outside their natural environment; they can cause no end of mischief if they get into norm communities. You've heard of basilisks? So, we generally spend some time chasing down the escapees. When you get a wild and drunken crowd like we had on the Head, it can get a bit freaky. We got them all, but I ended up with a nicely crisped left wingtip (courtesy of Fancy, and I'm not sure I buy "I thought you were a pine tree"), and two stubbed talons. Luckily, we heal pretty fast, and I was good to go when I was sober enough to fly.

~ * ~

I didn't regret it the next morning (the Li sisters!), but I might have if my head hadn't hurt so bad. Still, duty calls, and I trudged in to work just the same. I don't have a big clientele, but Portland's a book-loving place, and I'm all the way across town from the big Powell's bookstore, so I survive. I'm on Southeast Division, so I get the new-alternative crowd, including a fair selection of 'thropes. On this day, thankfully, it was quiet. By the time Hank loped in around noon, I'd had my hand-roasted Turkish coffee, and was well on my way to 'normality'.

Hank is a puppy. A 'werewolf', the norms would say as they ran for the door. He does his best to play it up without coming out completely, but the sad fact is he's a pretty non-threatening figure even in wolf form. As a man, he's positively cute—long, shaggy blond hair, bright eyes, and a permanent smile. It's got to be that that gets him into guys' and girls' beds alike, cause mentally, he's no great shakes. Doesn't work on me, though, no matter how often he tries. I like a mate with a little brain on them. Still, he's nice enough, and his visits keep me from noticing how few customers I have.

"Hey, Hank. Eat any good norms over the weekend? I heard about this thing up on Killingsworth..."

He spun around, though any real wolf would have already smelled out any norms who might be listening. And on Division, no one would notice anyway. "No," he said at last. "Not me. I was down on the...I mean, I was here in town. Up on Mt. Tabor reading poetry. Alan Ginsberg." He winked.

He makes the same joke just about every week, and I'm starting to think that "Howl" is the only poem he's ever read. He certainly never buys anything from me. "I've got a nice beat anthology, if you're interested."

He shrugged. "Maybe next time." He fidgeted for a while.

"Something on your mind?"

"No! Nothing. I just, you know, heard something I thought you might be interested in."

"What's that?" It seemed unlikely.

"I heard there's, like, a sex tape going around. A *wyrm* sex tape."

I laughed. "I don't think so, Hank. Wyrms are pretty private, you know?" Not counting other wyrms.

"No, man, it's for real. Saw it myself." He glanced up at me. "If you want, I could ask around, see if you can buy a copy. Some hot stuff on there," he said leering.

"No thanks. I'm not really into porn." Probably some sort of anime thing, I guessed. Or a couple of folks in rubber suits. You can never tell what'll turn the norms on. I guess maybe Hank thought it would work on me too.

"Say, what do you look like as a wyrm, Wolf?" Hank trying to be subtle is...well, it's hard to describe, but you can't mistake it for actual subtlety.

"Really, really big, Hank. With really, really sharp teeth. And fire breathing." I was starting to have a bad feeling about this. "Why do you ask?"

He'd gone kind of pale as he backed away. "No reason. Just curious." He banged into the glass door to the shop, setting the little bell going. I watched as he fumbled for the door handle. It's hard to fumble casually, especially when you're nervous.

I vaulted over the sales counter. There's no real need for it; there's a little gate I can lift. But it impresses the shoplifter kids, so I stay in practice. It impressed Hank, especially when I gave him my biggest, toothiest smile and breathed hard. When I put my hand on his shoulder, I could feel him trembling.

"Let's have a talk, shall we?" I pulled him away from the door and flipped the sign to 'Closed'.

He told me everything about how he saw the film. It was just as bad as I'd thought. Some were-fox from Ethiopia, Hank thought he was cute, failed to hit it off with him, and had stalked him to the coast.

"Just north of Lincoln City," he told me. "He had a bunch of camera equipment and stuff. He set it up in the morning, and I, ah, bumped into him by chance when he came to take it down in the evening." Knowing Hank, the guy was no more convinced than I was.

"What day was this, Hank?" I let a tiny curl of smoke trickle out of my nose, more because I think it's cool than because he needed more scaring. It took me years to master that trick as a human, and I just don't get enough chances to use it.

"Sunday! Saturday! No, Sunday! Yesterday! What day is today?" Maybe the smoke was too much.

"Did you see the film, Hank?" I used my calm and soothing voice, something dragons really are good at. You have to be, to get the humans close enough to eat. Historically, I mean.

"No. I mean, just a little. A clip. He was making a teaser, like. A promo bit, to sell the tape with."

"What, last night?" This was moving fast.

"This morning. I, uh, you know, we spent the night together." He was bashfully proud of getting laid. It was cute, or would have been if there weren't film of me and my friends getting laid too.

"And I helped him with the titles."

So help me, titles. I raised an eyebrow at him, which is hard to do while you're wincing.

"*Dragon Crossing*"

I winced even more.

"Yeah, I know. I voted for *Worm Squirm*."

"Say those words again, Hank, and you're an appetizer."

"Sure, right, of course. You mean, um, his title, or, um, mine?"

"Any of it." Something came to mind. "Hey, so, you saw this tape, and you came to, what, *sell* it to me?"

"No! I mean, I figured, you know, we're friends, right?" Sort of. "You know, *Howl*. But, you know, I mean, I figured, how to find out whether you were there, you know? Like, whether you were *on* the tape."

The thing was, he was probably telling the truth. Hank didn't have a lot of friends. He was just one of those guys other people took advantage of. It's a cruel world, that way. For all I knew, his little Alan Ginsberg joke with me was the highlight of his day.

"Okay. You're a good guy, Hank. I don't know whether I'm on the tape or not, but my friends may be."

"And you *could* be on it, right?"

I thought about the Li sisters. "Yeah. Yeah, I could be. So. Who is this guy? *Where* is he?"

"He crashed at my pad." Hank would love to have lived in the '70s. "But then he took off. I don't know where. Said he had to meet a buyer."

Sometimes the smoke just comes on its own. Leaves a terrible burned smell in the nostrils. I shut my eyes and counted to ten. I got to four before I grabbed Hank by the shoulders and shook him. "Where'd he go? And what was his *name*, furball?"

"Harry. It's Harry."

"That's his name? This Ethiopian fox? Harry?" It didn't sound Ethiopian to me.

"Haeran," he blurted.

I let him go. "Okay. Haeran. What does he look like?"

"Oh man, he is hot! Like, totally beautiful."

With a little time and patience I worked out he was medium height and muscular, with short, curly black hair and mocha skin.

"Tell me anything else you remember about him, Hank.

Anything."

"Nothing. I mean, like, I could tell you what he liked in bed. There was…"

"Get out." How was I going to find one guy in Portland? Miss Marple always has more clues to work with.

Hank scurried to the door, visibly relieved the hard part was over. "Oh yeah," he said, holding the door open. "He mentioned something about Hollywood."

I was fast, but Hank was gone even faster. I debated chasing him down the street, but one thing puppies are is fast runners. He probably didn't know much more anyway.

Hollywood was a long way, and foreign to me, but Hank said the guy had a buyer in town. I didn't really know who that would be, but there are a few supernatural-fantasy-type shows that film in town One of them even used my bookstore once, as the backdrop for some scene or other. I let myself back behind the counter, and dug through my little mound of dusty business cards.

Half an hour later, I was having green tea with Ria Dos Santos, Assistant Producer, under a highway overpass in Northwest Portland.

"I'm so happy you called me," she said. "I was just thinking about you."

"Me too," I said. What else can you say? And we had had a good time. I couldn't really remember why we hadn't hit it off. Maybe just the difficulty of explaining. I guess that's why weres mostly stick with weres; it's easier.

"I remember you used to have this thing for dragons and stuff." She'd been to my house, and you do tend to collect a certain number of knick-knacks over time. "A guy came in this morning with a video you might find interesting."

"Really? What's it of?" Surely it couldn't be this easy. Despite my natural pessimism, I started to relax.

"You won't believe it." She giggled. "Dragon sex!" Pornsters 0, Fighters for Truth and Justice 1. "I thought you might want to watch it with me." She was giving it her best, but she wasn't a natural flirt, and the blush was starting to come through. She was more nerd than vamp, but I liked her for trying. My conscience reminded me I'd looked down on Hank for the same thing.

I waggled my eyebrows suggestively, to put her at her ease. It's funny, what eyebrows are good for. "Sounds...*hot.*" Guys in rubber suits. But she relaxed a bit, awkward flirt successful. "Who's the guy? I mean, dragon porn. Where do you get that kind of thing?"

"He's this Ethiopian guy named Harry. So, maybe, ah, dinner, sometime?" The blush was back.

"Absolutely. Dinner and a movie." I did the eyebrows again. "So, where'd he get this stuff, anyway? Maybe I could meet him, see if he's got more. Dragon stuff, I mean." Because how much porn does a person really need?

"Actually, I'm meeting him tonight. Dragons are not really our thing, you know?" I didn't know; I'd never actually seen her show. "But I know some folks who might be interested. The video quality was really good. There's this one scene, with what must be three or four dragons, all intertwined and writhing, and...you know. It's like a living Celtic knot."

There'd been me, the Li sisters, ...Had Dumitru joined in at some point? It was hard to remember. It didn't matter. There was film, and if it wasn't me, it was someone I knew.

"Can't wait to see it," I said, mostly to stop her from saying anything more descriptive. We talked for a while longer, and I agreed to meet up with her and Harry at a new vegan place near my house. "Division Street is the new food paradise," I assured her.

"I'll tell Harry," she agreed, and we left it at that.

~ * ~

Chanterelle is a new place focused on, as you might guess, mushrooms, and they do a terrific job of it, too. I got there early so I could scope out the exits. That's what they do in all the books, but Chanterelle is a store-front kind of place—one big garage-door opening in front, and I guess an exit in back. I didn't actually check; I'm not that much of a scoper.

Haeren and Ria came in together. They made a nice couple, and I had to admit he was good looking, if you like the compact, muscular type. Some of the other diners seemed to. So did Ria, from her body language, and it made the scales flatten on my neck. Then I had to think calming thoughts, because most humans don't have scales.

It was him, alright. A spicy mix of dog and wolf. He'd made me from across the room, of course, having a better nose for it. Ria was almost dragging him along, and I could tell he'd forgotten something in the car, had to make a phone call, needed to look for the restroom, etc. Apparently he didn't convince her.

"Just say hi first," I heard, and then they were there.

"Wolfgang, meet Harry. Harry, Wolfgang."

We shook, and I held on to his hand for just a moment. "Nice to meet you, Harry. I look forward to a long talk."

"Sure, sure." He was sweating. "Just need to make a call first. I'll go outside."

"I'll come with you." I got up and took him by the arm. "We'll be right back, Ria. Order some appetizers, would you? The pickled boletus with arugula is nice." She looked at me strangely, but sat down. Maybe she thought I was going to give him a 'That's *my* girl' talk.

Out on the sidewalk, I got straight to the point. "Okay, Haeren. Hand over the video, and we'll call it quits, got it?" I still had him by one large bicep, and I gave it a little squeeze just to underline which of us was the strong, dragony one here.

He shrugged off my hand, and did a little flex of his own, just to show tough. The sweat soaking his collar kind of undermined the effect. "I don't have it, whatever it is. Even if I did, what could you do about it?" He kind of edged away from me. In a foot race, the puppies win every time. Takes a while to get the wings out.

I just smiled "See where we are, Harry?" I waved at the micro-brewery across the street, the now-legal pot dispensary next door, the specialty courier-bag store— 'hand-made from local hemp!'. "I could go wyrm right now. These people wouldn't bat an eye if I ate you right here on the street." He looked like he might be a bit stringy, but I've never actually eaten human. No, really.

He took a look at the fangs starting to grow out of my grey-green snout, and gave it up. "Yes, yes, of course. Here." He dug in one pocket and gave me a flash drive. "But it is a copy." His nice white fitted shirt was starting to look distinctly clammy.

"Where's the original?"

"I gave it to the client. The woman. Like you."

I shook him a little. "What do you mean, like me?" I had a suspicion, though.

"A worm." I shook a little harder; no one likes an insult. "A wyrm. A dragon."

This was definitely getting weirder. Why would a wyrm want wyrm porn? We get excited by pheromones and proximity, mostly.

"Who?" I did my smoke trick, just to move things along. It kills the sense of smell, but pretty soon, Ria was bound to come out and ask what was going on. I wanted to have this business done with by then.

"Nancy." No prevarication here. "Nancy Delavue."

I let him go. Nancy? Nancy was behind this? But she'd be on the film herself.

"Are you sure?" I could tell he was.

"Yes. Smelled like a worm. Wyrm. Short brown hair, green eyes. Thin, small." That was Nancy.

"But why?"

He shrugged. "How do I know? She sent an e-mail, paid in advance, told me where to go and when."

"How to make a copy?"

"Well." He head-shrugged. "But that is the only one. What you have. Maybe a few clips here and there." He nodded to the restaurant. "Your friend has one."

"Right. We're going to go back in there, and be friendly, and you're going to say you decided the video quality is not good enough, and you decided not to sell yet. Okay?"

"Okay." And that's what we did. Ria and I had a great chat over slabs of portobello and then a delightful coconut and tapioca dessert. She'd read *The Plague Dogs* and *Marune* and a bunch of my other favorites, and I promised I'd come by her place with take out on the weekend.

Harry didn't say much, and he didn't touch his food, though I ordered him some very nice straw mushrooms with basil. I volunteered to drive him back to his motel, and there I checked his cameras and his computer, and wiped every file newer than one week old. I made some standard 'track you down and hurt you' threats, but I think by then, he was just looking to write the whole thing off as a bad experience, and go home to wherever. He was careful not to say.

By then it was dark. It had been one hell of a long day, and it was already hard to remember the whole thing had started just after lunch, with a visit from Hank. There was no point in putting things off any further, though, so I drove myself over to Nancy's place in

Southwest.

~ * ~

Wyrms like to hoard, and we like a good cave. Instinctive, I guess. Some of us do it better than others. My cave is my bookstore. Nancy's is a dark stone mansion in Dunthorpe. Of course, she's got a much bigger hoard to put in it. Her cave has a wall and a gate, but she let me in without a question.

"Hey, lover," she said. She was wearing a very pretty not-much that clung to her like cobwebs, and I could feel my human side getting interested despite myself. "I was hoping you'd come by."

"What?" Surely she didn't already know about Haeran. Of course. He must have called her. Somehow that hadn't occurred to me. "Oh."

"Come in and make yourself comfy." She showed me into the parlor, and settled next to me on the sofa, legs curled up and under.

I hadn't really thought this far ahead. I'd kind of expected to storm in, surprise Nancy with my discoveries, and call her to account. Instead, here she was, temptressing for all she was worth, and pretty effectively, too.

"What's going on, Nance?" When all else fails, get to the point.

"It's not working, is it?" She set her legs back on the floor and stretched over them to look at the carpet. It was a nice Persian type. "You're not seduced." It was more a mumble than a statement.

I'd been getting quite interested in how she looked, but I couldn't say that, could I? "Tell me what's wrong, Nance."

She just kept staring at the carpet, so I looked too. It was kind of an off-white with a red border. It was only when a tear dripped onto it I realized she was crying.

"Hey! Nancy. Come on, now. Tell me what's wrong." I put my arm around her in the awkward way of everyone who ever comforted someone weeping.

"I'm not pregnant!" she cried, and turned to drip snot into my shirt.

I wanted to ask why that was bad news, but I'm not quite that insensitive. Hollywood has told us for years pregnancy is good, and non-pregnancy is bad. But what else could I say? "Um, have you, …have you tried?" Obviously she had.

"Of course I have." She pulled her head out of my shirt enough to cast a baleful eye at me. "I tried with you, didn't I?"

So she had, and I had turned her down in favor of the Li sisters. It was a decision that seemed to be haunting my day. Maybe they're right about things too good to be true.

"What about that, um, that guy from Seattle?" Hadn't I seen him down at the coast?

"Hunh!" It's amazing how much scorn you can pour into one syllable. "He's good enough at sex. Better than you are." Gee, thanks. "But his drang couldn't light a piece of charcoal." Not an image I'd needed. "Besides, I can't get pregnant." Head and shirt reconnected. "Hardis said so." That's the doctor we all go to for were-specific issues. He's a were-tortoise, of all things. "He said my heat threshold is too high."

"Oh Nance, I'm sorry." I'd seldom felt so inadequate.

"I thought, you know, your sperm are so potent." They were? "There was Liana eight years ago, then Dixie three years ago." Two clutches in ten years. Thats pretty good, by wyrm standards.

"But, …How did they, um figure it out?" Wyrm mating is a 'come one, come all' kind of thing, and no smirking in the audience, thank you.

"Oh, we know." She'd pulled back from my chest again, after wiping her eyes and nose on my shirt tail. "There's a little group of us that keep track, and Jinghua did a whole statistical analysis."

"Jinghua? Not…"

"Jinghua Li. Do you know another one?" Her eyes widened. "Oh! Oh my goodness." She started to laugh. "You didn't…Did you think they wanted you for your great physique.? Your dull literary jokes?"

How is it some people can turn the tables on a conversation without making an effort? Here I'd been trying to comfort her in my best 'poor little thing' way, and suddenly I was the butt of a joke. I didn't like it, and in fact I didn't think it was very nice.

"Oh, come on, Wolfie. You knew you weren't just getting lucky. Jinghua wants a clutch, and Jingfei agreed to help her get one. I want one too." The hunger in her eyes doused my irritation a bit.

"But you said…"

"I know what the doctor said. Okay, so I can't have a clutch. Or he could be wrong."

"Yeah, okay. But…but what about the film?" That was what I

had come for, after all.

She shrugged. "If I can't have a clutch, maybe I can have a baby. I thought…well, I thought maybe some film of the two of us in action might be exciting. To us as humans." Humans are easily aroused. "And then it turned out to be film of you and the Li sisters, but maybe that's even better. I don't mind." I could see she did. She ran one hand through her mussed hair. "Would you like to watch it?"

Appealing as she tried to look, tear-tracked, nose-dripping, vulnerable types are not really my thing. I put my arms around her and said "Not now, honey. Not now." We cuddled for a while on the couch, each crying from time to time, and doing some pretty good talking, too.

"I just don't know that many people," she said, as she had several times before. "People think the entertainment business is all networking, and it is, but they're not friends. Not people you want to have children with."

"Well, that's the thing, Nance," I did my own repetition. "Siring a clutch is one thing. Having a baby is another. I…I like you, I really do. But…we're not in love, are we?"

I could see her wavering between snark and sincerity, but in the end she went with honesty. "No." She smiled. "You're nice, Wolfie, but you're not really my type, I guess. I mean, I think you'd make a great father, gene-wise, and a good parent too, but I'm not sure you're husband material. For me," she added hastily. She really had this complimentary putdown thing nailed. "I need someone happier, and more…biddable. And a bit more buff, to be honest." That was when the scales of justice suddenly came into balance.

"I think there's someone you should meet," I said.

~ * ~

They hit it off far better than I could have hoped. In fact, I'd thought a little strife might do them both good, but they're depressingly cheery. Nancy makes the money, and Hank does whatever she tells him to. He likes it, though, says it gives him direction. And he's a hell of a good father, to tell the truth. They've got twins—one boy, one girl. Just humans, of course. Still, they've each got a copy of the were genes, and if they marry another recessive, they could have were-babies.

Hank tells me there's one of each—a wyrm boy and a wolf girl. He says he can smell the difference, though to me they just smell like diaper. Maybe it grows on you. Here's hoping, because Ria and I have been getting pretty cozy. She even hinted about moving in together, at my place, because that's where the books are. There's a lot I'll need to tell her first, of course, but it so happens I've got a movie that might help explain some of it, and I understand it got pretty good reviews.

~ * ~ * ~

B. Morris Allen is a biochemist turned activist turned lawyer turned foreign aid consultant, and frequently wonders whether it's time for a new career. He's been traveling since birth, and has lived on five of seven continents, but the best place he's found is the Oregon coast. When he can, he makes his home there. In between journeys, he works on his own speculative stories of love and disaster. His story collection *Chambers of the Heart* came out in April 2022.

Find out more on Bluesky @BMorrisAllen.com and on his website: www.BMorrisAllen.com.

Mens Comedentis

R. Joseph Maas

The lights in the theater had been off for quite some time. Too long perhaps, as the crowd was getting restless. Before the room had gone dark, we had been told the next specimen they were going to bring out was something extraordinary. That it was sensitive to light and sound. And while the audience had held quite still, the unease was growing. No matter how great the creature we were about to be shown, whoever was presenting it was likely going to struggle to regain the attentions of some of the scientists who were doubtlessly waiting now only for the light to be raised so they could find their way to the door.

A shuffling of clothes and the patterned plopping of boots upon the wooden stage was all we had to tell us something was indeed happening before us, but what exactly was a mystery. Cameras and other electronics had been taken at entrance to the symposium, a shame since the last beast on display was a creature with what appeared to be bright eyes and a big smile. All of it camouflage for its prey. Our Pareidolia made it adorable, but its "eyes" were really ears, or at least the extraterrestrial equivalent, and the smiling "mouth" was meant to emulate a wormlike creature native to its planet. Anything foolish enough to try making a snack of it would be quickly mauled to death by the claws the creature hid underneath its body. We were treated to a demonstration involving an earth lizard, and it was...unpleasant. It rolled onto its back when approached by the young bearded dragon and was launched flailing into the air only to fall helplessly into the maw of the creature. It popped back upright and, despite appearing not to move at all, the crunching of bones was loud enough to be audible from where I sat. Now it seemed the confiscation of some of our personal things had been more to avoid anyone from using an external light source more than keeping us from recording the bizarre things they brought before us.

From the dissatisfied grunts emanating from the man directly behind me, I knew another minute or two of this and he was going to risk groping his way in the dark to find the exit. But this next specimen was supposed to be the showstopper and the delay was only making me more curious. No one except the hosts knew what we would be seeing next. The movement on the stage stopped and a whisper started to move through the crowd. The woman to my right muttered the creature might have gotten loose. Other whispers seemed to confirm this and worry began to overtake boredom for some. A clattering in the back of the theater made it clear at least a few people believed the rumor and had chosen to hasten their departure.

I wasn't worried.

I was patient.

I sat.

And I waited.

After twenty or so minutes of darkness that felt more like an hour of hushed worry blanketed in shadow, a dim light started to grow on the stage. Our eyes had grown used to the darkness, so the light was low but plenty. The presenter stood mostly hidden behind a tall legged table that was high enough to stop just above her stomach. Upon it sat a sealed dome glass fishbowl. Other than two packets of some indeterminate nature held by what appeared to be magnets to the underside of the upper areas of the bowl from above, the bowl appeared entirely empty.

The presenter gestured for quiet. She began, "What lays contained before you is not from a distant galaxy. It was not scraped from the exterior of a rocket. It was not culled from a sun bound asteroid. It is, I am quite sorry to say, comparatively terrestrial in its nature." Another few onlookers began to gather their things and leave including the grunting fellow from behind me. We had been promised only the greatest and most bizarre. It was apparent something from home soil just didn't fit that criteria for them.

"I beg your patience," she continued. "Despite its relatively humble origins, this creature is not one you have seen before." The man immediately to my left waved his hand at the stage as though he was rebounding her very words in some kind of linguistic table tennis match. He gathered his attaché and headed for the door making sure his departure was known to everyone by letting his case impact every chair to his right on his way up the aisle in complete disregard for the calls for quiet. She continued through gritted teeth, "What is in here is killing people. And we have finally caught a live one!"

He paused for a moment. But only a moment. When he and his noisy attaché had finally left, the tension in her jaw relaxed.

I looked around, and better than half of what had been the audience seemed to have left. The presenter was visibly frustrated with the change. She straightened her back, tugged at the lapel of her lab coat, and pressed on. "This creature is, for now, invisible. It has had countless victims over its existence, taking from celebrity, wealthy, poor, and common folk alike. Every tier of society has been touched by this monster, from queen and king to baker and candlestick maker."

She paused for solid minute before popping the magnets off the top of the jar. The two packets opened within and some kind of glittery powder began pouring slowly into the chamber, gently like falling snow. As the falling particles mingled, small flashes of light like a combustion of some kind appeared to be happening within the bowl. A precipitate began to form along the edges of the container. Soon, a thin layer covered the entirety of the glass while managing somehow to not obstruct the view of the creature inside. "Now that so many have left, please, come closer. You'll want to see this, I am certain. But do be careful as it cannot survive for long unattached and in open air."

I jumped from my chair and rushed for a seat at the front as quietly as I could. Terrestrial or not, I knew what I was witnessing was rare. Something in the glass was moving, dare I say, struggling to remain hidden. As it worked to try to hide itself, it was rubbing against the glass. Every second, its form became clearer. The more it fought against the powdered substance, the more the powder seemed to cling to it.

"What is it?" a large man with a small voice two rows behind my new seat asked.

A wide smile grew across the face of the presenter. "Its scientific name was chosen carefully and decided upon by committee. We call it *mens comedentis*."

Though I have studied it, I have never been particularly proficient in Latin. Thankfully, the woman I had been sitting next to before moving handled translating from her new spot behind me and to my left, "Mind Eating?"

The presenter continued to effuse sheer glee as she corrected, "Mind Eater. Yes. Every time anyone has heard that terrible voice in their mind, this is the beast that caused it. If you have ever heard a voice in your head tell you how you aren't good enough, you aren't worth it, you should shut up, or you should just die," her smile fell away as she paused contemplatively. "…This monster has been the how and the why."

I sat, with the rest of the room, in total awe and confusion. There has not been a single person I have ever known who has not heard this voice at some point. Every colleague, every brother, every sister. Everyone. Always. This thing has been there.

I was transfixed so much that as a doubter spoke, I didn't turn to look to see who. "There ain't no way that damned thing is in my head. I hear the voice, sure. That thing is so big, it would have made cavitations that would surely have been on every CT scan, MRI, or what have you in history."

"Ah yes, you are right. But also wrong. And much like you, this thing too exists in a superposition. Ladies and gentlemen, *mens comedentis* is the first living quantum being ever encountered in science." She paused again for everyone to soak in the implications. "The combination of conditions we created in this jar allowed our sample to be observed. As such, this is only the…" she paused while counting on her fingers, "…tenth or eleventh time one of these creatures has been seen by the human eye. We have been able to duplicate the findings from a number of tissue donors both living and recently deceased. Our paper on the subject is being reviewed now and it is expected to be published in the next few months. Within, clear instructions will be given to duplicate the experiment, but for now, we ask for your understanding in why we aren't sharing those details today."

It continued to squirm within the jar. Approximately two centimeters long and almost as wide at what seemed to be its "body" for lack of a better descriptor. It resembled a bacteriophage in many ways, though significantly larger. How something even in a quantum state wouldn't cause more damage just through its sheer size seemed unlikely given where it had to reside.

"H-how d-d-d-does it wh-wh-work?" I managed to stammer. The voice in my head had used my stutter against me innumerable times. It seemed unlikely it could pinpoint my hurt so quickly. A bespoke torturer.

"It eats, just as the name suggests." Her smile was now completely gone. The proud captor had been replaced by a sad storyteller who had been given the task of recounting the victims lost to flood or hurricane, some natural yet profound horror. "We haven't completely ruled out dopamine, but it seems to subsist at least predominantly on serotonin and norepinephrine. Many current antidepressants have been successful because of the way they keep serotonin available to the brain. Too much for these little bastards to eat in one go. But as they get stronger, the medicines become less effective. When changes are made to dosage or type of medication, this once again upsets the balance the mind eaters rely upon and they struggle until they adapt. Doctors for decades, centuries even, have done all they can to fight these creatures without even knowing of their existence. Now that we can see them, we can study them. There may be real hope for people like…"

She didn't finish the sentence and there was no need. It could have ended with any name, any relationship, from friend to spouse or child.

The woman I had been sitting next to asked the next, best, and only other question, "How do we fight them?"

"For now," the presenter spoke as though her heart were tied to the floor with a short rope, "we can't. They feed off the very thoughts that make us our best and turn us against ourselves until we are our worst. If there is anything this knowledge can do for us for the immediate future, it is knowing the voice of self-hate is not just 'all in our head'. They are very much actually 'in our heads'. For now, I beg you to love each other as if they were under constant attack from within. Because they very much are."

"We as a society must do better to care for each other. And someday, when science has helped to free our minds from being a quantum nesting ground for these monsters, we may truly be at our best."

The lights dimmed again. Within a few minutes of shuffling lab coats and boots, the lights came up again to an empty stage and empty chairs.

I stayed seated while everyone else departed, trying to speak with the monster in my head about the friends its kin had taken.

About the time this one very nearly took me. I knew it was futile because I spoke in words and it in chemicals. The only replies I got were in my mind, in my voice, and so dismissive and hurtful they made me want to cry. A watchman closing up the school shook me from the cycle of self-hate and I finally went home.

~ * ~ * ~

R. Joseph Maas has been writing since he was 7 years old. After decades of practice, his first published work was released in March 2014. He is father to an amazing young lady who claims to be his biggest fan. When he isn't playing with her or pretending to be a grown-up at work, he is writing. Follow along with his exploits at www.facebook.com/talesofthegodhand. Feel free to ask for updates on all of his projects there.

Fighting Stock

David Castlewitz

Though endearing as a hatchling, Ozo didn't stay that way. It changed, as Rynhart knew his pet would. The soft hair across its wide back fell out, replaced by overlapping cartilage that resembled an armadillo's armor. The boney buds at the corners of Ozo's mouth matured into formidable maniples with sharp points. Skinny antenna grew from the top of a long ant-like head, and Rynhart often witnessed Ozo stabbing the air with the tips, practicing an instinctive fighting technique.

Mental pictures often paraded across Rynhart's mind like an invading army's march through a village. A cornucopia of thoughts ambled behind his eyes, presenting fuzzy images he struggled to understand. When he saw money signs, he imagined Ozo in a pit, surrounded by bare wooden boards, with hard-packed sand for a floor.

Once Rynhart realized these images were his pet's attempt at communication, their appeal grew like favored plants. He enjoyed flickering views of what Ozo saw when it sat on the windowsill, the pictures of life in the alley behind the street where they lived above an abandoned store in downtown Evanston.

These empty storefronts provided a low-rent refuge, one handled by an agent for the owner, who didn't care that a tenant kept a manufactured hybrid as a pet. The lab that produced Ozo called its animals "Gryphs", after the mythical Gryphon, though they resembled neither a lion nor an eagle.

The business of creating genderless creatures with recombinant DNA was squashed by ethical types. Labs were shut down. Eggs and larvae were destroyed, but chicks like Ozo, already adopted, were allowed to live out their lives.

Walking along Dempster Street, Rynhart kept the leash taut, unwilling to let Ozo sprint ahead on its fast-moving six legs. They had to look like a man and his pet out for a walk, not like an excited fighter intent on getting to the arena. Rynhart was always careful to not attract attention. Ethic-minded people, some of them agents of the health department or animal control, but just as often vigilantes looking for a payday, might notice a too-eager Gryph and his smiling owner. Pitting Gryphs against one another in staged fights was only semi-legal, only frowned upon when a creature was killed, either by accident or in a death match.

The thought about vigilantes brought on an image of a snarling bug's face, eyes red and antenna folded down across its high forehead.

"Sorry," Rynhart muttered out loud. "A passing thought."

The arena didn't advertise itself. No blazing murals painted on nearby walls, no huge outdoor sign inviting the public inside, and no one at the door drumming up business with solicitations to "come on in and take a gander."

Located in the basement of a retro-arcade, which didn't advertise itself either, the arena sat nestled next to a storeroom full of old-time pinball machines and video game kiosks. Spectators stood on risers around a fenced-in pit.

"Not going to make a fortune here, Ozo," Rynhart muttered after checking the green slate chalk board for the posted odds. This arena didn't offer high-stakes bouts. No death matches here. Just two Gryphs slugging it out until one of them fell.

"Ethics," Rynhart said, his outburst drawing a few glares from those nearby.

Careful. You don't know who's listening.

That wasn't Ozo speaking to him; just some voice in his head, one he manufactured whenever he saw a mental image he thought was sent by his pet.

"We'll stay," Rynard announced in a whisper. "You need the practice." He picked Ozo up and went to the registration desk.

Rynhart gently placed Ozo in the trench where other fighters waited. "Go get'em!" he said with an encouraging smile and got back a mental image of a Gryph standing upright on its back legs.

I'll get'em alright.

Happy to hear that, Rynhart worked the room to take on bets.

~ * ~

What happened wasn't anything Rynhart expected. The killing had been accidental. Ozo slicing open an opponent's throat when they fought for the day's championship and the one-hundred-dollar purse brought cheers from half the spectators and groans from many others. It also brought an animal welfare agent to his home.

Standing in his small kitchen, watching Ozo slurp breakfast—a mix of ground rat meat soaked in almond milk—he wished his pet showed some signs of remorse.

"Tell me, Rynhart, do you fight your Gryph in death match-ups?" the agent asked. A short heavyset woman with the gray hair of someone who'd been at this job for fifty years, leaned against the wall just outside the kitchen and made notes with a stylist that raced across her eSlate's screen.

"You'll need to pay compensation," she said.

"With what?" Rynhart said. "I didn't even get the prize money."

"I'm just telling you our conclusions and recommendations."

"Your conclusions? Why don't you conclude it was an accident? Recommend no further action required."

The gray-haired woman straightened her back and stood away from the wall. "Sounds like you've been through this before."

"No. But accidents like this—"

"Don't happened every day." The woman glanced at Ozo peacefully eating its breakfast. "They do happen. More and more, it seems. Like maybe these factory products are maturing into sense-less killers."

"Ozo didn't ask to be made,"

The gray-haired woman sighed. Rynhart studied her wrinkled round face for some sign of understanding. Her small hard mouth barely moved when she spoke.

"They show a propensity to violence, these things. You trained it to fight, so you must've known."

Rynhart kept quiet. Yes, he'd trained Ozo to be a fighter, but that wasn't the same as being a killer.

"Your pet owner's license could be revoked."

Rynhart let the woman's warning sink in. Revoking his license would condemn Ozo to death. Dangerous animals weren't kept as pets.

"What's that?" the investigator asked, pointing.

Rynhart let himself smile. Murph, a wandering alley cat, had just jumped onto the open windowsill from the fire escape outside. Ozo glanced sideways, antennae waving, and stepped back from the near-empty bowl on the floor.

"Murph likes to come by," Rynhart said. The striped black and brown cat, which was fat and healthy for a wanderer relying on handouts, leapt to the floor. It padded quickly to Ozo's side and the two animals nuzzled one another before Murph turned to chomp on what was left in the breakfast bowl.

"See? They're buddies. Would a killer-Gryph be like that?"

The agent scribbled more notes, made a non-committal *hmmm* sound, and then left the apartment. Murph licked Ozo's face before hopping, back onto the windowsill.

Bye now, Rynhart sensed from Ozo.

Murph meowed.

~ * ~

But they were friends.

Rynhart refused to believe Ozo had anything to do with killing the wandering alley cat, even though he found Murph's body in the kitchen the next morning, with Ozo lying nearby, face buried in its front paws. Which Rynhart interpreted as:

Sorry.

"Not good enough, Ozo! This is bad. Very bad."

Ozo stood, its six legs cocked at the knees, and walked to a corner of the small apartment, slipping under the sofa that folded out into a bed. At the sound of the buzzer, Rynhart spun sideways and nearly fell. He looked back at Murph dead on the linoleum kitchen floor, head in a pool of blood.

"Yeah? What?" Rynhart barked into the intercom.

"We're downstairs. Crawford and Green. From Control. Can we come up and talk to you?"

Rynhart wanted to say no, but where would that lead? They'd barge in behind a squad of Evanston police with a battering ram.

"Give me a minute to get dressed."

Rynhart covered Murph with a ratty towel, but didn't like the giveaway bulge on the floor, so he wrapped the cat's body in a bigger towel and stuffed it into the oven he never used. The blood on the floor posed a problem, but all he could do was cover it with a thick bath towel and claim he'd spilled something if asked.

He opened the door at the sound of a single knock and greeted two men in tight fitting suits, a fashion better suited for the young and trim, not this pair of roly-poly functionaries.

"We're here to collect your pet," one of them said, before introducing himself as Green. His near-identical partner said, "Crawford," as his introduction.

"You gotta be brothers, right?" Rynhart said, and smiled.

"Where's your Gryph?"

"I didn't get any notice, you know."

"We're your notice." Green—he had shoulder-length blond hair while Crawford's hair was cut military style short—showed Rynhart his eSlate. "You should've gotten this already."

"I don't have a slate," Rynhart said. Ozo's ant-like face beamed at him from somewhere at the back of his brain.

"Don't matter," Green said, stepping into the apartment. "We got a warrant to search your place."

"Where's the Gryph?" Crawford asked.

Ozo scooted out from under the sofa and into the kitchen, then bounded onto the windowsill. Green pointed a stubby finger at the open window. "Get him."

"Wait a—" But Rynhart couldn't stop the two men from barging into the kitchen and tripping over the blood-soaked towel on the floor, while Ozo jumped to the fire escape landing.

"There it goes," Green muttered.

"I'm telling you," Crawford said, "they got like a sixth sense. They know what's up."

"Sure, sure. Sixth sense." Green turned to Rynhart. "If it comes back, make it easy on yourself and your pet and call it in."

"It'll probably run to the sewers like some of them do," Crawford said in a sad voice. "Get eaten by the alligators or swarmed over by rats." He turned to Rynhart. "You want that for your pet?"

Rynhart bit his lower lip. He struggled not to look at the bloody towel next to Green's soft brown shoes.

"Not pretty what happens when they get in the sewers," Crawford said.

"We'll send a follow-up to your eSlate," Green said.

"I don't have one," Rynhart said.

"It's best to call it in." Crawford kicked at the towel on the floor. Green curled his lips in disgust and stomped off.

"I don't think he's coming back," Rynhart said as the two men left.

You think I don't know? Ozo leapt onto the windowsill. Rynhart imagined it laughing. A full belly laugh, front claws on the underside of its ribbed abdomen.

"Now what do we do? You going to the sewers? Running off like they said?"

What do you think I should do?

Rynhart answered with a long sigh, feeling like he did as a child when he fought back tears after a scolding.

You think I want them to take me? They'll kill me if they do. You know that.

"I know it. You know it. Okay. We know what happens to—"

Say it. It's what happens to killer Gryphs."

This isn't good, Rynhart thought with a glance at the closed apartment door.

Unless I escape.

"We need one last match," he said, ashamed of himself for thinking of his bank account.

Why?

"I need it. Then I'll help you get to wherever you want."

One more? You got it.

~ * ~

The brackets on the green chalk board filled quickly. Thirty-two fighters would compete, with the early rounds designated as "First Blood" or "Beg-Offs." Only the final four and the championship match were to-the-death, no quarter asked, no quarter given.

Rynhart bent close to Ozo in the narrow pen where it would wait its turn to fight. "Don't kill any of these guys until the—"

I know, I know.

Prize money would shore up Rynhart's dwindling finances. But not the small change offered by the prelims. The championship fight promised a thousand eBucks to the winner. More money could be made with side bets. The house ran a pari-mutuel, but bookies abounded. Rynhart intended to augment his winnings by placing wagers with whoever gave him good odds.

The early rounds went well Thirty-two Gryphs paired off. The round of sixteen led to the round of eight. As Rynhart expected, Ozo won a slot in the Final Four. The killer round. *Okay*, he thought, *you can let the blood lust out.*

I know, I know.

The Final Four combatants took their places in locked pens at the corners of the arena. Ozo pawed the floor, its nails digging shallow trenches in the densely packed sand. Rynhart wiggled through the crowd so he could stand behind his pet.

"They're big brutes," Rynhart whispered.

Big and slow.

Ozo proved himself right. A veteran of dozens of such fights, Ozo had a knack for finding an opponent's weakness. With blood on its back, his armor plates chipped and oozing white fluid, it emerged from the first death bout bruised and winded, having dispatched a much bigger opponent.

Settled down with its pointed chin resting on his front claws, its nails still extended, Ozo watched the next pair of fighters. Rynhart had the queasy feeling of watching the bout through his pet's eyes. Big, husky monsters, both with long thick antennae that they used to whip the air, railed against one another, head-to-head, mandibles engaged.

Bet against me.

Rynhart grinned. "Never will. You got this."

Someone jostled Rynhart. "You think it understands you, buddy?"

Rynhart shook off the intruder's comment.

The second bout of the Final Four round concluded with one fighter getting off a final blow—sharp nails ripping across its opponent's eyes.

"Five-minute rest," the arena announcer said on the PA.

"You got this," Rynhart said again, crouching close to the pen where Ozo rested.

"Fighters out," the arena announcer said.

Ozo and its opponent stepped out of their individual pens and onto the hard-packed sand.

Will you take me away? Afterwards? I don't want to be gassed.

"Who said anything…about gas?"

That's how they do it. Animal Control. I read their minds, Green and Crawford. They gas killers.

"You got this." Rynhart wanted to stifle talk of gassing or defeat.

~ * ~

After the fight, Rynhart took Ozo north by train, then to a cheap motel a mile's walk from the RR station at Route 176. He carried Ozo in a paper bag. It was the only thing he could find after scrounging around in the dumpster outside the arena.

"Not the best transport, huh?" he said when he settled onto the hard mattress in the tiny room.

Ozo lay on its side on a thin green blanket across the bottom third of the mattress. Rynhart wiped the blood from his pet's long face, his fingertips lingering at a corner of its mouth, touching the place where a mandible had been blunted during the fight.

That's sensitive.

"Sorry."

Ozo turned over onto its back and wiggled its legs, opening them to expose a ribbed belly. Rynhart placed his hands across the ripples of flesh and massaged Ozo, who purred.

Is it time?

Rynhart glanced at the lace curtains. Twilight. A late summer night. A breeze might pick up later, especially close to Lake Michigan. That's where they'd go now. Ozo claimed to know where to find safety. It was a place the other fighters talked about while waiting to enter the pit.

Do I have to go in that bag?

"Can you walk?"

Ozo shook its long head and crawled into the paper shopping bag.

"You're sure of this, right?"

This is what I've been told. That's why those two comedians, Green and the other guy, thought we run off to the sewers and get eaten by alligators.

Rynhart shared a laugh with his pet.

I'll be okay.

They reached the forest three miles away from the motel and walked in. Where Rynhart entered with Ozo in the paper bag tucked under his arm, the woods were thick. He found it difficult to push through the foliage. Bushes with sharp thorns scratched his face. Weeds on the ground seemed to come alive and grab his ankles.

He came to a clearing where a shallow river flowed a few yards away. It smelled of chemicals, a mix of oil and waste so thoroughly blended Rynhart couldn't identify any one thing.

"And you're sure about—"

Don't keep asking. This is what I want. They'll take care of me. It's better, really. Better than getting gassed if Control takes me.

Rynhart put the bag on the pebble-strewn ground near the river. Raw sewage poured out of a narrow pipe into the green-brown waterway. Ozo crawled out, struggling until Rynhart helped.

They'll take care of me.

Rynhart wondered if that was true. "I can wait until they come." According to Ozo, other fighting gryphs had told him about the secret forest community, how it welcomed escapees, especially fighting stock.

They don't like intruders.

Blood trickled from Ozo's sides where it'd been slashed. The bleeding had stopped earlier. Now it resumed. The internal injuries, Rynhart feared, were worse. Unlike insects, hybrids such as Gryphs had ribs and a backbone. Both had been damaged during the fight. It was why, once it killed its opponent, Ozo went into a pain-fueled frenzy and engorged himself on the dead fighter's flesh, much to the delight of a cheering crowd.

Just go.

Rynhart backed away, leaving Ozo lying on its side, antenna limp across the sides of its face. He intended to return to the apartment in the morning. He'd deal with Murph the cat he'd left in the oven. He'd handle inquiries from Control. He'd say he didn't know where Ozo had gone when he ran off. If Control knew about the fight in the arena and the champion ripping into its opponent, Rynhart would claim innocence. No one could prove a thing.

He hoped Ozo was right about the forest community of Gryphs. He liked thinking of Ozo running with a pack, happily hunting with its own kind, no longer someone's pet, no longer just fighting stock to be pitted against other Gryphs.

He sheltered in the thick forest and looked back at where he'd left Ozo. Gryphs emerged from the drainage pipe leaking waste-water into the river. One nudged Ozo with the front of its head. Another pushed Ozo's body. More Gryphs joined the first two. Rynhart turned away, didn't look back, didn't want to see if these forest Gryphs attacked his pet or gently carried him to safety. He preferred the latter.

But he had to know. The need propelled him back to the drainage pipe. Several Gryphs surrounded Ozo, who raised a paw, swiped at the air with one antennae, and kept the largest of those around him at bay.

Ever the fighter to the end, he thought with admiration. Ever the fighter! The words booming through his mind became an out loud shout. He sprinted forward. The Gryphs backed away from Ozo with short high-pitched barks and grumbling menacing growls.

Leave me be.

"I'm taking you home."

So they can grab me and gas me? No. I want to go out like this, fighting to the—

"It's not a fair fight. Look at you."

I'm hurt. I know. I don't care. Don't you get it? I'm a killer. This is how killers die. Now, get out of here. They'll be back, and there'll be enough of them to kill us both.

Threatening eyes peered out from the darkness of the drainage pipe. One pair joined by more pairs, until it looked like eyes everywhere watched what Rynhart did next. As if he had a choice, he thought, and backed away, obeying Ozo's wishes.

~ * ~ * ~

After retiring from a long and successful career as a software developer and technical architect, **David** turned to a first love: writing fiction, particularly SF, fantasy, magical realism, and light horror. His stories have appeared in many anthologies and online as well as print publications. David lives on the North Shore, outside Chicago, where he enjoys long walks, the occasional bike ride, and other outdoor adventures.

The Physics of Equus Monoceros

Benjamin M. Weilert

The roiling Greenland Sea forced me to hook both arms around the railing on the side of the heaving boat as I plugged one ear with my finger and smashed the satellite phone against the other ear. I could barely hear the voice on the other end ask, "How did you get this number?"

"I'm Doctor Katrina MacGregor. My ma, Fiona, used to do research at your university."

The pause seemed longer than normal, given my voice had to travel to space and back to the ground before they could respond. "She hasn't worked for us in over twenty years."

"Aye, I know that," I yelled over a gust of wind. "I've uncovered some of her research recently and would like your support in seeing it completed."

"Sounds familiar. Hold on." I couldn't tell if their voice was garbled over the connection or whether they were shuffling papers. "Ah, here it is. Your paperwork seems in order, but you'll have to forgive me, Dr. MacGregor. While your mother was a beloved member of our faculty, we can't just hand out grants to people with wild theories—fairy tales, some have said."

"That's just it, though!" Nausea hit my stomach as the boat leaned over a steep wave. "Imagine the notoriety your university could claim if it's true!"

"Thank you for your interest in partnering with our university, but I'm afraid we'll have to pass on this opportunity." Three short tones beeped before the connection went quiet. I pulled the phone away from my ear to see they dropped the call.

I squeezed my eyes shut and shouted the loudest obscenity I could muster. Four days of navigating old contacts scrawled in a notebook that was practically falling apart. All while out at sea. At least the University of Glasgow had the dignity to just hang up instead of laughing at me.

Opening my eyes, I saw a deckhand approach in my periphery. He motioned for me to follow him into the bridge. I untangled myself from the railing and shoved the sat phone into the messenger bag slung across my chest. Warily, I clung to the metal bar of the railing as I shuffled to the door he held open for me.

The door slammed shut behind us. The relative quiet was as disorienting as the fog on my glasses. I took them off and wiped them on the sweater under my raincoat as I approached the captain. My chest tightened as thoughts of him throwing me overboard for being unable to pay for this 10-day journey swirled in my head.

My Icelandic was terrible, but his English was passable. He pointed at the radar. "Storm's clearing soon. Should be calm by night." Summer in the Arctic could hardly be called "night," but I knew what he meant.

"And ya're sure we'll see a pod out here?" I asked.

"Others seen larger groups days ago. Odds are good."

I nodded and smiled. He nodded back, silently acknowledging our agreement.

The sea was already settling as I fumbled my way to my cabin and closed the door behind me. My hair was still tied in a tight bun, which didn't help with the headache I was getting from the cold mist. With a quick snap, I pulled off the hair tie and let my copper-colored hair fall to my shoulders. I collapsed face first onto the tiny bed in my minuscule living quarters. The softness of the pillow I brought with me was an instant comfort.

My soul failed to find comfort, though. I flipped over onto my back and took deep breaths to allow the sighs ample opportunity to keep the wall of tears from breaking through. A steady stream flowed down the sides of my face and into my ears. My stiff lips quivered as a sob broke through. I slowly exhaled a shaky breath, followed by a steadier one. I pulled my legs up onto the bed and closed my eyes.

The memory of my pa and ma together in the kitchen making breakfast when I was six years old gave me a modicum of solace. Wherever they were, I hoped they were together again. I hated seeing pa's downward spiral over the last 20 years—it's definitely what killed him.

Other memories weighed heavy in my chest until I heard two quick knocks on my door. I jolted awake and saw my brief nap lasted almost three hours. The muffled voice on the other end was unintelligible, but I knew what it was telling me. With a groan, I rolled out of bed and fumbled into my dry suit.

The waves had calmed enough to make launching my sea kayak a breeze. I paddled toward the coast of Greenland as a cloud low on the horizon blocked the sun, shooting rays of light out from behind the silver lining. My research subject had been active only a few minutes ago but was hiding when I coasted into the area where the deckhands first saw it. Now it had disappeared.

A burst of water and air from a blowhole surprised me as the rubbery hide of a narwhal surfaced nearby. I always imagined them to be larger—more like whales than manatees. This one was only a little longer than the kayak I was using. It must have been a younger member of the pod, as it had no fear of me when I reached out and stroked its forehead. Other blowholes spouted nearby to let me know it wasn't entirely alone. "Okay, little one," I said, easing my hand down to its tusk. "Let's do an experiment, shall we?" My trip to Zimbabwe proved inconclusive, so hopefully this narwhal would give me the data I needed.

It boggled my mind academic institutions didn't want to spend a little grant money to prove micro-singularities existed. Ma's hypothesis was that single-horned animals like rhinos and narwhals descended from a common ancestor that carried a black hole at the end of its horn. She was more than qualified to prove her theory with degrees in evolutionary biology and physics—an educational path I had mimicked in my own life. Unfortunately, nobody took her seriously when she made the logical leap into more mythical creatures.

With my free hand, I secured my paddle and opened my dry bag. After removing the measurement device, I sealed the bag, stowing it and my gloves back at my feet. Ma's notes described the apparatus she needed to prove her hypothesis, but it was prohibitively expensive to reproduce. I jury-rigged something that would have to do, considering the entire lack of funding I had for this expedition. Fortunately, certain technologies were much cheaper now than 20 years ago, so I didn't break the bank making it. Five clicks later, and all the laser pointers were operational. The small cameras clicked on, their feeds streaming to the tablet on my lap.

The water was icy cold, but I needed the dexterity of my fingers to attach the collar around the narwhal's tusk. I lifted it gently out of the sea and strapped on the lasers and cameras. The baby narwhal squirmed a little, but didn't struggle.

There wasn't enough particulate in the chilly air to allow me to see the beams of the lasers, so I turned my attention to the tablet. Infrared videos from the cameras revealed slight diversions in the paths of the lasers, converging at a point a couple dozen meters away from the tip of the tusk. My breath was shallow with excitement as I took a screenshot to document this first step toward proving ma's theory. Now I just had to hope the scientific community would believe evidence from an uncalibrated device I threw together over a weekend. If it led to finding a live specimen of *Equus Monoceros*, all the better. How I'd manage that was beyond me, though.

I heard yelling from the boat and turned to see a deckhand waving my sat phone in the air. Hope swelled in my chest, and I scrambled to remove the measurement device from the narwhal's tusk. I shoved all the loose equipment down toward my feet and grabbed my paddle. My arms burned with exertion and my hands ached from the cold. I didn't have time to put my gloves back on—this was the call I needed to answer.

Despite my best judgement, when I got close to the boat, I motioned for the deckhand to toss me the phone. He begrudgingly obliged, and I almost fumbled it into the sea as it hit me in the chest. It chirped in my lap, and I allowed myself one deep breath to calm my nerves. I brought the device up to my ear and said, "Dr. Kat MacGregor."

"Doctor! I heard you need research funding." The voice on the other line sounded familiar, but not from any of the universities I had been contacting over the last few days.

"Aye, I am. And which university, may I ask, is interested in this research?"

"No university. Do you not recall our travels in Zimbabwe together?"

His clipped English finally registered. "Tumaini? Is that you?"

"Oh! You recognize me. You sound garbled. I did not know if I was coming through clearly."

"No, I hear ya fine. It's just…"

"Why am I calling you? Well, you are not my only client for finding the rhinos. They have caught wind of your planned research and would like to provide financing."

Chills. How were these people able to learn what I was after? "And what's in it for them? Most institutions I contacted would want credit. Nobel Prize claims for their alumni magazine—that kind of stuff. I don't even know who your clients are."

"These men are less interested in the science, and more in the exotic animal tied to this science. They will pay sizeable sums for a live specimen."

"Tumaini, ya have to be straight with me. Do they want to do sex stuff with it?"

"I am paid enough in commissions to not care what these men do with the animals I obtain for them."

"And how much would your commission for this one be?"

"I gave you quite the discount when we found your rhinos. I normally ask for ten percent. A single specimen from your research would bring me one billion U.S. dollars."

My ears started ringing and my vision narrowed. I felt like I was going to pass out. The warmth of my hope had steadily turned to icy fear. Nausea gripped my stomach again, and I reached out with my hand to steady myself on the fishing vessel nearby. My financial woes were the least of my worries now. Was my life in danger?

"Doctor? You there?"

"Aye, I'm here, Tumaini," I said. "How soon do your clients want an answer?"

"I think they can wait until you obtain a specimen, but they are notoriously impatient."

I sighed. "Let me get back to land and I'll think about it."

"Please do. You know how to reach me, Doctor. And get some rest. You sound tired."

Aye. I was tired. Even a Rip van Winkle nap probably wouldn't help at this point.

~ * ~

It had cost extra to have the captain change my drop off location, and the two-way trip from Reykjavik had originally cost £7,000.

Something about being unpredictable made me feel more comfortable about my predicament. I probably should have gone to Edinburgh instead, but I badly wanted to get back to a comfortable place as soon as possible.

I was fortunate my pa's friend was willing to drive me there and back and not ask for any gas money. He said I could ask him for anything when we re-connected at the funeral months ago. A couple hours of driving wasn't asking for much, but I had already sold my car.

The hour-long drive back from the nearest Western Union in Aberdeen was bittersweet. My inheritance was gutted. I had sold almost absolutely everything of value my family owned and just barely had enough to pay off the rest of my £15,000 debt to the captain. The financial burden had lifted, but now I had painted myself into a corner with no assets.

Back at my pa's house in Ballater, I snuck in the back door and immediately locked it behind me. Technically, this was my house now that both my parents were gone. It was all I had left. Well, to be completely accurate, I had the house, a small box of priceless heirlooms, and a single mattress. I didn't even have a phone anymore, which was just as well because Tumaini had been calling me more regularly, awaiting my decision.

Not that there was a decision to be made. Normally, I'd fault myself for being paranoid—this time, though, the hair stood up on the back of my neck far too often for it to be coincidence. I'd either accept these poachers' offer or they'd coerce me into it.

I wandered into the empty living room and kneeled into the corner, allowing the two walls on my back to feel like a hug from behind. My oldest coping mechanism. Pa did the best he could after ma disappeared, but sometimes he had drunk himself to sleep when I still needed to be comforted.

Tears blurred my vision as I took in the unrecognizable space. There were so many memories in this house and now I had nothing to anchor them to. The couch where I first kissed a boy was gone. The turntable credenza where my pa would play his silly accordion records was sold to an antique shop for a mere £50. Even the china from my parents' wedding couldn't fetch more than a £5 note despite only having been used once. Pa was sentimental like that, a trait I unfortunately inherited from him.

Deep, steady breaths helped keep me from breaking down completely. I had to get out and clear my head. Ma always took a walk into the woods nearby when she felt overwhelmed. Then, one day, she never came back. After weeks of searching, we just had to accept she was gone and move on with our lives. This unsolved mystery now felt much more sinister considering the mess I had gotten myself into on her behalf.

I let out a deep sigh and brought myself to my feet. The afternoon light streamed through the windows as I headed out the front door, locking it on my way out. It only took a few minutes to walk across town and over the River Dee to arrive at the thick forest that bordered the southeast portion of Ballater. I crossed the road and turned left to follow the hiking trail into the woods.

My feet remained on the path as my mind wandered. I mentally tried to sort out all my problems into ones I could solve and those I could not. One category was significantly larger than the other. I panicked and had to bend over and force myself to breathe.

A deep breath full of fresh air, filled with the dewy scents of the trees and soil, broke me out of the negative spiral. I turned my eyes up from my feet and gazed into the thick woods. Its sheer size made me feel small and its age made my problems feel insignificant. Now I understood why ma would come out here so often.

I took a few more steps along the path when a glint of something caught my eye. Dried tears from my eyelashes speckled my glasses, so I cleaned them off with the hem of my shirt. The gleam was still there. Something was off about this beam of light, which curved in a way that was slightly unnatural compared to the rest of the sunlight streaming through the canopy of the forest. I left the trail to pursue this odd phenomenon, plunging myself deeper into the woods.

The bend in the light became more severe as I zig-zagged my way toward it in my attempt to determine its parallax. Eventually, it refracted into a rainbow that grew stronger with each step I took. I squinted, unsure if I was hallucinating. This rainbow appeared to be emanating from the hindquarters of a white horse. I couldn't see the rest of the animal, which was highly peculiar. Tiptoeing toward the horse's flank, more of its body appeared from the nothingness that lay beyond it.

My heart skipped a beat and my breath stopped.

I blinked.

I blinked again.

A pinch to my cheek confirmed I was not dreaming.

Standing at the shoulder of this horse was none other than my ma. She had not aged a single day from when pa and I lost her. In fact, now I was as old as she was. With a small notebook in hand, she was making rough measurements with her hands, jotting down each dimension before moving on to another aspect of this animal.

That's when I noticed the horn.

It was a unicorn. *Equus Monoceros.*

I audibly gasped, which broke ma out of her concentrated frenzy of measurement. She spun around and saw me. The blue eyes behind her glasses squinted with confusion but steadily opened wider with surprise after each moment of recognition. "Kat? Is that you? Ya're so—"

"Ya're so young!" I interrupted. "How…wha…wher…" I stuttered through the beginning of all the questions, trying to get any of them out as they clogged my tightened throat.

Her embrace was sudden and comforting.

I hugged her back hard, fearing she would disappear again if I let go. The faint smell of her perfume overwhelmed my eidetic memory as tears flowed freely onto her scratchy sweater.

"I've only been gone for an hour," she said. "How did ya get so old in that time? I know puberty can happen fast, but…"

"It's been much more than an hour, ma. Ya've been gone for over twenty years."

She let out a short laugh. "Of course it's been that long out there. I was so caught up in discovering this micro-singularity I forgot to account for time dilation." Ma paused for a moment and added, "Makes sense, considering the lore about unicorns keeping people young."

I pulled away from our embrace and turned my attention to the distortion of space and time that existed at the sharp tip of the unicorn's horn—likely a result of it passing beyond the nearby event horizon. "That's why I couldn't see you until I got close! The gravitational lensing of this black hole bent the light around you so all anyone could see was the forest beyond this unicorn."

Ma raised her eyebrows. "Aren't you a smart lass? Roy musta had his hands full while I was gone."

I diverted my gaze to the ground nearby, pursing my lips against my teeth to hold back my grief. "He's gone," I whispered.

Looking back at my ma's face, I saw the shock hit her as she tried to comprehend it. "But…but he was only…" her eyes darted above her, trying to do the math.

"Liver failure."

"He only drank socially, right?"

I shook my head. "It was how he coped. Not me. I tried to be just like my ma."

An almost manic giggle escaped ma's throat. "And look where I got myself. A widow with a daughter who might as well be my twin sister."

I reached out and grabbed her hand. "But we're together again. We can still live our lives together. Except…"

"Let me guess. Poachers?"

"How did—?"

"Ya don't start trying to find a mythical animal and expect those types to ignore it."

"I wish ya had mentioned as much in your research notes."

"I'm sorry, but they had just called that morning before I went on a walk into the woods and found this fella."

"After they threatened me, the thought crossed my mind they had made ya disappear. I'm just glad that's not true."

Ma came in close. "What kind of threat? Are ya not safe?"

"It was more intimidation than anything," I said, waving my hand to brush away this genuine fear I had, so my ma wouldn't worry.

Ma was skeptical until a wry grin crossed her face. "We still own the house, right?"

"I do, aye."

"No debt?"

"Nae. Just paid everything I had to a boat captain."

"Then we just have to wait these poachers out." A quick glance up at the unicorn's horn let me know what she was thinking. "My daughter hasn't seen me in over twenty years, and I want to hear about her life. Could take a couple hours. Maybe more." She winked and sat down cross-legged and patted the leafy ground beside her. "Come and tell ma all about it."

~ * ~ * ~

Benjamin M. Weilert is an award-winning multi-genre writer from Colorado who writes whatever stories pop into his head. He is on a mission to write something in every single genre…eventually. So far he's tackled science fiction, fantasy, memoir, children's picture book, short story anthology, guidebook, and cookbook with many more on the way. He currently lives in Colorado Springs with his supporting wife and children. You can find him online on social media as "BMW the Author."

Working Both Sides of the Street

Charles Kyffhausen

"Come one, come all," the carnival barker proclaimed. "The intergalactic portal opens to the far side of the Galaxy, whose denizens are eager to meet you. You will find them far stranger than any form of life on our planet, or even in the imaginations of science fiction and fantasy writers."

"Is this worth the hundred-dollar price of admission?" Helen asked her date. "I remember the 'centaur' that consisted of two men in a horse costume. The original Mechanical Turk, a purported chess-playing robot, had a man inside. The Piltdown Man, the purported missing link between apes and humans, was a pure fabrication."

"John and Susan assured us this one is for real," Mike replied. They paid for the tickets and went into the sideshow's tent.

"Don't get too close," a stagehand warned indicating a swirling globe of colors and flashing lights. "That thing has four dimensions rather than three, and nobody knows what happens if you make physical contact with it. All we know is the other end is on another planet, in real time. Any light or radio signals from that planet won't arrive here for another three million years."

"It looks earthlike," Mike said. "How do we know this isn't just another place on Earth…" He froze staring at the portal. The trees had vine-like limbs, and they were moving. One of the big plants walked over to a pool of water and inserted its roots for the apparent purpose of ingesting some.

"Evolution took a strange turn on that planet," the barker said. "There is enough ultraviolet light there to sustain intelligent plant life. Nobody knows exactly how plant neurons operate, but these creatures obviously have them. They don't have muscles like ours, but their vascular fluids move their branches and limbs. Not only that, they can actually move from place to place as you just saw.

They can apparently drive their roots into the ground to get other nutrients, and then pull them out when they want to go somewhere else."

"They also can see with arrays of leaves that somehow generate composite images," the barker continued. "That one's leaves are arranging themselves to focus on the intergalactic interface. They are obviously looking at us the same way we are looking at them."

"This is amazing," Helen said. "We will have to recommend this show to all our friends. It's well worth the price of admission."

Three Million Light Years Away

Come one, come all," the carnival barker proclaimed. "The intergalactic portal opens to the far side of the Universe, whose denizens are eager to meet you. You will find them far stranger than any form of life on our planet, or even in the imaginations of science fiction and fantasy writers."

"Is this worth the price of admission?" Chlorophyllius asked Arboria. "I remember the one of a plant with violet leaves, which they achieved by having him/her ingest water with a harmless violet dye. They scammed a lot of people with that one before folks caught on. Then there was the eight-legged pollinator, with two very clever fake legs that appeared, however, to be part of the insect."

"Our friends assured us this is for real." They paid for the tickets and put their sensory vines into the tent.

"Don't get too close," a stagehand warned indicating a swirling globe of colors and flashing lights. "That thing has four dimensions rather than three, and nobody knows what happens if you make physical contact with it. All we know is the other end is on another planet, in real time. Any light or radio signals from that planet won't arrive here for another three million years."

"It looks a lot like our planet," Arboria said. "How do we know this isn't just another place here..." They froze staring at the interface. The four-limbed creatures in the globe had no branches or leaves, but they were obviously alive.

"Evolution took a strange turn on that planet," the barker said. "These creatures apparently eat life forms like us, but don't be alarmed; chlorophyll-users on their planet do not have brains, let alone central nervous systems."

"How can they live if they cannot turn light into body mass

and energy?" Chlorophyllius asked. "It's a biological impossibility, at least according to what I learned in high school."

"They put nutrients into those holes in the centers of the tops of their bodies, which somehow react the nutrients with oxygen to make carbon dioxide and energy. Our infra-red sensors show they are substantially warmer than their surroundings, and the only way to achieve that is through oxidation."

"They do it backward, then," Arboria said. "Everybody knows intelligent life uses sunlight to convert water and carbon dioxide into nutrients, and only then do we use oxygen to turn some of it into energy. Air, sunlight, and water are free, so whatever they do looks very inefficient."

"They also say they have too much carbon dioxide on their planet," the barker added. "I'm not sure how less than half of one part per thousand can be too much, though, as our atmosphere contains twice the concentration. It's possible to have too much carbon dioxide, but we are well short of that amount."

"I feel sorry for those poor plants of theirs, they must be positively starving," Arboria replied. "If they really have too much, though, it's a shame they can't send it to us."

"This is truly amazing," Chlorophyllius admitted. "This is definitely worth the price of admission, and we will have to tell all our friends to visit this show."

~ * ~

After the show was over, the respective barkers looked into the swirling globe. "What was your take?" Sungatherer asked his Terran counterpart.

"We brought in fifty thousand dollars for one night, and we didn't even have to do any work. How did you do?"

"We got roughly the same amount in our money for exhibiting your people to ours. Working both sides of the street, or both sides of an intergalactic portal, is highly profitable."

~ * ~ * ~

Charles Kyffhausen is the SF/Fantasy pen name of the author of stories published in anthologies from WolfSinger Publication, Dragon Soul Press as well as magazines like *The Lorelei Signal* and other places.

Scut Work

Gregg Chamberlain

"Okay, Sully, let's go over the checklist."

"Right."

"Steel-toed boots?"

"Check."

"Shin guards?"

"Front AND back!"

"Good. Some of those little Green Hell Amazon buggers can really sneak up on a body."

"Yeah, tell me about it, Jake."

"Uh huh. You got yer hockey pants?"

"Used, but still got all the stuffing."

"Okay, should be good. You made sure to stuff the leg holes too? Remember what happened with Mitchell?"

"Yeah, don't worry. Used up all the dirty socks in the laundry bag."

"Well, if nothing else, the smell should make any creepy-crawlies clear off."

"Hardy-har-har. Funny like a broken crutch you are."

"Just remember when you're around the unicorn…"

"I know, I know, never turn my back on him."

"Yeah, and he's got the 'Itch' now too, and he ain't feeling too particular. So don't bend over neither."

"Uh, right."

"Lessee…chest protection. Says here Kevlar vest best option."

"Yeah, right, as if."

"What? Thought you were gonna borrow one from your cousin the cop?"

"I asked. Bugger said he'd see then next day he up and says no way he can get without proper requisition b.s. paperwork. And forget the local Guns-R-Us army surplus. No way I can afford what they want, even for a used flak jacket."

"So? What's under the sweatshirt?"

"Got my kid brother's motocross chestplate. Industrial-strength molded plastic. Hard enough to bust your knuckles on."

"That the rig looks like Star Wars stormtrooper armour?"

"Yep. Pretty much, almost the same thing, really. Even Erich's claws should have a tough time scratching through."

"Erich? What's he doing in the Pen?"

"Blue moon month. My craphead cousin the cop loaned me his nightstick. Least that he could do, the putz. Got some silver wire wrapped around the end to tap Erich with if he gets owly."

"Okay, guess it should work. Arms?"

"Football shoulder pads and hockey elbow pads."

"Gloves?"

"Yeah, bit of a problem there. Hockey gloves are okay when I'm using the shovel or pitchfork. But, y'know, if I gotta do something that involves manual dexterity, well, there's a reason those guys throw down their gloves when they wanna mix it up on the ice."

"Yeah, okay. So?"

"Well, I thought about those leather half-gloves like some of the biker guys wear. But my fingers feel all exposed, right? So, I gotta pair of those heavy-duty rubber gloves like chemists use when they're handling beakers of acid."

"Okay. What about the head?"

"Motocross helmet with detachable face guard and a pair of heavy-tint goggles."

"Right then, okay. So, you got your shovel, pitchfork, buckets. What else?"

"Uh, lemme think. Two sling bags. Right side, I got three, no, four small bleach bottles with spray-nozzle caps. Left side's where I got the hair spray canisters. Half dozen should do, I think. Four Bic lighters strapped around my left wrist with rubber bands, and a Zippo inside the pouch of my sweats."

"Y'know, Doctor Prospero doesn't much like us using the homemade flamethrowers in the Pen."

"Hey, what the Doc don't know won't hurt me. Some critters—like that damn cockatrice—little taste of fire's the only thing they understand enough to back off."

"Whatever. Your funeral if he catches you using them."

"My funeral I go in there without 'em."

"Mm hmm. What else?"

"Water pistol full of fresh-squeezed garlic juice."

"What? No holy water?"

"Ever try to sneak a squirt gun into a holy water fountain?"

"Ah, yeah, right."

"Got a bag of rock salt in the right-hand sack too."

"Not slug bait? Shoggoths take a little more than a bit o' salt."

"Gardening shop was out. Been a wet summer this year."

"Well, I guess. Just remember to wing the stuff where the face is supposed to be."

"Yeah? Which end's that?"

"Hey, if you're close enough to tell the difference, then you're too close already."

"Managed to score a couple vials of anti-venin."

"Well, that won't work fast enough if the basilisk gets you."

"I don't plan on getting close enough for ol' Fangface to get me. But he spits worse than a camel. First sign he's getting ready to hawk one, I stick myself and run."

"Got a mirror too then?"

"Little sister's compact."

"Wha'?"

"I use the mirror to look around and behind me. Then close my eyes, spin, blow a big puff of face powder into whatever big ugly's there, and hightail out."

"Okay, that's not too shabby thinking."

"I get an idea now and then."

"Must die of loneliness sometimes."

"Oh, you're wasted here, man. Oughta be writing for Leno or Seinfeld."

"Well, that's the checklist. Got maybe three hours until show time. Ready?"

"No, but I'm going in anyways. Gimme a hand first putting these earplugs in."

"Nah, you won't need them. Siren's got a cold and can't sing for spit. But you might wanna play deaf around the Sphinx."

"How come? She's a pretty nice sort, most times. Not hard to look at neither. Leastways, half of her is."

"Ah, her and Doc Prospero got into a riddle contest last night. Doc stumps her with this one about whether or not a tree makes any noise if it falls and there's no one around to hear."

"Well?"

"Well, what?"

"Does it?"

"How the hell should I know? Ask the Doc, 'cause the Sphinx didn't know an' he wouldn't tell her either, an' it's put her in a right pissy mood."

"Man, I hate doing scut work in the Pen."

"Could be worse. Mitch got stuck with spring cleanup in the Doc's office."

"Ugh!"

"And you know what Harry's doing?"

"What?"

"Scrounging around for a really big pair of pliers with the longest set of handles he can find. And a big case of the cheapest whiskey he can afford."

"Pliers and rotgut. What's his deal?"

"Erich's been complaining about a toothache."

"Oh, shit!"

"Oh, yeah."

Originally Published in
Ricky's Back Yard Weekly Dump of Arty Goodness in the spring of 2017

~ * ~ * ~

Gregg Chamberlain, a community newspaper reporter now retired after five decades in the trade, lives in rural Eastern Ontario, Canada with his missus, Anne, and their cats who allow their humans the run of the house. He writes speculative fiction for fun and zombie filk on a whim. Past fiction credits include *Abyss & Apex, Daily Science Fiction, Apex, Pulp Literature, Mythic, Polar Borealis* and *Weirdbook* magazines, and various original anthologies.

Gregg likes circuses and one of his favourite songs is "Send in the Clowns".

More Books from WolfSinger Publications

The World of the Moho — Tyree Campbell

Aldon (Allie) McIntyre, a white American geologist with a thirst for adventure, and Thadie Mayane, a Black South African mining supervisor with a commanding presence, are exploring the depths of an abandoned mine when the floor collapses, hurling them into an extraordinary realm known as Below. Nestled between the Earth's crust and mantle, this vast world is home to breathtaking landscapes, intelligent species—some friendly, others predatory—and dangers unlike anything they've ever imagined.

Forced to rely on each other for survival, Allie and Thadie must navigate treacherous terrain, fend off alien predators, and face the looming threat of capture by those who see them as little more than slaves. As they search for the legendary passage back to Above, their uneasy alliance will be tested by the perilous environment—and the prejudices and mistrust they each carry.

Will they overcome the trials of Below and find their way back Above? Or will this stunning and dangerous world consume them entirely—if they don't destroy each other first?

Mars in Carnage — William Paul Lazarus

Humanity's dream of colonizing Mars quickly becomes a fight for survival. Mission director Lt Col. John Hathaway sends astronauts Aadya "Kate" Khatun and Hamza "Arti" Artsruni to explore and establish a foothold on the Red Planet. One astronaut is killed, during what appears to be an alien attack; the other makes a solo, dangerous return to a hero's welcome on Earth.

Over a century later a Martian colony has firmly established— the underground city of Katarti, Cecil Townley, a tour guide for visitors to Mars is captured by a band of terrorists trying to end what they believe are horrible governmental actions on Mars. Hiding in underground tunnels, they begin their attack with Townley forced to be their guide. Their actions introduce him to a world he never knew existed, far from the innocent tale he had been telling newcomers for years.

Cowboy Up – edited by Carol Hightshoe

Cowboy Up gathers stories that celebrate the timeless tradition of rodeo. The dust, the grit, the glory—it's all here.

From the echoes of the past to the rodeo arenas of today, these stories will take you on a wild ride through the highs and lows of rodeo life. You'll share in their triumphs and their heartbreaks. From the unbreakable bond between rider and horse to the courage it takes to get back in the saddle after a fall, this anthology is a tribute to the spirit that keeps rodeo alive.

But this book isn't just about telling stories. It's about giving back. Eighty-Five percent of proceeds from Cowboy Up will be donated to the Justin Cowboy Crisis Fund, a non-profit organization dedicated to helping injured rodeo athletes get back on their feet. Your purchase helps support those who risk it all in the arena, offering them a lifeline when they need it most.

So saddle up. Dive into these tales of resilience, heart, and the cowboy way. With every story, you're not just reading about rodeo —you're helping to keep its spirit alive.

Homefall Search – Dana Bell

Charged with finding the best place for a new Homefall, Jehna Talon searched on Saris, a world located in the Tashiti Nebula. Along with her Arial shapeshifter companions, she goes into the Ghost Mountains to find a specific valley, only to become trapped during a storm and encounters a native dragon.

With local rancher Harrison Talbot she negotiates the price for the land. Brides, for him and his hands. As her uncle taught her, there's always a need to be filled. Traveling to Aris and with the help of a local contact, she finds women willing to brave the frontiers of space.

Returning to Ronia, home of the Talons, she learns opposition from the other clan leaders may stop the dream she had of becoming a clan leader. They argue there are too few Rovers, and she'll never succeed.

Could they be right, despite her already finding the ideal location?

The Dragon's Hoard 3 – edited by Carol Hightshoe

In this anthology, twenty-six authors weave enchanting stories of dragons—from the fierce and fire-breathing to the wise and benevolent. Enter a treasure trove of tales where dragons reign supreme and hoards are more than mere gold.

Discover hidden gems of wisdom and magic within these lairs. Feast on tales that shimmer with magic, adventure, and the timeless allure of dragons. Explore the myriad treasures dragons hold dear and the legends that surround them.

From heartwarming tales of friendship and loyalty to thrilling adventures filled with danger and magic, these tales offer something for every dragon lover. Whether they are guardians of treasure, seekers of knowledge, or forces of nature: the dragons in this collection will ignite your imagination.

The Dragon's Hoard 2 – edited by Carol Hightshoe

Welcome to realms where dragons reign, treasures abound, and every adventure leads to magic. Explore stories that spark the imagination and might just awaken the dragon within. Are you brave enough to face the dragon and claim your prize?

From the unyielding grip of ancient magics to the cunning of those who seek dragons, their treasure or both—each story weaves a rich tapestry of magic and lore.

Whether it's a battle for survival, the forging of an unlikely alliance, or a humorous twist on hoarding habits, our authors invite you to delve into realms where dragons not only hoard gold but also secrets, spells, and sometimes, even friendships. After all, in the world of dragons, not all treasures are silver and gold—some are stories waiting to be told.

The Hounds of Ardagh – Laura J Underwood

Ginny Ni Cooley never desired more than the simple life she had, living in Tamhasg Wood and using her magic to occasionally assist the folk of Conorscroft while putting up with the machinations of the ghost of her former mentor Manus MacGreeley. But her peace is shattered one night with the arrival of a lad who is fleeing a pack of red-gold hounds led by a hound-shaped demon known as Nidubh.

So much for peace and solitude. By rescuing Fafne MacArdagh, Ginny becomes wrapped in the fabric of an intrigue involving a family feud, a traitorous son, and a blood mage named Edain who is determined to keep her soul. It is she who cast a spell on Fafne's family and household and transformed the MacArdaghs into hounds.

Ginny gives Fafne her word to take him to Caer Keltora so they can report the matter to the Council of Mageborn. But Edain is determined to keep her secret and her soul intact and moves to thwart Ginny at every turn.

For Ginny Ni Cooley who has faced many bogies, dealing with a demon, a bloodmage and the Dark Lord of Annwn will be no easy task. But she will do what she must to undo Edain's spells. If not, Manus' soul will become part of Arawn's Cauldron of Doom. Ginny will become a demon's feast, and poor Fafne will join the Hounds of Ardagh.

Wee Folk and Wise: A Fairies Anthology

– edited by Deby Fredericks

All over the world, fairy tales are told.
There are big fairies and little fairies.
Ugly fairies and pretty fairies.
Wise fairies and silly fairies.
Sweet fairies and scary fairies.

Seventeen authors share their own fantastic fairy tales in this magical collection. What kind of fairy will you meet here?

Infinity – Ted Pennella

In the distant future, when peace between humanity and the artificial intelligences their ancestors created has been settled, Conrad Conner tries to live a quiet and unassuming life in orbit about Jupiter on the city-station Socrates' Odyssey. When Conner's attempt to create a prototypical communication artificial for use by the Sol-Humana Confederation's Stellar Fleet gets derailed by the attempted murder of the very artificial he's created, his life spirals into a mad flight back to Earth to try and save at least his sister's children, if not his sister herself. Past failures and heartaches resurface as seemingly unconnected dots become a plot by the First Admiral to steal not just power over the Confederation, but a secret Conner holds within himself.

A secret not even Conner knows about.

Flatlanders - Mike Sherer

Young theoretical physicist Mickey Haiku has fallen into Eden's trap. She is a much smarter scientist who is intent on saving her own dimension by destroying his. Unbeknownst to either, beings from several yet higher dimensions have their own strategies. This sends the mixed-up pawns off on a wild odyssey through a dozen weird, twisted dimensions. As if this hyper-dimensional odyssey isn't challenging enough for Mickey, he has the additional difficulty of embarking on this whacko tour as a (pregnant!) female. Which means Eden is stuck in Mickey's body. The two are soon forced to cooperate since each holds the other's body hostage.

The strangest relationship this side of the 11th dimension develops between the two.

And more – check out our books at
www.wolfsingerpubs.com

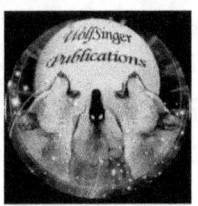